THE CARNIVORE

ALSO BY MARK SINNETT

FICTION
Bull (1998)
The Border Guards (2004)

POETRY
The Landing (1997)
Some Late Adventure of the Feelings (2000)

THE CARNIVORE

a novel

MARK SINNETT

ECW Press

Published by ECW Press
2120 Queen Street East, Suite 200, Toronto, Ontario, Canada M4E 1E2

Library and Archives Canada Cataloguing in Publication

Sinnett, Mark, 1963-
Carnivore / Mark Sinnett.

ISBN 978-1-77041-034-3
Also issued as: 978-1-55490-998-8 (EPUB); 978-1-55490-898-1 (PDF)
Originally published in hardcover in 2009 (ISBN 978-1-55022-898-4)

I. Title.

PS8587.I563C37 2011   C813'.54   C2011-902955-3

Editor: Michael Holmes / a misFit book
BackLit editor: Jennifer Knoch
Cover and text design: Ingrid Paulson
Cover image: City of Toronto Archives, Fonds 1257, Series 1057, Item 2002
Typesetting and production: Rachel Ironstone
Printing: Webcom 5 4 3 2 1

This book is set in Adobe Caslon

The publication of *The Carnivore* has been generously supported by the Canada Council for the Arts, which last year invested $20.1 million in writing and publishing throughout Canada, by the Ontario Arts Council, by the OMDC Book Fund, an initiative of the Ontario Media Development Corporation, and by the Government of Canada through the Canada Book Fund.

Printed and bound in Canada

for Lucian, Willa, and Sam

There was between them a fusion of the kind that occurs in great public panics, where hundreds of people who an instant earlier differed in every way make the same motions, utter the same mindless cries, gape wide their eyes and mouths.

— Robert Musil, *The Man Without Qualities*

RAY

In the beginning there was only darkness and heavy rain. Sudden black waters that ruffled and swarmed like a plague over the roads and fields, poured like Guinness into abandoned stairwells. Downtown, at the intersection of King Street and Spadina Avenue, a young man in hitched-up plus-fours tried fording one of the deepest sections of road on his bicycle. The wheels slid out from under him and he disappeared, then rose again sputtering and indignant. Cop or not, I laughed along with the sodden crowd. Two unshaven men carrying a spineless mattress from one building to its neighbour had it ripped from their arms by the current. One of them, a showy and well-muscled lad, dove in theatrically and performed three or four impressive freestyle strokes before standing again, suddenly waist deep. He flopped aboard the ruined springs and feigned exhaustion. Bravo! I thought. Bravo!

No one took any of this splashy weather very seriously, even though there were reports of similar scenes all over the city. The CBC's meteorologist reported matter-of-factly on the radio that a hurricane was blowing itself out over the Appalachians. His confident forecast was for a little more rain that evening, then drying out after midnight. But the sky was fierce with fat, scudding armies of cloud. And at the lake, a debris-laden surf was beginning to wash in. There were logs and curled roofing shingles, wretched baby toys with broken or missing limbs, dislocated umbrellas and battered hubcaps; a buckled American stop sign.

Commuters were clutching at lampposts and hats, yanking overcoats tight and yelling to each other quite cheerfully, almost proudly, that they couldn't remember the last time they'd seen a rain like this. The buses were packed and glowed like lanterns. Their drivers honked at the more timid drivers to give way. If it stopped soon, I thought, then there wouldn't be much of a problem (though I had seen a few refugees evacuating basements already, clutching their record albums and a favourite pair of shoes, or a squirming, terrified cat), but another hour or two and it would lose its comic edge.

Worst was the traffic. Motorcycle cops were attempting to guide drivers towards the shallowest sections of road. A couple of detours had been established. A drunken crowd that had gathered on the roof of the Gladstone Hotel on Queen Street had taken to lobbing beer bottles into the rising sea. The fact that instead of smashing they simply bobbed west seemed to strike them as miraculous. One idiot was scrawling messages on paper napkins and stuffing these inside the Molson's bottles, as if he had been stranded in this overrun cattle town long ago and had finally sensed the possibility of rescue.

When I found a moment I telephoned home to tell Mary that I wouldn't arrive until later, when things calmed down. She was disappointed — she had wanted us to spend the evening together, packing. We'd planned a trip to Niagara Falls. She whispered (as if she might be overheard) that she pictured us in bed together tonight, riding out the storm, if I got her drift, and so I told her about the boy on the mattress.

"Do you think we'll still be able to go away?" she asked me.

"You said the Queensway was flooding."

"We'll drive around it," I said. "Or we'll rent a boat." I was feeling strong, cocky even. But I was a respected policeman with a pregnant wife, and that struck me right then as the epitome of good citizenship. Everything about my predicament felt crystalline and pure. It was just the adrenalin kicking in, I suppose.

I told Mary I loved her and her throttled little gasp excited me. I would have to do that more often. But then, feeling suddenly delinquent in my duty, somehow adrift, I said only, "Mare, I have to go."

"Go! Go!" she commanded, and I felt oddly as if I was being ordered once more out of an Italian trench and across exposed muddy fields towards tangles of barbed wire. And I also felt, with an unsettling certainty, and with the wet telephone still in my hand, that I was about to die.

The reporter — a lovely young Chinese woman, Katie something — was bored, I think. She had talked herself into our home but now she wanted none of this florid indulgence; it was unusable. At best she would reduce it to a dozen melodramatic words: *Fifty years ago today, Detective Ray Ignacius Townes spoke briefly to his wife before the full force of the hurricane struck Toronto. He had time only to tell her that he loved her. . . .* What she really wanted from me were the so-called heroics. She had a deadline (and perhaps a dinner date), and her appetite for the story's peripheral details was limited. The day after tomorrow something else would demand her attention. A killing at the Eaton Centre. A police strike. Tuberculosis in the shelters. Any of the sordid thrills Toronto routinely offers. Quite reasonably she might have been thinking that I should understand those things, that I should help her.

And it really was a dreary retelling. I've done it much better elsewhere. At cocktail parties and at the occasional speaking engagement arranged by the public library. Every few years a relative of one of the deceased will track me down with questions and I'll try to tell them what they want to hear.

And even now, hours later, lying here in my own bedroom with my notebook pressed against my knees, my heart isn't in it. I've given up on my plan of repeating everything I said to Miss Katie Whatsherface. Mary crept away up the stairs an hour ago. I heard her pull a bottle of Chardonnay from the refrigerator and take it with her. I have driven her to drink. Saying goodbye, Katie kissed my cheek (a social nicety, that's all it was, but a fly-away strand of her hair was for an instant, I swear, *inside* my mouth). Once she was gone, Mary began to shake. At our age such a rage is alarming, seems freighted with risk. I can imagine all too readily an aneurysm, blood flooding her brain, or her heart clenching too tightly around her disappointment. Her eyes did pool with tears but words were beyond her. She kicked lightly at my oxygen tank to make sure it was full and that its hoses were attached properly to the valves, and then she sniffed away. She has shrunk in recent years, become shorter, and in a long-ago moment of levity I even suggested we scratch a set of lines into the wall, begin an ironic measure of our annual decline. And as she passed into the kitchen tonight (though it might have been an illusion, I suppose, some trick of perspective) I don't think she reached much above the halfway point.

Dinner arrived late and stone cold. She had eaten alone presumably, wondering whether to starve me altogether. I think it entirely possible I will die before we are civil with each other again.

And I do understand her anger. That hurricane changed everything. It put our house under a cloud and caused a permanent turbulence to clatter through its rooms. Mary only knows half of it and that's apparently more than enough for her to never forgive me. She should have, but she didn't. And as a result we have wasted much of the rest of our lives. Why in God's name did she stay with me? Was it the memory of love? The faint hope it can be rekindled?

I remember one night (it must have been around the same time as the hurricane — just a few days or weeks before it hit) I found her hunkered down in bed, the covers hiked around her neck. I sat at her feet and rested my chin on the cotton-covered mound of her drawn-up knees. "You okay?" I asked her.

"Sure I am," she said.

"It's just you seem, I don't know, more tender today."

"I'm always tender, Ray." She stuck out her bottom lip. "Why don't you get yourself in here and feel just how tender I am."

I clambered over legs. "I think maybe delicate is a better word," I said. "Like the world was having its way with you."

She feigned indignance. "Now you're making me sound downright promiscuous. Which is the last thing I am. Now you hold me. Just like that. You dare tell me I'm not the tenderest woman in the world. No don't let go. You just hold me."

You see, if we had separated long ago perhaps I would have lost innumerable moments like this. And given the pain they cause us, the pain they cause *me*, the infinite regret, I would choose that. Yes, let us consign the beautiful bits to oblivion, I say, rather than have them cower here, fetid little ghost children, illuminating nothing more than this dank shadowland we have picked as our lot in life.

MARY

I said to Jenny, our daughter, "I'd like to strangle him, Jen, I really, really would." And she laughed, of course, but the sadist in me, as well as the judge, wants at the very least to pin him down, sit on his chest and force him to speak transparently. To tell the goddamn truth. But one cannot do that, especially, it seems, to a retired policeman. The indignities involved in such a scene are unthinkable. And how do you even argue, how do you berate a man who cannot catch enough breath to argue back? He knows, of course, that his illness protects him, and damned if he doesn't exploit it. The man, what little is left of him, is totally without shame.

But did he really think I wouldn't find out? I change his sheets every second day, for crying out loud. You can't just slip a notebook under the mattress and have it remain a secret. He's like a dumb teenager with a greasy stash of girlie pictures.

It wasn't much more than twelve hours after that girl left — that stupid, fawning reporter. I helped him into the shower we'd installed behind the kitchen so he wouldn't have to negotiate the stairs. Then I came in here to clear away the dishes. I shouldn't do that for him, I know. It makes him more dependent than he needs to be and besides, I feel diminished by the act. But old habits, just like Ray, die hard.

And when I found it I read it. I don't know why. On another day I might have just handed it to him unopened, asked what it was. But today, perhaps because I was still smoldering, I riffled through its mostly empty pages until I came to his nearly illegible scrawl. Then I sat. I squinted. I slumped and I ached. And when he called for me, when he wanted my arm to lean on again, I dutifully led him from the bathroom's hot mists into this cool, well-stocked room. But then I sat him down and I said, "So what the hell is this, Ray?"

He took the notebook from me and closed it. Maybe he hoped I hadn't had time to read all of it. He left his mottled, quivering hand on top of the cover, to shield it from my gaze, but the impression was of a man about to swear an oath. Finally he shrugged. "I don't really see that I owe you an explanation." His robe (it is new and black and absorbent; it is so much better than he deserves) parted over the revolting white knob of his knee. There might as well be no skin on him at all.

"Then how about just telling me the half I don't know? Isn't that what you say in there, that I don't know the half of it?"

He stared. He'd forgotten that admission, I think. I saw panic in his face as he scrambled to remember what he'd written. His breathing, shallow and worrying at best, tore around the edges, lost its predictable rhythm. Both of us eyed the tank. "Yes?"

He nodded meekly and so I wheeled it over and pulled the mask over his face. He thinks he looks like a fighter pilot like this — or so he has claimed — but in reality he is simply an old man near death. I remember that during a replay of that awful footage of George Bush on the deck of an aircraft carrier, all dolled up in pilot's uniform and with his breathing apparatus swinging as casually from his shoulder as a camera, Ray's eyes lit up so brightly it was as if new batteries had been installed. Apparently he saw something of himself in that dumb, offensive scene, and I pitied both of them.

I gave him a minute or two. He was fine and just buying time; pretty soon I would screw down the valve.

He lifted away the mask. "I only meant that we have always left the fine details unspoken," he rasped. "We agreed a long time ago there was no need."

Rubbish. Absolute rubbish. I could just *scream*. But you know, I have never been able to believe him. Even when we met, the first day, the first date, it was clear that he was a deceiver. He was an hour late, and his excuses were pitiful. But back then, so long ago, I found it obscurely charming. He was a raconteur, I told myself, a handsome spinner of fabulous yarns. I was young and I was impressionable and I was also utterly naïve. I thought somehow that an exemption would soon be granted to me. That because love was involved I would be treated more often than not to the truth. I didn't know that I was wrong, not categorically, until October of 1954. But by then we were married, we had a house, it was just about inconceivable that we might part ways. Do I wish I had been smarter and recognized him for exactly what he was? Of course. And would I, as he asks, have left him then? I don't know. I like to think so, but those answers are so patently unknowable that the questions become ridiculous, merely a form of torture. We endure and we go on.

And that's how it was for me this morning: I endured and then I went on with my day. He sputtered and blustered mightily. He denied everything — the malicious intent, the negligent cruelty I accused him of; he even denied the relevant facts of history. And as he regained his footing he began also to mock my outrage. But we have fought this fight so often that much of it is conducted on some sort of autopilot, so I eventually found myself in a daze and vaguely disinterested.

I told him firmly, though, that he had to stop. "I have no interest in your rewriting our history," I said. He duly pocketed his notebook and struggled upward. He paced breathlessly before me. Now that the stairs prove such a trial this parlor has become also his bedroom and he feels it is a space he can dominate. "A lion's den" is how he has described it.

And so I stood up, too, which forced him to make a detour around me, and then we regarded each other warily through the dust-specked gloom. "You gave that girl completely the wrong idea," I said.

"I gave her what she wanted."

"I'd wager that what she wanted was the truth."

"Nothing I could say to her would have made you happy."

I told him I would be happy to list a dozen things he could have said. A hundred things. "But once again you succumbed to your ego, Ray." He opened his eyes very wide. "No, I'm serious," I said. "You need to know that's how I feel. Your problem here, the fatal flaw, is that you can't change the truth." I poked him in the chest, where his heart should have been. "So when you read in the newspaper in the next few days that you're a hero, just remember that I'm in the next room reading it too, Ray. And with every lie —"

"I didn't lie."

"— with every *omission*, you shrink in my eyes. And already you're about this big." I held my thumb and finger an inch apart.

I left him grumbling and muttering. On my way out I drew back the curtains so he couldn't hide all day in the dark. I kicked a rubber wedge firmly under the door to hold it open. When he looked up to see what that noise meant, I said, "And by the way, dear. She found you pathetic. I'm surprised you didn't see that." Then I made a second pot of coffee because he would see me making it and not bringing him any. I didn't care that it was petty and ineffectual. It was something.

He is eighty-four (I am seventy-nine) and he has end-stage emphysema. In other words, he is dying. No one expects him to make it to the end of the year. Our darling Jenny is with us for a few days, and everyone knows why. We all wonder if father and daughter will see each other again after this visit. There have been half-hearted words about Christmas, but Jenny is on her way to Africa. She does important work there and to return again would take her away from that. And besides, like all aid workers, she is woefully underpaid; an airline ticket could cripple her financially for months and she is too proud, too frustratingly stubborn, to accept our help. This morning she secreted herself somewhere on the second floor. A middle-aged woman hiding like a teenager. I'm sure she heard us fighting. She knows far more than I would have liked about the kind of marriage we have. But the good thing about that is that I can talk to her a little. It would break her heart if I told her everything I know, everything I feel, but whenever the steam inside threatens to take off the top of my head, I will telephone her, or e-mail. Sometimes, when she is working, it is a week or two before I get a response and by then I have usually defused whatever it was that got me so heated. But just knowing she is out there, on my side, is a great comfort. And for that I am grateful.

He wants to mythologize those days. In his mind he is already polishing the statue he fantasizes they might erect in his name. He'll try to find an audience for his ravings, you watch. I worry that this newspaper thing is just the start. Why in God's name couldn't he leave it alone? I have dreaded just this sort of eventuality for years. I knew the fiftieth anniversary might bring the papers sniffing, but I always thought I would be able to intercept these disruptive forces. He almost never answers the door or the telephone, and it is me who sorts the mail. He is nearly invisible, mostly unreachable. And we have, in recent years, attained a sort of middling peace. I had just about come to terms with our life together, our disappointments. And so had Ray, I thought. We smile at each other, if only half-heartedly. My coping mechanism has been to dwell on the several pleasant-enough months and years we have had together. And Ray? Well, I don't really know what tricks he has used to get him through the rough spots. Wilful blindness? A total insensitivity? I'm not really joking, but of course that can't be all of it. What I have known, for many years, is that whereas I think of the good times as lily pads, slippery havens floating in an enormous pond, Ray finds those memories depressing, cruel in how they set our tensions in such stark relief. But anyway, the point is, I felt this coming, I really did. Another horrendous storm; a dark ghost of that first weather-bomb.

It is so odd, so mysterious, how the events of a few remote days have shaped much of the rest of our lives. And to that limited extent I suppose I understand Ray's need to revisit them now, to figure out exactly what makes them so vital, and so mortally wounding too. I mean, millions of couples recover from similar events. Why didn't we?

I sometimes think that if he hadn't succeeded for a while in hiding his misdeeds our lives might have been entirely different. That if he had slipped up earlier, or simply admitted everything and thrown himself at my feet and begged for forgiveness, we might have recovered, gone on to lead brilliant lives together. But no, he stuck to his guns. He created mad, panicked alibis, and by and large he has stood by them for the rest of his life, even in the face of an Everest of contrary evidence.

When he was still with the Force, Ray was fond of telling me that what put away most criminals was the fact that, at some point, they changed their stories. They buckled under pressure. They admitted to an investigating officer that other scenarios were more likely, or more defensible. "Bang!" said Ray. "Soon as that happens, you lock 'em up." He would shake his head and smile wryly, condescendingly. Because being the brilliant man that he is, Ray wouldn't crumble that way. Even when we are sequestered in dark rooms, miles away from another set of ears, and even at the best of times, when I think there might be a chance for us, he looks me in the face and lies. He has done it over and over.

The fool.

To my mind this catastrophic slide of ours all started a good month earlier than Ray will admit, on the day I took the street-car along Queen Street to St. Mike's hospital. That was September 15th, 1954.

So here they are: *the goods.* It's one of Ray's terms. He means the irrefutable facts of a case. Well this is them, whatever he says to the contrary.

So yes, I was on the streetcar heading east, towards Yonge. It was windy and early turning leaves were being hassled from the trees, and a Canadian flag lashed at its pole outside the insur-ance building. By lying to my supervisor at the hospital I had got the day off. It was my parents' wedding anniversary, I said, and Ray and I were taking them out to dinner. But first there were going to be cocktails and a reception at the house, and everyone knew what sort of preparations *that* required. There were the flowers to buy, and the carpets, well they desperately needed something fresh to happen to them, I said, and the freezer was on the fritz, so I would have to buy ice and get it home without melting. It would have been so much easier, I complained — getting caught up in my own lies — if Ray and I could have visited them in Hamilton on the weekend. But my mother, Ruth (who no one from the hospital had ever met, because she didn't think it was a sanitary environment), had once said you needed to mark these occasions properly, or else there was no point marking them at all.

I was early (I've always been early; I've wasted days, weeks of my life waiting for people who arrived on time) and so I contemplated riding the subway north. There was time, I thought, for a roast beef sandwich at Clem's, my favorite lunch counter, at the far end of the line. I loved that ride, still do, the way the train emerges into the light for some of its journey before diving again, like a sea monster. Many of the riders were still visibly excited by the fact that Toronto had a subway at all. For so many months there had been just a terrific wound between the sidewalks, ruining business for the store owners, who were only somewhat placated by the notion that the train would bring in thousands of new shoppers. I should do it, I thought. *Go north, young girl!* They would have the radio playing up there, and there would be progress reports from Lake Ontario. The American girl, Florence Chadwick, had given up in her attempt to swim across Lake Ontario, but the Canadian teenager, Marilyn Bell, was still going strong; they said she would make land by nightfall. The city's attention hadn't been focused on one thing like this since the subway opened in May.

But no, a trip to Clem's wouldn't work; I was too distracted. The possibility that my world might change had made it impossible to concentrate properly on anything else. Even a sixteen-year-old girl braving twelve-foot waves and swarms of black eels. God, it was all so exciting.

I should have talked to Ray about it weeks before, and I wasn't at all sure why I hadn't. He would have been pleased, of course he would. But whenever I thought about it, I always decided to wait a day, and then a week, and now . . . well now it didn't make sense to talk about it at all until it was a certainty.

What I should have done, I decided, was make myself a nice sandwich at home and leave an hour later. I twisted my hands in my lap. This was so unusual, the way the anxiety writhed inside me. I hoped fervently that none of my friends or co-workers would appear in the streetcar's doorway. Because then the lies would start again: I was looking for a particular cheese my father liked; I had heard they sold it at the St. Lawrence Market. Adding to all my discomfort was how even the fleeting thought of cheese nauseated me.

I stayed on the streetcar, watched a stream of shoppers shuffle through the revolving doors that marked the entrance to both Simpson's and the subway system. Those are the people I might have ridden with, I thought. I might have sat opposite him, for instance, and he would have stared at my knees the whole way. Or I might have elicited a smile from that young girl. Her, there, with the ribbon in her hair, behind the woman with the bird in the wicker cage. Girls, I thought. I like little girls better than little boys.

It's so alarmingly *clear* to me, that old train of inconsequential thoughts. Amazing that at the same time I can't remember what I wore yesterday, however hard I try. I do remember slapping the biscuits down onto the table between Ray and the reporter, though. I can even see my thumb wrapped over the lip of the plate. But do you think I can summon the colour of my sleeve that day? Not a chance.

I went two more stops and then hurried into a meager, dusty park in front of a church. I sat on a bench in the shade of a maple. Two crows argued above me while I nibbled on a Digestive. Sunlight settled weakly on the back of my hand. I held out my arm, twisting it back and forth, as if it were under water. I wondered idly where Ray was, whether he was safe and whether he might have thought fondly about me at any moment today.

I pulled in my hand. I was being ridiculous. My brain had turned to mush. I would have to be careful it didn't become a permanent state.

At ten minutes to one I announced myself to the reception-ist in the waiting rooms of Dr. Pierce at St. Michael's Hospital. I had seen Pierce once before, but only from a distance of fifty feet, and on that occasion there had been at least one hundred other nurses in the room. As well as being a general practitioner, Pierce was an expert in the management of fever and swelling, and he had delivered a lecture in the spring. There were both doctors and nurses in the audience. The doctors had sat on one side of the room, mumbling quietly or reading their newspapers, and usually keeping an empty seat between them. They seemed to begrudge the education. But across the aisle we nurses had coagulated into an excited mass.

Pierce had turned out to be an appealing, good-humoured man, though slightly peculiar in his appearance. He was prob-ably younger than Ray but his hairline had already crested the top of his skull and even begun, either side of centre, to gallop for the back of his neck. His lips were too pale and too thin, and his nose . . . well, equine is the euphemism we would use nowa-days. His eyes, though, were blue and attentive, and always seemed, I remember, slightly wet, as if he lived in an eternal state of fresh sorrow, or joy — at the mercy anyway of great lurches of his heart. The flyers they handed out said he was American, born and educated in Boston. Only a few of the nurses were single. But his seaboard drawl, his expensive, slightly too large suit, his retreating black curls, as well as the cheerful absence of a tie — "I use ties to impress my patients; you lot would see right through me" — had somehow made the buzz inside the hive of nurses rather intense. His odd appear-ance seemed to work well for him. My best guess is that it suggested availability. What I liked most about him, though, and what had brought me halfway across the city to see him again today, was that he hadn't addressed his remarks to only one side of the hall. Because, as my mother was fond of saying:

"Finding a man who doesn't talk down to women is harder than finding a chained dog that doesn't bark."

Ray, it must be said, was better than most, but when he was explaining something about police procedure, for instance, (often at my instigation, because I wanted to show I was interested in his life), he could make me feel about six years old. He didn't do it on purpose, and he was quick to apologize, even to blush, when I told him what was happening, but that didn't mean I could expect it not to happen again. It is part of men's souls, I think. It is a flaw that proves heaven is somewhere else. My mother has always said that men need to see women as weak, as somehow lesser creatures, and that I might see there was some truth to that sentiment if Ray was one day to pull me from a burning building, or fight off a knife-wielding intruder. It infuriates me. "And what if it's *me* who pulls *him* out and, what's more, nurses him back to health afterwards? What do you suppose *that* would prove?"

All the same, sitting in the newfangled plastic armchair in the waiting room and trying to look composed, I wouldn't have minded one bit if flames had licked under the bottom of the door and someone, be it man, woman, or child, had thrown me over their shoulder and carried me out of that infernally humid room.

"Mrs. Townes. Mary Townes?"

Dr. Pierce was in the hallway, beaming at me as keenly as if we were old friends. I was instantly petrified. He was wearing a bright tie, but possibly it was the same suit, and he had thrown over that ensemble a decently pressed white lab coat and gleaming stethoscope. He took my hand in both of his. "Come in, come in." The effect at that moment was of being solicited by an overgrown and irrepressibly cheerful gnome.

And so there I was, the future tugging me into a room perhaps twelve feet by ten feet, with more than half that area taken up by the steel table and sink, and the cupboards full of sheets and syringes and b.p. gauges and tongue depressors. During training I'd stocked a thousand cabinets just like these. I knew where the rubber hoses were, and the alcohol swabs. Nearby there would be another space that Pierce shared with the other doctors, crammed with well-thumbed reference books and soiled ashtrays, tennis rackets and cast-off clothes. And if I should present with anything out of the ordinary Dr. Pierce would excuse himself for a moment and seek guidance in one of those smoky volumes. He might even seek out the opinion of a colleague, before returning to me with a reassuring smile and a confident-sounding diagnosis, or a suggestion of more tests.

But none of that was necessary today. I knew in minute detail how the next few minutes were likely to unfold. Through the window I could see the top of the maple I had sat beneath. It was possible the doctor had seen me down there, that between appointments he stood before the glass and surveyed the world in which he was regarded as nearly a god. My gaze settled finally on his leg. He was perched on the leather-topped stool, eyeing me benignly.

"It's an unusual feeling, isn't it?" he said enthusiastically. "Being a patient rather than a caregiver."

"I keep telling myself to get over it," I told him. "To relax." I laughed uncomfortably.

"And does it do any good?" he asked. "We can control these things to a certain extent, you know. Stress is what I'm talking about. Deep breathing works. So does distraction. And denial, of course." He laughed self-consciously.

I smiled. "I tell my patients the same things, doctor. But putting it into practice is much harder. So this is a good lesson for me."

"Yes, a lesson." He brought his hands down on top of his knees and spun away from me to collect an unblemished chart from his desk. "So," he said, and waved the papers like a fan. "Not much to go on here. You live on Aldringham. That's in the west isn't it? Not very far from St. Joseph's, where you work. As a nurse."

"I came for the anonymity, doctor. I want this to remain my business a while."

"You think you might be pregnant."

"There are a lot of things I might want to keep private," I reminded him rather hotly. I hated that it was so obvious. "But yes. I do."

"And just how pregnant do you think you might be?"

"Completely pregnant," I told him, and was so relieved when he laughed.

"I'll have to come up with a different question," he said. "See, you've made me a better doctor already. More precise."

I told him I had missed my last two periods. And now there was the nausea. This morning I had burst into tears. "And I never do that."

"Is this a planned pregnancy?" Pierce said. "Have you told your husband?"

I chewed a little at the inside of my cheek. "He'll be very excited," I said confidently. "Ecstatic. I just don't want to get ahead of myself because . . . well, you're right, it is a surprise and it's thrown me for a bit of a loop." I forced myself to take a breath, to look out the window again. There was another tree, with immense leaves and seedpods as long as babies' arms. The word catalpa came to mind, but I had no idea whether that was right. "So no, I haven't told him yet," I said. "I want everything to be perfect before I do that. I don't want him to feel ambushed."

"Is that likely?"

"No, but I think it can happen, if the relationship's not real. If you're just playing along."

"Is that what you're doing?" He looked suddenly flustered,

like someone who has waded out of his depth and the sandy bottom has just fallen away. "You don't have to answer that, of course. It's not part of the —"

"The exam," I said. "*It's not part of the exam*. Did your teachers make that distinction: You need to remember *this*, and you don't need to remember *that*. I always thought that was a silly thing for them to do."

"I think they might have, yes."

We looked at each other, momentarily lost. He liked me, I think. I have relived this first meeting with him a thousand times and long ago came to the conclusion that we were flirting with each other. It makes no sense to me (it was 1954, after all, and I was pregnant, and as well as being far less attractive than Ray he was also my doctor!), but I'm sure that's what it was. Nowadays I would just say we were in the inexplicable thrall of some chemical event, some pheromonal tradewind. But then, that day in his presence, what I felt was completely drunk.

He told me he would need a urine sample and, if I agreed, a physical made sense. To make sure I was otherwise healthy. And possibly, if I had already missed two periods, he might be able to determine something with an abdominal. "But you know all this," he finished. "What do you think?"

I said that sounded perfect, just what I'd hoped for, and he handed me a sample cup and pointed the way to the bathroom.

I sat in there for a long time, clutching the warm vial of my own urine. And afterwards, while Dr. Pierce pushed with two extended fingers into my stomach and I stared up at the smooth underside of his chin, I resolved to tell Ray I had been here, whatever the outcome. If it turned out I wasn't pregnant, maybe we could talk about trying. And if I was, which I already knew would take two interminable days to determine, we could talk about changing some things at the house. Emptying one of the bedrooms and maybe repainting it. I had seen a rug that would look nice (it was orange, and soft) and a rocking chair for the corner. Putting out the word that if anyone had a crib they were finished with, I would be more than happy to pay a reasonable price.

"Well, I can't tell you anything categorically," the doctor said, easing me back to a sitting position. He snapped off his gloves. "And if you weren't in the business, I wouldn't tell you anything at all. But there is a tightness there, a certain tension. And you know as well as I do . . ."

I left his office in a giddy daze. He shook my hand again, I remember that much, then walked me through reception and wished me well. Did he place his hand in the small of my back as we rounded the last row of those too-blue chairs? That I can't be sure of. But he did say I should telephone him for the confirmation, and then I could decide whether I wanted to continue seeing him, or to transfer to a doctor at St. Joseph's. His voice came to me as if from the end of a long hall filled with cotton wool.

Tightness. I thought about that. He had discerned a tension in me that might indicate new life. Well, of course. I was *abuzz* with tension. If the true indicator of a pregnancy was tension, then I must be carrying twins. I grinned, felt the muscles in my cheeks tighten and brought a hand up to my mouth, in case someone decided I might be mad and dangerous, and called for a policeman.

What I needed was somewhere quiet to think. I didn't want to go home yet. I was on Yonge Street again, heading north, and in the muddy shade of the Imperial Cinema. It seemed as good a place as any. The red velvet seats. The darkness. The womby comfort of the place. I fished around in my purse for the seventy-five cents and passed it through the hole in the glass.

"One for *Niagara*," the bored girl said. "Enjoy the show."

When the film was over (it was wonderful, I adored it) I strolled south to the streetcar stop. After ninety minutes of flickering darkness, the soft September light was calming. I picked my way between dawdling shoppers. I would try to find out in the next day or two whether the Rainbow Cabins really existed. I thought it was possible. In the scenes where Marilyn Monroe is standing on the forecourt, pleading that her room not be given away, the falls are visible between the log buildings. And they are very convincing. There is no sense that another film is being projected over her shoulders, as there is when Marilyn is first arriving at Niagara in the car, and the road unspooling behind her is patently fake.

This mattered to me because I had decided, quite impulsively, that Ray and I should holiday in Niagara, even if only for a weekend. And what's more, we should stay at the Rainbow Cabins, if they were real, so that I could loll around seductively on the bed just as Marilyn Monroe does, the sheet pulled up over her breasts and her lips painted cherry red. There would be nothing wrong with the world if I was able to play that part for an hour or two. Perhaps I would let Ray in on my game and perhaps I would keep it to myself. Afterwards we could don those black slickers and ride the Maid of the Mist. We could clutch each other's hands and be astonished together by the power of all that water. It would be a dreamy few days.

As I've said, I was *so* innocent.

A crowd swarmed the streetcar. Children were waving small fabric pennants out of every window and trying to out-holler each other. Queen Street, to the horizon, was clotted with families singing their way west.

I fought through the crowd and pushed through Simpson's revolving doors. I asked the woman at the perfume counter what was happening.

She looked at me with astonishment. "You from Mars, Missus?"

I shook my head, in case the question wasn't rhetorical.

"Well it's the Bell girl, isn't it? She's getting real close. Just a mile or so now. They say she'll make it before dark if she don't have a heart attack or drown. We had the radio on, but when people got wind of what was happening they started to leave. I reckon our manager's just upset with the world because some lady ran wild with her dogs upstairs, broke a lot of fancy china."

I bought a scarf I didn't need and, as far as I remember, never wore, and then I telephoned the police station. It wasn't something Ray encouraged; he said it got him laughed at. But he also said most men were just jealous, particularly the ones who had seen me. "Just make it sound serious," he said.

"You're right, Mary," the duty sergeant told me. "I expect he's down there already. And you know Ray, he'll probably be the last one to leave too. Maybe you can keep some dinner warm for him, love."

I hung up on him. I didn't care if he thought me rude. I had recognized his voice. His name was Albert something; he was fresh from England. A constable in Coventry who had developed "a yen for something more exotic." His wife hadn't made the trip yet, Ray said, and Albert was making the most of his freedom. Which meant drinking it up every night with the Italians. He was loud and opinion on him was sharply divided. I was worried that his wife would actually arrive in Canada and willingly shackle herself to this ogre.

I decided to follow the crowd to the cne grounds. How in the world had I forgotten about the girl swimmer? I walked for a while alongside a group of boys in a brown uniform — were they boy scouts? — listening to their bright chatter brimming with vengeful ghosts and bottomless lakes. They jostled each other good-naturedly, and when one of them fell over they all stopped and waited for him to recover. Their energy and good spirits made me even happier than I'd been when I left the theatre. This is what people must mean, I thought, when they talked about going from strength to strength.

My plan, such as it was, was to either wait for Marilyn Bell to wade ashore or, if she floundered, take a bus the rest of the way home. History, though, was clearly in the making, and I thought that when the baby — if there was a baby — was old enough to understand, I would like to be able to point to faded newspaper clippings and say: You see that woman coming out of the water? And you see the crowd behind her? Well if you look very carefully, just to the right of her cap . . . there! You see that woman waving? That's me, waving at you because I had just found out about you, and I wanted to say hello. Seriously, love, I looked for the photographers, and I put myself in a place where I might get recorded. At the precise moment this photograph was taken I was thinking how much I loved you already. More than anything. And I still do. I always will. Look again. Right there.

I repeated it to myself all the way to the fairgrounds, kept pace with its rhythms: *I loved you already. More than anything. I still do. And always will. Look again.*

The crowds were phenomenal. If the radio had announced the arrival of visitors from space it would have looked the same down there. There was no hope, I realized, of finding Ray. I would just have to find a good vantage point for myself, one where it was at least possible to see glimmers of the lake.

But then, quite miraculously, he was there, standing out from the crowd as obviously as if he had been made of gold. I felt it was an omen.

I've said it before: he was a good-looking man. Not particularly broad-shouldered but I think he gave everyone the impression of solidity. He had the build of a football quarterback — he was fit and strong, agile, quick on his feet. Another way of putting it is that he resembled a movie star hired to play the part of a policeman. His stomach was flat and there was a single tough knot of hair at the centre of his chest that I loved to wind around a finger until he cried out. He looked good in shorts too, and for another twenty years women would clutch regularly at my forearm and ooh and aah over him pitifully: *What a dreamboat, Mary! What a winner!*

At the lake, I clung to him. He was distracted, but I understood that; he was on duty, and with so many people there anything could happen. The important thing was for us to see her come in together. The three of us would see her rise like a spirit from the soft swells.

And then it actually happened and there were so many photographs taken that even the darkest corners of the world were brightened. The air smelled sharply of magnesium and a blue-white cloud drifted over all our heads, as if from a nearby battle. But in the following days I scoured every newspaper and never saw myself in any of them.

Ray drove me home when I know he thought he shouldn't, and I appreciated that. I fell asleep beside him on the drive, and dreamed of I don't know what. I think, I really do, that it was the last time in my life I slept without even a smidgen of fear or worry. I felt sure that the world, as I sank into it, was a perfect place. I thought Ray was the perfect man for me. It remained that way until I woke up.

RAY

What the hell was I supposed to say? How about: By the way, Katie, I was having a torrid affair back then. Do you think you can find space for that in your article? Or this: Mary thinks I'm a terrible cad, Katie. In fact, she wouldn't mind a half-hour with you when we're done, so she can elaborate. Or should I have struck a piteous note: Please leave me to die in peace, my sweet girl. It turns out my acts aren't worth the paper you'll use to publicize them. Yes, I'll show you out. So sorry to have wasted your time.

Perhaps the last option is the best. With that one I might still have felt her cheek against mine at the door. A bit embarrassing, though, I must admit, to have Mary read it all.

And I should be ashamed, she's right. Lust isn't becoming in a man my age and in my condition, which is to say married, and also hacking hard at death's door.

But I'm not sorry. Were I in a more robust condition I would climb onto the roof and shout it loud enough for all the neighbours to hear — *I'm not ashamed! I'm not, I'm not!* Because it's too late for that. Yes, I'm sad, even depressed some days, sure, and scared (to death) of the coming days and weeks. I'm horrified by the shambles we made of things and I have regrets. Yes regrets, I have a few. Isn't there a song? But never ashamed, however much Mary would be pleased if I was.

The emphysema (such a breathless word, don't you think?) means that there are long stretches of each day now when I can't breathe without help. There are great modernist renovations afoot in my lungs. Walls are being torn down to make more room. It's all open-plan and empty spaces in there. But the blood runs in those walls, you see, and draws oxygen from the adjacent open spaces. So you take out the damn walls and presto, the blood can't get close enough to the air. Eventually this new architecture will kill me. So about now self-pity strikes me as more appropriate than shame. And I do give in to that. Late some evenings I haul out the Scotch Mary hasn't found yet (I don't think) and I sit shuddering in the window that looks over our garden. She would be thrilled to know that. He's human after all, she would say. Or who knows, perhaps she would just laugh and turn away.

Her problem, the five-decade sticking point, is Alice. My denial of her for so long. The mere mention of her name is still enough to start Mary on a fevered hunt for the carving knife. You see, Mary has always held that I must have been with Alice while she — Mary — was at the doctor's office that day in September. That I was destroying our lives even as she was confirming the origins of another. We have walked these fight-filled streets so often we know each other's every step. And, though I have never admitted it before, not once, she is probably right. Yes, while she was being examined on that table, legs wide, I was most likely descending in a humid department store elevator with Alice, praying the doors would never open. And while Mary wandered the streets in a daze afterwards, Alice and I played like children in the shallow waters at the bottom of a ravine. In fact, that very evening, Mary fell asleep in the same passenger seat that Alice had occupied only an hour or two earlier, whispering her crude endearments into my ear, her tongue like a lizard's.

Alice wanted me to handcuff her (it makes me sweat even now to recall this). But first she wanted me to track her through the dappled parkland and bring her to ground at the edge of the stream. *Chase me!* she implored. She would get quite dirty, she hoped, and she ran her hand suggestively over the front of her skirt to indicate where she wanted the grass and mud to end up. There would be leaves in her hair, and when I pulled her to her feet there would be mud smeared like camouflage across her face. "And you would have me by the arm, here, above the elbow, Ray. Not rough or anything, but so if I tried to twist away from you it would hurt. And probably it would leave a bruise, two bruises, one small one where your thumb was, on the inside, and then a longer one on the outside from the rest of your fingers."

What honest man could resist?

Our day had begun in the elevator at Simpson's. I was there because an old woman had allowed her poodles — giant, ornately coiffed dogs with sopping grins — to run amok in the china department. She was one of those women who thought the world belonged to her; but the department manager was even more unlikable, a sniveling, greasy man with a good suit and too-long fingernails. I remember I asked the woman — Beaton, I think her name was — to wait in the manager's office while I tried to talk him out of pressing charges. Her dogs put their paws against the glass like idiot twin brothers surveying a factory floor. When I went in to talk to her she was rifling through the man's desk. She scowled at me, daring me to challenge her.

I offered her an amicable smile.

"He's a little shit," she began. "Isn't he, William?" One of the poodles stopped pawing at the glass long enough to give the impression he was paying attention. "I used to eat men like that for breakfast." She lazily pushed around whatever was inside the desk. "Such a ditchwater sort of life," she said. "Don't you agree?" She held up a dull-bladed penknife, a small silver flask. "I mean for this poor fellow. I suppose I can understand why he would need to exercise some small authority once in a while, just to feel like a man." She pushed the drawer closed. "But to waste a person's time like this is unforgivable. And by the way, do you know that woman out there? She does seem rather interested in you."

I looked over my shoulder and there was Alice, luminous at the centre of a grove of leggy teak carvings that bore titles such as *Entwined Lovers* and *Friends*, and which I had already dismissed as kitsch. She stared at us blatantly and I am sure I must have blushed. "I think maybe she's just amused by all of us," I said gruffly, aiming for indifference.

We watched Alice sashay for the elevator. The manager was on all-fours, coaxing splinters of glass onto a sheet of paper, his backside protruding rudely through the vent in his jacket. "This isn't one of that man's proudest hours," I said. "No one likes to be brought to his knees."

"How very clever of you, detective. You also read books, I suppose. And perhaps you even cook. Or is that beneath you?" I feel she was probably mocking me slightly. She evidently found me stiff, which disappointed me, though I can't imagine why it mattered what she thought.

That room smelled intensely of her dogs and of the carpet, which was frayed along the edges and crooked, as if it had been cut and laid too quickly. I opened the door for her and her dogs trailed her so obediently across the floor it was hard to conceive of their running amok without being told to do so.

I pocketed my notebook, and waited for the elevator. I watched the bronze needle ticking from two to three to four. Then the doors opened and there she was again — Alice, I mean — in her fetching green suit. A light buried in the elevator's ceiling lit up her hair so that she appeared nearly angelic. I stepped aside to let her pass but she remained where she was. The doors tried to intervene and she raised a gloved arm calmly to stop them. "Get on," she said.

I stood behind her and the two of us gazed upward as the needle reversed its crawl. "I could stop it," she said.

"Stop what? Following me?"

"The elevator. I could trap us between floors. These old machines are very cranky. We could be stuck for hours."

"You shouldn't do that," I said.

She faced me. "But it would be so perfect, Ray. You could save me, eventually, by breaking us out of here. Couldn't you climb out through the roof or something? Shimmy up the cables?"

I eyed the solid lid doubtfully.

"Perhaps the floor," she said and stamped a heel into the carpet. We were almost to the ground.

I tried to be stern. "That woman noticed you."

She placed a hand against my chest (I feel it still). "I frighten you."

"You do a lot of things to me," I admitted.

"I didn't know you were up there," she said. "I swear."

"I hope not."

She brought up her other hand and took hold of my lapels. She pushed me against the back wall and I felt the brass rail against my hips.

It was wrong, I understood that. It marked an escalation, a spiraling. In her lemony one-bedroom above the furniture store on Roncesvalles it all made perfect sense. Lying on my back with her astride me, her pale slip gathered around her waist and falling from one shoulder, it was ideal. But here, with the doors about to open, revealing us to the world, it was foolhardy. I very nearly summoned the energy to push her away. But whether impaired by lethargy or desire I didn't quite manage it. Instead I allowed her to lean into me — her hips deftly slotting between my own, her minted breath flowering in my mouth, her hands on my arms, guiding them around her.

In the wilds of High Park, a little later, I asked her, "And why would I be chasing you?" The idea of bruises, a physical evidence of my transgressions, made me uncomfortable. I was turned around in the seat so I could see her in the back. There was plenty of room but Alice had angled her legs to the side as if she was jammed into a tight spot. Her skirt had ridden up so one stockinged thigh was exposed, and I was having a hard time concentrating on her face. Alice had her hands behind her back and was demonstrating what she'd look like after I caught her. Bedraggled didn't quite do it, so calculated was her disarray. So completely disarming.

"Because that's what you do, Ray. You chase people down and you handcuff them."

"Only if I have to."

"You don't *have* to do anything, Ray. But I thought you might want to." She swung her legs impatiently. She wanted me to play. "You might even have to remove some of my clothes — for safety."

I didn't know if I wanted to play. There were so many obvious reasons why it shouldn't happen.

"Just show them to me. Let me feel them. Let's pretend the chase part is done already, and you've bundled me in the back here, and the steel is cutting into my wrists."

"The cuffs?"

"Yes, where are they?"

I leaned over and dug the handcuffs out of the glove compartment. I showed her how the mechanism worked, how once they were on her wrists she wouldn't be able to remove them without this key. Which I dropped into my pocket.

Alice twisted in her seat so her back was to me, and knotted her hands together. I was reminded of those teak creations in Simpson's and wondered if that was where she'd got the idea. "I want them behind me," she said.

I glanced at the shadowed park around us and, when I saw no one, I slipped the loops around her wrists. I felt the tendons jumping around, saw the buried track of her veins. Her pulse thumped once into my hand, like a small bird gliding into a closed window. And when I snapped the cuffs shut and she winced, part of me wished that I could drive her to the station and book her into a cell and never see her again. That wish, I knew, was a symptom of regret, regret for what had already passed between us and for what was surely still to come.

Alice fell back against the seat. She grimaced again as her own weight put pressure on her arms. "I like it," she said haltingly. "I like that you did it. I like how it feels."

I told her I was glad, even though I wasn't, not really. But would she turn around again, I said, and let me free her, because this whole situation was making me nervous.

"I will if you'll at least walk with me down to that stream there, Ray." She indicated with a toss of her head the sandy path that wound between pines.

I told her that wasn't a good idea.

"Then I stay like this." She pouted. "A prisoner of your unwillingness."

And so I thought about it, and constructed three or four scenarios in which I might have to accompany a pretty woman to the edge of a stream, all of them more or less believable.

But all the way down to the water she rubbed her wrists dramatically. Wanting to remind me of what I'd done to her. I tried to counteract this by pointing out gravel flats where salmon would spawn, and said that even though this stream was only eight, ten feet across, I knew how to go about fishing it. How there were perch in here, and even pike up to four or five pounds. Sunfish, I said, and smallmouth bass. All of them hunkering down about now for the winter that was just around the corner.

She was amused by me. She sat herself on the heaved-up rootmass of a birch that had fallen across the stream and rested her head in a cradle made of her hands, her elbows on her knees. She smiled impishly. "I think I might be falling for you, Ray Townes. Did you know that?"

"I didn't, no. I think you are just toying with me, and any day now you'll move on."

"Would you be sad if I did that?"

"I don't know," I said truthfully. "At first, of course." I reached up and tore an oak leaf free of its branch. I set it gently onto the surface of the stream and watched it glide around the next curve. "But I suppose I'd be relieved too."

"Because of your wife."

I didn't like to talk about Mary with Alice and I knew there was nothing unique in that. "Of course. If we stopped this now, Mary would never have to know."

"And now that I might be falling for you," she said, "how does that make you feel? Does it make you happy, or does it make your life too complicated? Because I can stop, you know. Just like that!" She snapped her fingers.

"The vain part of me is very happy," I said.

"How big a part is that?"

"I'm quite vain," I told her, and crouched down so I could

look at her levelly, and also so we weren't as visible from the parking spots above. I tossed a flattish stone at the water, wanting to see it skip to the far bank, but I got the angle all wrong and the stone drowned itself. "Hell, all this excites me, Alice. I don't want to stop. I just don't know how we can manage it. And if you fall for me, then you'll want more from me. And I can't give you more. As it is, I'm going to wonder for the next week whether anyone besides the old dear in Simpson's saw us together."

"You can't worry about that. Or you can, but then we may as well stop seeing each other. People do these things precisely *because* they're risky," she said. "Men do anyways. That's what gets them all fired up. It's a thrill, Ray. Don't you think?" She left her perch and brushed off the dry bark that clung to her legs. She pushed me onto my back but I sat up again and put my hands out behind me. She said, "Don't worry, Ray, I'm not going to attack you."

"Attack me *again*, you mean," I said, trying to make her smile. "Like you did in the elevator."

"That was fun, though, wasn't it, Ray? I wanted it to be fun." She kicked at the soles of my shoes.

I was frustrating her. The afternoon had become tinged with sadness. Analysis was the enemy of our relationship. I was so much better in the safe half-light of her apartment. "You got me going," I said. "There's no denying that. Now help an old man up so he can properly show his appreciation."

She grabbed my arm and leaned back so I could cantilever upright. I held her around the waist and she looked up into my face. I kissed her lightly.

"We can do whatever you want," she said. "Everything or nothing. And not just this afternoon. I'm not trying to scare you off. I like you more and more, Ray. Your wife's a lucky woman."

"She wouldn't think so if she could see us."

"But she can't, can she?" Alice broke free and skipped away from me. She scooped up a handful of leaves and twigs and threw them at the water. "There's no one for a mile right now. That's why I suggested this place. I'm not crazy. I wouldn't risk everything."

"I know you wouldn't," I said untruthfully. The headlights on the Buick were just visible, like a steel monster that had crawled to the edge to watch us. "So come on. I have to get down to the lake."

I followed her up the slope and opened the rear door for her. I had disappointed her and I was sorry for that. She was trying hard to make the risk worthwhile for me. I sometimes felt that she was trying so hard to please me that I didn't know who she really was.

One of my favourite things to do was sit in the pastry shop where she worked and just watch her. To nurse an oil-slicked coffee in the back booth as she worked the cash register or wiped down a table, or took the silver tongs and rearranged the pies and turnovers with the precision and concentration of a surgeon. Even the way she responded to the bearish advances of the owner, a barrel-chested Portuguese man named Joseph Tavares, made me laugh. She let him crowd her by the display cases, and even reach around for pies no one had ordered, nearly suffocating himself in her cleavage. Because that was what Tavares demanded of his employees, and she would be out of work if she complained. But when Tavares walked away Alice would stick out her tongue and grab the tongs and jerk them upwards sharply. "I'd like to stick them up his ass," she'd say. "And then open them *like this!*"

I watched her for weeks in June before finally talking to her. For those first, nearly innocent conversations, at the end of her shift we used to decamp to the much grittier and less illuminated coffee house next door. She told me she had moved here from Cornwall, along the St. Lawrence River, where her father ran a dive named Olympia Billiards, and her mother had died nine months ago in a car accident. Her father, she said, had driven off the road into a drainage ditch while he was drunk. He was either knocked unconscious by the impact or he had passed out. Whichever it was, her mother had drowned when the car tipped onto its side. "She made dents in the ceiling trying to get out," Alice told me. "Her boot prints were on the window."

"But your father escaped."

"I don't think he even got wet. They found him in the morning, still passed out. You know something? He never cried. He never said sorry. And he expected me to move back home and take care of the house."

"You were living somewhere else?"

"I lived in Brockville. I worked at a bread factory, monitoring the slicer. I rented a room downtown. I was dating a boatmaker from New York State. I truly thought I had escaped. My mother would take the bus down to visit me every second week. In the summer we would sit by the water and talk. I would bring the lunch and we would watch Tom work — that was his name. In the winter we sat in my room or we went to the library, or even to a movie together. We would talk about why she should leave Dad, and then she would explain why she couldn't: she was too old; he was too dependent on her; what else would she do? *I'm in the service of the Gord*, she liked to say. That was Dad's name: Gordon. She was a wonderful woman, but she worked too hard to make everyone else happy, and didn't pay enough attention to herself."

"So did you move back?" I was looking at her hands, still studded with sugar from the doughnuts I had watched her scoop from the fryer half an hour earlier.

"Uh-huh. For a month. Thirty-one hellish days. Until I realized that he was a lost cause."

"Too bad your mother never saw that."

"She thought she had to save him or he would just drown in the bottle." She stared through teary eyes at the napkin dispenser. "Ain't that an ironic sentiment?"

A week later she stepped off the bus in Toronto.

"And now, every day the sun rises, I think that I get a chance to live the life my mother was afraid to."

"Does your boyfriend know where you are?"

"He knows I'm here somewhere. But he'll get the idea. Tom's not someone to sit by the telephone."

"How about your father?"

She crumpled the napkin and set the tight ball on her saucer, resting against her coffee cup. "Nope."

"Fair enough," I said.

"I told his lawyer, though. Because one day he's going to kill himself the way he killed my mother, and I can go back for his funeral and I can close down that poolhall of his, and sell that dingy little house he wouldn't let them move out of, and I can rescue my mother's belongings. And then I figure if he wasn't in debt up to his ears maybe I can buy a little place here in Toronto with the proceeds. Don't you think that sounds like a good plan?"

"It's a very comprehensive plan considering the man might live another thirty or forty years."

"Yeah but at least I'll be ready," she said, and stared at me fiercely, challenging me to contradict her, or tell her she was a callous young woman, neither of which I was inclined to do.

"Tell me about you," she said. She had ordered a slice of lemon meringue pie and was separating the snowy cap from the filling, letting the breakaway floes melt down to nothing on her tongue. "You gotta be married. Sure you are. There's the ring, right there." Pointing her fork "Tell me about her." She laughed at my discomfort, offered me a bite of her pie ("Not the top, though, don't you dare; just the lemon and the pastry"), which I was too afraid to take.

And so, feeling queasy all the while, I told her about Mary. I wondered a lot about that afterwards. Did I just not want to have to lie to her the way I was going to have to lie to Mary, if anything came of this? Was I trying to build some sort of fence between us? Or the opposite: paint a desperate picture of my marriage? I didn't know the answer. But watching the meringue melt between her lips, I knew one thing too well: the torture begins right here.

Back in the Buick with her, bound for the lake and my handcuffs hidden away where they belonged, I thought that Alice probably had some respect and admiration for this girl, Marilyn Bell, who the radio said was nearing the shore now. But Alice said, "Nah, she's different from me. I'm not that tough. I'd let the eels have me, then I'd just sink quietly to the bottom."

I told her I didn't believe that for a minute, which seemed to please her.

I dropped her off before I went through the intersection at Lakeshore Boulevard. I knew how disappointed she was. She would have wanted to walk arm-in-arm through the crowd with me, and who could blame her. But there were limits, I said. And even being in the car with her, with all these people swarming about, was definitely brushing up against one of those limits.

"But the Buick is unmarked," she protested.

I laughed at her. "Everyone knows from all the aerials that this is a police car. I don't want people being pleased with themselves for identifying me, and then wondering who the impressive dame is."

And so she left me, trapped in a long line of traffic. She picked her way along the grassy median. Someone hit the horn as she passed and she smiled, as if she appreciated that sort of attention. Encouraged, the man followed up with a whistle but that brought a quick reproving scowl. All down the line I saw men's heads shifting left so they could watch her walk.

But it's *me* she's falling for, I thought, so satisfied at that moment with my complicated life. None of you obvious fools. Just me.

By the way, it seems Mary has abandoned me, at least temporarily. And taken my daughter with her. A few minutes ago I heard the prolonged electric whine of the garage door. I shuffled promptly to the refrigerator and removed some cheese, a half-glass of her wine. I defrosted an olive and rosemary bun in the microwave and brought everything back here to the desk. I feel furtive nowadays, like a criminal in my own home. In all the important ways I am completely alone. We both are.

My official duties at the lake didn't amount to much. Wander, mostly. Keep an eye on the crowd. Check licence plates against the list I kept in the car. Easy.

When I joined the force in 1947 at the age of 23, I walked the beat along Queen Street from Dovercourt all the way over to Roncesvalles, usually at night. The job bored me but I was calmed by that boredom. Not once did I feel I was in danger, and that was a marked change from my stint in Italy when every day was utter shit.

I spent most of those first months on the force checking that doors were locked, shining my flashlight over the midnight inventories of drug stores and butchers. Walking through piss-stinking alleys to make sure no one was suffocating on their own vomit. Hauling drunks out of the Gladstone so the night clerk could get on with adding up the day's receipts. The route never changed and after a few weeks I felt like I was sleepwalking.

In the early days I arrested plenty for disorderly conduct, thinking to establish myself as a no-nonsense sort of cop, but that number dropped off when I twigged to the fact that each arrest meant a daytime court appearance, which meant cutting into my sleep and not getting paid for the privilege. From then on, I was a more tolerant (and more respected) cop. I became known as something of a diplomat and as an arbitrator between men fogged in by whisky or beer, or simply bewildered by the horrific fact of being alive when so many of their comrades had died. Which isn't to say there weren't those who spat on the sidewalk behind me — that was the nature of the work — but the respect most showed me was responsible for getting me onto a motorcycle, and then, in near-record time, out of the uniform altogether.

At the lake I checked plates and came up empty. I scanned for Alice from the top of the bleachers. All day I had heard radio updates, and boys from the *Telegram* and the *Daily Star* were hawking the latest editions from every street corner, but I was still taken aback by the size of the crowd. There were people five or six deep all along the shore, and more were streaming across from the fairgrounds. Children had been allowed to congregate in front of the adults, while other more industrious or indentured kids were selling chocolate and cigarettes from trays slung around their necks. Free newspapers were being distributed and every few seconds a flashbulb popped and someone else's grinning mug was preserved for posterity. A television camera had been set up on a hulking tripod so it looked like a giant spider. A man in a sober grey suit, but with no hat, marched back and forth with a microphone, swinging his arms and rehearsing his lines.

Out on the water a small flotilla had gathered near the

shore. The oily rumblings of outboards and the metallic slap of rigging was like applause. And perhaps a half-mile away was the collection of craft that people said was surrounding the swimmer herself. These included a boat from the *Telegram*, which had sponsored Marilyn's swim and another from the *Star*, which had foolishly put its money behind the American, who was now recuperating from her failed effort somewhere in New York State. A third was delivering Marilyn's coach. And indeed, when I strained I could make out, or so I imagined, the intermittent splash of a tired young woman crashing her way home.

Some people were beginning to point, to yell out, as if their encouragements might somehow travel out to her, act as a beacon so that the eventual landing would occur directly in front of them. On the bleachers, men were stamping their feet in unison. Beneath them, on the bent grass and beset by empty bottles and hotdog wrappers, a baby girl had managed to find sleep in her father's arms. This man had given up all hope of following the excitement. Instead he leaned contentedly against one of the steel uprights and hummed quietly. I envied him, or was warmed by the sight of him. Something anyway. He stopped me in my tracks for a moment. It was a little past seven o'clock in the evening.

I skirted along the back of the crowd. There were pickpockets here, there had to be; purse snatchers working alone and in pairs. The Exhibition grounds were where they spent their September afternoons, putting in long days so that they wouldn't starve when the more impenetrable coats of winter appeared.

I introduced myself to a constable and for a few minutes we chatted. He was twenty-one years old, he said, and I realized that the kid must think me an old man, nearly. After some brief exchanges about the swimmer and the crowd, the weather, the impending darkness, we fell silent and just watched the girl get closer. There were concerned whispers that she was tiring and wouldn't make it, that her coach was shouting himself hoarse just trying to keep her going. I didn't see how anybody could know those things. Surely it was just that the undeniable fact of her being there, not a quarter mile out now, her white cap appearing and disappearing in the gentle chop, seemed too good to be true.

I threaded between prams and cameras, fedoras and skirts, to the seawall. Two kids, one from the *Telegram* and one from the *Star*, were trying to outshout each other. And then one threw a punch and they fell like skinny kittens to the ground. Neither of them could have weighed more than sixty pounds and I was content to let them go at it.

The cbc crew hauled their camera and tripod over and that seemed to distract the boys from their fury. They grabbed their empty satchels and sped away from each other. I thought I recognised Pierre Berton, the writer from *Maclean's*, interviewing a crowd of children. He was a gangly young man back then, in brown suit and a low cap, down on one knee with his notepad open and scribbling mightily. We had met once at City Hall when Berton was reporting on the creation of the Municipality of Metropolitan Toronto and had just finished interviewing the chairman, Big Daddy Gardiner. I had been escorting a lawyer across to the courthouse. The lawyer and Berton had known each other, and when I got a chance I expressed my admiration for the reporter's work. Berton had seemed surprised that anyone should recognise him. "My wife," I explained. "She reads me everything you write."

"You poor man," Berton said. And then he suggested with a grin that maybe it was time I learned to read for myself. We trotted down the front steps together, before Berton waved and disappeared into what looked to me like a Jaguar parked at the street.

Now, at the side of the lake, I looked about, hoping

someone else might confirm the man's identity, or the reporter would lift his face clear of the cap's shadow. At my side, though, and grinning up at me just as brightly as I remembered Berton doing, which is to say as if she had just managed a major coup, or saved someone's life, was Mary.

I was panicked at first. Pierre Berton was a distant memory. I felt leaden, rooted to the ground. There was the sensation of being completely obvious, as if when I looked into her eyes, Mary could see Alice's face. And so I looked down at her hands instead, saw them fumbling for mine, bringing them up to her lips. I had no idea, of course, that she had come from the doctor's office, and that she suspected she was pregnant and was just bursting to tell me. I was ignorant of all that.

"I'm *so* pleased to see you," she gushed. "I didn't think it was possible. Isn't this crazy?" Marilyn Bell had swum to within a few hundred yards and the noise of the crowd was rising.

"What are you doing here?" I shouted.

She kissed my hand again and so I brought her hands up to my own lips and held them there. Then I said, "I'm just shocked." In case she was wondering.

"I couldn't get away from it," Mary said breathlessly. "I was out, and it was on the radio all the time. The streetcar drivers were talking about it, and there's that picture in the newspaper of her waving as she goes into the water. I just didn't want to miss it. And I knew you were down here *somewhere*."

"There are nearly a hundred thousand people down here. They go all the way west to Sunnyside. It's a miracle you found me."

"I didn't expect to," she said. "But I'm so glad. We'll be together for it. Do you think this is where she'll touch?"

"I think it might be, yes."

There were more flashbulbs popping now, and darkness was gaining on us. Mary craned to see where the photographers were. She was still smiling. "That's so exciting," she said.

I looked at her, really looked, and even though her gaze was directed out over the water, at the hundreds of lit-up and tinkling boats that had parted subtly to let the swimmer and her escorts through, I could tell that Mary was aware of me looking. She raised her chin slightly and her lips parted involuntarily, in a pure expression of love for this moment. The camera flashes outlined her silhouette so starkly that I was reminded, with the deep blue sky behind her and her face so pale, of those Wedgwood plates her mother had collected on a high glass shelf in the sunroom in Hamilton.

She was going to cry, I realized, and marveled that an event like this could affect her so intensely. I put my arm around her shoulder and she nuzzled into me and together we watched as the girl drew closer.

When she was inside one hundred yards, two Toronto Lifesavers skiffs advanced on her as if to intercept. They were being rowed by boys in dark caps. One of them was shirtless but in dungarees. What light there was reflected off his muscled shoulders and the polished oarlocks. Mary whispered that he would be in the newspapers dressed like that and wasn't it a shame, but I thought those were undoubtedly the boy's favourite pants, chosen specially for the event. The boys swung around to escort Marilyn Bell to dry land. It was a shade past eight in the evening now and as fine a way as I could imagine to earn a paycheque.

The moment the swimmer rose up out of the water, her white bathing cap rising like a moon, and the water running from her bathing suit as if it had no right to be there in the first place, the audience seemed to still for a beat, to lose itself entirely in what was happening. There was an instant, I thought, where a little space was created, a fold in time almost big enough for a man to crawl into. And when the crowd erupted into cheers a fraction later, and hats were thrown high into the air, many of them never to be reunited with their owners, and children shrieked with excitement and begged to be told what had just happened, and women, including Mary, dropped a few exultant tears onto their husbands' shoulders, I considered this inability to somehow slip through that open seam and move about the stilled crowd unnoticed, to be an opportunity missed.

Marilyn's coach hauled her into his low launch and another cheer went up. The girl waved and blankets were wrapped around her. The coach held his student to him tightly, as if she were a child he had lost many years before and had now redis- covered, unexpectedly, in the shallows of a darkening lake twenty-one miles wide. The magnesium lights burst almost constantly for a few more seconds, and then through great blis- ters of static a radio announcer proclaimed this one of the great moments in the nation's history. Women counted their children while their husbands congratulated each other and seemed to take full responsibility for this stupendous success.

Mary kept a grip on my hand as I led her slowly back to the parking lot. I was tired and excited — I was not immune to what had transpired — but I was nervous too. It wasn't that I thought Alice would announce herself, but it wouldn't have sur- prised me to see her shadowing us, just as she had trailed me at the department store. The risk involved in such action would seem negligible to her, and yet at that moment the idea was almost more than I could bear.

Mary asked me what I was looking for. Did I need her to go home alone? It was okay if I did, she said; it was only a mile and it was a lovely evening. "It is a lovely evening, isn't it Ray?"

I reassured her that it was, and that I had only been looking for a young constable I had befriended. No, of course I would take her home.

"Did you want to find him? I can wait in the car." She was

always slightly too considerate, I think. It has made it easy for people to take advantage. "No, I want to leave with you now," I said. "I want to take my beautiful wife home." That was all that was important.

Before we had even crossed Lakeshore Boulevard, or begun the long gentle climb through the back streets to our new house, with its stiff young sapling on the front lawn, Mary had fallen asleep. Stopped at a traffic light I saw that one of her shoes had come off and lay on its side in front of her foot. I pulled over to the side of the road and shifted into neutral and then pulled back hard on the handbrake. I knew how that foot would feel in my hand, could summon the memory in immaculate detail. I bent over the gear shift and reached down. She stirred at my gentle touch and then was still again. I leaned over a little further and kissed her kneecap.

So there it is. What you've wanted all these years, Mare: some of the *nitty gritty*. More will have to wait, though, because I hear the plastic splashes of shopping bags as they hit the floor; you have returned home. With more shoes, I wonder? One of you will poke your head in soon, check that I didn't die while you were away. The sight of the wine glass will annoy whichever of you comes, and I must quickly say that I have always thought that such a ludicrous instinct in people. For heaven's sake, give the man dying of lung cancer a cigarette; pour a glass of plonk for the poor sop with his pickled liver. What more harm can it do? Deprivation is pointless now. As is so much of what we feel. But enough: footsteps.

MARY

I have been thinking about our neighbours on Aldringham, a young Italian couple, Frank and Gina. He was a fireman (which gave him and Ray plenty to talk about), and Gina worked in the mayor's office. I liked them both, but her more than him. He was bit too quiet, broody; I felt scrutinized a lot. And he was also a drinker. Many times Gina had to pretty much carry him home.

Gina, though, was truly brilliant, by which I think I really mean that she was smart, yes, but also that she was beautiful and glamorous. I was jealous of her, and of the way Ray looked at her. But I repressed those feelings, discounted them because I loved having her as my friend. The day we moved into the house she appeared at the door with flowers and a vase to put them in. My niggling fears about the neighbourhood evaporated immediately. I was so grateful to her. They were over at our house for a while on the same night I told Ray about the baby.

Frank had such big plans. He was telling us how Aldringham was nice and all, but they weren't going to settle for this, not him and his Genie.

He was better than us, that seemed to be his message. Only he didn't look like he quite believed it. There was a desperate look to him, a bruised quality. I held an ice cube in my mouth, kept it there when the more comfortable thing to do would have been to shoo it back into the glass. He was making me sad, I remember that. He wanted everything to change just when I wanted to keep everything as it was. Whatever we had done to get here, I wanted more of it.

Frank, though, as if he read my mind, was already trying to clarify. He wasn't intending to give up their house, he said; not at all. "We love you guys." He just wanted a place to get away. He had his eye on a cottage, he said. It was on one of the Toronto islands. One thousand dollars bought a one-hundred-year lease-hold on the property.

"What happens after the hundred years?" I asked. "Do you lose it?" I had never heard of such an arrangement.

"You're looking at the wrong end of this," Frank told me. He blew cigarette smoke into the centre of our circle.

Gina said she was going to at least look at the place. "Frank says when we're not using it we can rent it out."

Ray said he thought it was a damn fine plan. But he had that air of reckless high spirits that usually meant he wasn't taking the world seriously.

"The thing is," Frank said, "we'd like your opinion. Both your opinions. We thought we could get you over there. Maybe next weekend. The sixteenth or the seventeenth. You're good with structural things, Ray. And you, Mary," he added almost apologetically, turning to me, "you can give us an aesthetic judgment. You know: are we out of our minds, or is this a really great deal."

I said, "I'd thought about us going down to Niagara that weekend too, Ray. A visit to the Falls."

Ray looked at me, understandably puzzled. I hadn't told him yet that I'd seen *Niagara*, probably because seeing that film was so inextricably wrapped up with my first visit to the doctor. Doctor Pierce had confirmed the pregnancy two weeks before, but every time I thought I would tell Ray, something stopped me. Not doubt, I don't think, or any crisis, just a sense that the moment had to be perfect. That evening, though, I was determined. The moment our neighbours left, however tired we were, however much vodka Ray had thrown back, I would sit him down.

I said, "I just thought it would be nice. Romantic."

"We could all go," Gina said. "I'd love to see Niagara. One of the world's wonders, right?"

"So long as we look at the cottage first," Frank insisted. "We'll lose it otherwise."

And soon afterwards, with those plans more or less made (how awfully undone they came), Frank and Gina made their excuses.

"I want to talk to you," I told Ray when we had the house to ourselves again. "I bought some Scotch. Could you manage a small one? The man at the store said it was very fine."

Ray was immediately suspicious. He positively squirmed. "Not if you expect me to think straight," he said doubtfully. In hindsight I imagine he was petrified. My wanting to talk probably sounded like a challenge. Instead of nervous I must have appeared angry.

"Don't worry, Ray. I think you could drink the whole bottle and still not forget what I'm going to tell you."

So he sat obediently and accepted a tumbler. He downed nearly the whole shot. His eyes watered. I thought he might come down with a coughing fit, but he fought it off. I crossed in front of him twice, three times, gathering steam, trying to sort the words that must come. I felt like an elastic band being wound around a pole. "I've been to the doctor's, Ray. More than once."

"You're sick?" He perched on the lip of his chair. It's quite possible he was drunk, the room spinning a little around him.

I shook my head. Put my hand on top of his. "No. I'm not sick. But I'm not doing this very well either, am I? I was going to tell Gina, just so I could practice. But I thought that wouldn't be fair. And anyway, you're not supposed to say anything to anyone for a while. Just in case."

I fell back, and felt as I did so that this was what they meant by a swoon. I was closer to lying down than to sitting.

Anyway, Ray looked as if he was afraid to guess anymore, and had decided to let me talk. How poorly we knew each other. I was frustrated. I could feel the moment unraveling.

"And, well, I telephoned him again this morning."

"Him? Who is him?"

"Sorry. The doctor. I've had tests performed, Ray." I thought it *must* be dawning on him now. There were plot lines on television that were more subtle. He had to be drunk. I should have waited longer. In an hour we would undress in front of each other and I had wanted this scene to end with Ray lying beside me with a hand on my stomach. Perhaps even for him to touch that nascent bump with his lips. But as it was, it seemed more likely I would have to turn away from him.

Ray refilled his glass and sipped timidly. Above the rim of the glass his eyes narrowed and then widened. An owl, I thought. Ray put his glass aside, aiming for (and nearly hitting) one of the crocheted placemats my mother had given us.

"I'm thinking . . ."

"I see that." I was very faintly amused.

". . . that you're about to tell me you're pregnant." I held my breath, did it so I could listen to my husband breathe. The world had stopped revolving, I was convinced of it. Were it not for the firm grip I had on the arms of my chair the sudden deceleration would have thrown me clear into space.

"I shouldn't have had this." Ray held up his glass again and regarded it suspiciously, as if it might have contained hemlock, or morphine. He rubbed vigorously at his face. Grunted behind his hand. But eventually he emerged with a loopy, cockeyed grin.

He was . . . happy! He was thrilled.

"Wow!" he said, trying to sum up his excitements. "My God, Mare, you must have been dying. The suspense."

"Tell me again that you're happy," I commanded. I had no strength in my legs. There was a diamond sheen over everything. He had come through for me. My Ray.

"I'm over the moon," he said. His eyes were a fog of tears, his hands were shaking. He was what he said he was; the news had made a rag doll of him. "I knew something was going on," he stuttered.

I was happy just to watch him fumble through the emotions. I saw a ball dropping through a maze, finding its way home.

"Christ," he said.

I told him it was okay. Strength was coming back to me first. Ray was like a boy again. I would have to take care of him too.

"You're a marvel," he said.

I leaned over his chair and kissed him between the eyes. He held my hips, pulled me into him. I arranged myself on top of him, my head resting against his. Together we stared absent-mindedly into the room that would soon contain another. We would have to protect the infant from its sharp edges. Buy special food. Ray could push him on a red wagon through the brilliant spring streets, the maples budding deliriously above them. Because it would be April when he arrived. *Him*. I put a hand to the side of Ray's face and kissed his cheek.

"Thank you," I said.

"For what?"

"For being a wonderful husband."

RAY

The article was in the newspaper today. Jenny tossed it on the bed as casually as she could manage. But they talked about it, I'm sure; whether they could reasonably prevent me from seeing it. I had wondered whether I would have to telephone Katie, beg her to send over a copy. We don't subscribe, you see. We have always thought this particular newspaper too strident, too simplistic in its worldview. And far too full of advertising. On a Saturday it can weigh nine pounds (Mary dropped it on the scale one week: "More than the cat," she announced conclusively). Until today there had been nothing worth reading. *Hypocrite. Hypocrite.* I hear the word rustling in the walls like so many conspiring mice.

I wonder whether they fought over it. "Let him go out for it," Mary might have said.

"Mum!" Jenny would have countered. "He'll keel over dead."

And I might have, I really might. It has been a week since I ventured even as far as the end of the driveway. I have no interest in being seen dragging my oxygen cart around town like it is one of those ridiculous little dogs swaddled in a silver sweater. Occasionally I will allow myself to be driven to a film, but only a matinee when the theatre is more likely to be empty; I have a horror of being shushed when I steal a few puffs of the pure stuff. Or we go to a distant mall, where I can camp in the food court like a grotesquely shrivelled adolescent. It is all about vanity, I know that. But the bars of that particular cage are remarkably unbending. I have become the Elephant Man.

The article isn't at all bad. My pleasure is seriously dampened by our fresh domestic spats, but Katie has very much surprised me. Her vocabulary for starters. *Wrenching winds* indeed. And *mud-thickened waters*. Hardly Shakespeare, I'll grant, but hardly what I expected, either. One can nearly see the elms being torn from the river banks. And I am described in sober, entirely reliable ways. I thought a lack of talent would force young Katie to capture me in a primitive fashion, something more suited to a cartoon. I saw her creating a mad, disconnected night full of Superman-ish leaps and Herculean swims. I expected to sprout a jutting chin, to become altogether more *imposing*. But it is to her great credit that there is none of that. Well done, young lady.

The accompanying photograph of me, though, is a little alarming. It is the one that grim little man snapped as I left the station in the days after the storm. I was preoccupied and he surprised me. But the intervening decades have, I suppose, softened the implications of my unshaven face, my growling expression. Mary said at the time it was more mugshot than accolade. Today, I must have looked at that image of me for a full minute, trying to see in that young man's athletic slouch the panting wreck he was to become. It is not there, of course. There are ways to see ahead, definitely, but there are also blind curves, and this disease has always lurked around one of those.

The facts of the evening, the following days, Katie presents nearly as I gave them to her. They do seem scant to me, there is no meat on those old bones, but they have a breathless sort of vigour and verisimilitude that no one who lived through that night, save Mary, will point at and shout, Lies, all lies!

Speaking of Mary, she does come off rather less well. She becomes *petite* and *forebearing*, she is *supportive* (my God, did we spike Katie's tea?), and she is also *endearingly patient at this difficult time*. Whatever other kind mentions are present, whatever references to her noble work on the hospital ward, that tight little cluster of unwitting derogatives will not help matters at all.

After a very tense dinner tonight, Jenny received a phone call (staged, I am positive) from a friend she hasn't seen in ten years. As soon as she left to meet her, Mary turned on the television. In order that she might ignore me, she pretended to be captivated by scenes of a dozen bronzed and ratty survivors, marooned on yet another remote island, vying for wads of prize money, and trying to lop the heads off of coconuts with a rather blunt-looking scythe.

And so I withdrew to my cave, where I reread Katie's smudged account. It provoked such powerful memory-sparks — I simply closed my eyes and I was *there*. And I have been able to drift back and forth like that for hours now. A time traveler.

Here, fresh for me as morning's milk, is one of those glowing embers.

On one of the days just before the hurricane hit us (it rained the entire week) I told Alice we had to end things. She lived above a furniture store, and feeling brave, or brazen, I parked out front. There was a cheap bed in the store window made up with a pink bedspread and chocolate-coloured pillows. A young couple were trying out the springs. A salesman looked on, bored. All three of them glanced up disinterestedly as I ducked past and into the dank hallway that led to the stairs. I had been in the rain all afternoon, arguing with a retired colonel who thought it quite okay to shoot any dog that ventured onto his ravine property. I was filthy and had talked myself into believing Alice was better equipped to deal with me in that state than Mary was, after another exhausting shift at St. Joseph's. A lot of the mud had dried on me in the car and I brushed it onto the green linoleum. I took a smear of my own spit and rubbed it over my cheek.

There were brown water stains on the walls and the ceiling, like ropes flattened under the old wallpaper, which depicted a desert oasis, a family of camels gathered beneath palms to drink. There was also a brass fire bucket in the corner, and into it, from a hanging flap of ceiling plaster, dripped orange water that smelled of iron. I stood at Alice's door, the varnish long-gone through most of its mid-section. The hinges had been painted white at some distant point in the past, and rather than knocking on the door I leaned in and scraped as quietly as I could with my car key at the top hinge. Under the white paint I discovered a dull blue, and underneath the blue was a steel grey.

Alice drew open the door slowly, peered around it. "I thought it was a rat," she said, and broke into a grin. "And I was right, wasn't I? A rat who's abandoned me lately. Cruel rat!"

I was barely inside Alice's rooms, with their scents of sugar and vanilla and something floral, before she was tugging at the buckle on my belt. "How did you get like this?" she wanted to know. She freed the belt and was on her knees, undoing my shoe laces, chiding me as she might a schoolboy who comes home with a ripped uniform. "This foot," she said, tapping on the leather toe. I obediently lifted my foot and she slipped the shoe off, cradling my heel. "Okay, now this one."

We sat next to each other on her red Victorian sofa. There was classical music coming from the radio. I was in my underwear. My pants were hanging over a line next to the radiator in the kitchen. Alice didn't have a washing machine but she said my clothes would soon dry and then she would brush the mud out of them. "I'll take care of you," she promised. But she hadn't offered me anything to put over my bare legs and I felt awkward, as if it had been a mistake to come.

The door to the bedroom was ajar and the bedcovers were pulled back on one side, as if I had woken her. She was dressed, though, in a pleated red skirt two shades lighter than the sofa, and very similar in style to the green one she had worn to Simpson's. There was a cream blouse with the two top buttons undone. She had on no stockings and no shoes and I was excited by that, as well as by the tan her legs maintained and by the thought of her sunning herself on the gravel rooftop of this building. I saw her lying on a worn towel next to the chimney with a yellowed paperback and a bottle of Coca-Cola. And then I tried not to see anything at all.

I told her in a colourless way about my day. I suppose I planned to tell the story again later, for Mary (leaving out a lot of the mud and rain, which would have vanished), and I wanted to save most of the drama for her. I had made my decision: I would disengage from Alice that day. As quickly as I could, so as to minimize the risk of being found out, but also as slowly as was necessary to save Alice a precipitous sadness.

She was unimpressed with my afternoon adventures. I thought of her father, drunk and swinging a pool cue, ripping it through the green baize, and of the friends a man like that might collect. I said casually, "It was nothing special, I know," and drew my knees together.

She laughed at me, told me she knew me better than I thought she did, and I said there was no denying that. But there were things, I added, developments she couldn't know of, and I needed to talk to her about those.

"That sounds ominous," she said, and stood up.

She knew what was coming. It was as clear to her as a

power outage. Her world was about to go dark. I should leave now, I thought, before an explanation turned into a battle. How much easier things would be if we could agree to just *assume* the rest of it.

"I should tell you, though," she said — I could see already that she was trying to be brave — "that my opinion of you may change for the worse, Raymond, if these *developments* don't involve us going away on holidays together, waking up in the same bed, my loving cheek against your warm back."

"Mary is pregnant."

The room was stale, something to do with my pants hanging in the next room. The brocade that ran along the front of the sofa was tattered and turning black around the rivets. The carpet was threadbare. I had helped with some of these pieces. Carried them up the stairs for her, groaning melodramatically while she fell about laughing. These were the things I would leave her with. Along with the buzzing bulb over the sink that I had promised to change (and which she, kindly, had left for me rather than simply doing it herself). The paperbacks piled in the hallway. The bottles of beer I had put in her refrigerator, behind the milk and the day-old pastries.

She wanted to know if we had planned it, me and Mary.

I asked her if it made a difference. I felt miserable and, inexplicably, very pale; I wished there had been more time in the summer to sit around in a pair of shorts.

"If it was planned, then you knew a long time ago you would have to come here and get rid of me," she said. "But if it was an accident, I won't find you so cunning."

Cunning. Such a strange word for her to use. She marched in front of me, turning smartly on her heel each time she reached the end of the couch. An uncle of mine went mad when I was a boy and later his body turned up floating in the Rideau Canal. Before he disappeared he wore away a strip of tiles in his kitchen.

For the last few weeks he was unable to talk, and just grimaced, chewed away at his tongue, and ground down his teeth so that their yellow pulp was visible. "This wasn't planned," I said. "But I am happy about it." I placed a cushion over my bare legs. Alice asked if I was cold. She brought me a blanket from the bedroom and when I draped it over my legs she told me I looked like her mother.

I said, "So you don't hate me, then."

"What, because you remind me of my mother? That's quite a leap. But no, Ray, I don't hate you."

She sat cross-legged on the floor and sighed. She put a hand over each of my feet. I feel that gesture now, intensely, even an age removed. "So what do we do?"

It had never occurred to me that there still were decisions to be made, beyond whether I should have sex with her before I left, if she would allow it. I shrugged. "It's complicated."

"Not for me, it isn't."

"Then tell me," I said. If there was a way, I wanted to hear it.

"We carry on. We'll be more careful."

"Neither of us will be happy," I said.

"We'll have happy moments."

"And long stretches of misery."

"Not necessarily."

I didn't say anything. I supposed that she didn't really expect to convince me.

"You think I'm wrong," Alice said. She collapsed onto the sofa next to me, rested against its arm and brought her feet up, pushed her toes under my leg. "But I don't want you to go, Ray. Not yet."

"I can stay a while," I said. I looked for the clock but she had moved it. Alice was always rearranging, trying to find the perfect spot for everything. She said once that it had to do with balance and harmony. That it was like music. I asked her what she knew about music. "I know when it's gone wrong," she had told me.

"That's not what I mean," she said now. "I'm saying I can handle it for a bit. That I don't want us to be rash."

I didn't think I was being rash. Mary was pregnant. I loved her. I didn't think the math was very complicated. "I've been up front with you, Alice. From the very beginning."

"Honesty doesn't have much of a place between people like us," she said.

"Sure it does."

"How about between you and Mary?"

She wasn't being fair. I became increasingly aware that letting her hang my pants on a line in the kitchen had been an error.

She rubbed her face. "I told you I was falling for you, Ray. Did you know then?"

I swore that I didn't.

"Good. Because nothing's changed for me."

I began to say something — I wasn't sure what it would be except that it would be a protest of some sort — but she cut me off. "I think about you when you're not around. I daydream. At work they ask me if something's wrong. I think about you all the time. And the thought of you turns me on, Ray." She wriggled her toes under my leg. "And it's not just, you know, the physical side of things; it's because you listen to me."

I managed to say, "We've been pretending. Pretending the outside world doesn't exist. Pretending it can go on forever."

I had hurt her.

"Most people would give anything for a pretend world like ours," she muttered. And then she said, "I just need a little time to be ready. I want us to have some adventures together. I want to laugh with you some more. I'm not looking to hurt Mary, or ruin your life. I'm just looking to make both of us happier for a while."

"We were happier," I said. "I was happier. But I don't see how that can be true anymore. I'll be worrying about Mary and the baby all the time."

"Are you worried right now?"

I admitted that I wasn't. "But if there was an emergency and no one could find me . . ." I said. "If something happened while we were here . . ."

"Your wife's a nurse," Alice said. "She'd know what to do."

The discussion was useless and I said so.

She took my hand. "It's not only useless, it's *terrible*," she said. She was trying to amuse me, to chisel out a sliver of light. When I looked at her, she said, "I'm happy for you. Truly."

I thanked her. I said I was sorry.

Her eyes filled with tears and the music ended. The radio announcer read the news. Alice moved in next to me, still holding my hand, and we listened. Alice sniffed intermittently and cuffed her nose with the sleeve of her blouse. So that's it, I thought, it's over between us.

I remember some of that news broadcast. A woman in Belleville was about to stand trial for allegedly poisoning her husband to death with strychnine. I knew about the case. I had heard from the coroner that the man's piss was as black as oil and his arms and legs were rigid as planks before he died. His lungs failed, and then, finally, out of pity, his brain shut him down.

Workers at Ford's Oakville assembly plant were set to walk off the job.

We listened, as if waiting for our own names.

In Wilmington, North Carolina, 45,000 people were preparing for the arrival of Hurricane Hazel and its 130 mph winds.

So there it was, if only we could have known — our tomorrows were already on the radio.

"Turn it off, Ray. Can you turn it off?" She lifted her head from my shoulder. As I returned to the sofa I could still hear the radio dying behind me. I wanted to stop short, to announce my departure formally, from a distance. Alice picked up on my hesitation, though, and said, "It's still light out there. Plenty of time for you to comfort me a while."

I went to the kitchen and grabbed a handful of pantleg.

Alice said, "Still wet?" She looked remotely pleased and I understood that. I knelt before her, intending only, I think, to say a few final words. But then, impulsively, stupidly, I leaned over her lap and kissed her. Her lipstick tasted slightly sweet, and the texture of it was like butter. Christ. I was so wrong to think it would be easy; to think that I was that strong. I took her waist in my hands and shifted her so that she was lying on the couch. I could see falling for her too. Together we were like a fairground ride starting up. She brought her legs up and trapped me in them and her skirt fell around her hips. Oh, to have a woman lie on her back and hike up her skirt and raise her legs like that. The glimpse of heaven in that scene. I ran my hands over her thighs and closed my eyes. Alice gripped my torso more tightly. There were routines already in our lovemaking and that was fine with me. We were coming to know each other just well enough. Her hair was over her face, and her breathing was faster. I lifted my head far enough that I could look at her. She sensed me doing it and opened her eyes so that I could see that they had developed that frost she knew I liked so much.

"The bed," she whispered, and at first I shook my head because it would keep me here longer, but she bit her lower lip, said "Uh-huh," or something like it and the sound contained the promise of such delights that I let her pull me upright and into the darker softer room that she slept in and that I thought about too often when I was at home, out on the patio smoking, or in bed reading while Mary went through her mysterious routines in the adjoining bathroom. I loved the sounds of the street that percolated through the glass and the amber curtains. I loved the softness and depth of her mattress because it contrasted with the hard thin creation Mary had insisted on because her back always caused her pain. So much of what kept me there was the way the experience differed so dramatically from my life at home.

Outside there was the sound of a bus pulling away from the kerb, an angry bicycle bell and, in the distance somewhere, a police siren. Alice reached behind her and undid the steel clip that held her skirt to her waist. I waited for the intense ratcheting of the nylon zipper as it traced the curve of her buttocks. When it came I knew damn well there was no leaving that room and I began — even as she stepped out of the skirt and came towards me, unbuttoning her blouse and letting it fall from her shoulders — to concoct my excuses for Mary.

The chance to provide that last adventure Alice wanted came quickly, on the following Friday. The rain had intensified, and the wind. The downtown core was filling with water (this is where I began my narrative for Katie) and I had been directed to check on the stability of the Lawrence Street Bridge, which spanned the Humber River. It was becoming clear to everyone that this would be no ordinary night. I still thought it safe, however, even prudent, to collect Alice, since I had to drive nearly past her door, and bring her with me. This would settle our account, that was the extent of my scheme. This would be a cleansing storm. All of my trouble would be washed into the lake and away, in a white lather, to the Atlantic.

MARY

Before I could tell Ray, of course, the doctor had to tell me.

At Dr. Pierce's office neither of us had realized that two days from my first appointment (the length of time it would take to produce my test results) put us at the weekend. And so at eight on Saturday morning, at the nurses' station at St. Joseph's, I was annoyed, fidgety. It would be Monday before the lab opened again.

I asked a student to open a window before she left. "The one across from Mrs. Williams."

"She's hardly woke," the student said, concerned. Her name, appropriately enough, was Dot. "I changed her and still she hardly moved."

We checked on her together. I instructed Dot to take a pulse. Mrs. Williams' yellow wrist hung over the edge of the bed and the young girl took it cautiously, watching for any sign that the patient might grab, like a ghoul, at her hand. This one's afraid of death, I thought. (In the end, though, she surprised me and became an entirely competent nurse. We worked together for several years and I came to appreciate her; she was in my home more than once and I was always glad to see her.)

Mrs. Williams had been on ward for two weeks, slipping further from us each day. A week before, she asked me to sit with her and I said that was impossible, I would come back in an hour. When I returned, Mrs. Williams was livid. "I'm dying," she said. Her eyes were never still. "How did you know you had time to make me wait?" Her jaw trembled with the importance of what she was saying. "And if *you* knew, why didn't *I*?"

"It's faint," Dot said. "Thready." She leaned for my ear. "And she kind of smells."

I motioned at the window I had asked Dot to open, and Dot nodded, understanding now.

I put everyone's chart in order and waited for the doctor to arrive for morning rounds. I collected the last of the breakfast trays and walked the centre aisle. I was called over to admire the Italian's tattoo, and I checked for fever in a two-year-old boy who had fallen on his way up some stairs — "That's some feat," I told him, "falling up rather than down." He would have an unsightly scar after this, I suspected and I remember hoping that girls would find it rakish, debonair.

There were thirty-two patients. We were at capacity. The eighteen men were confined to one end and the fourteen women and children to the other. Why in the world these numbers have stayed with me, I don't know. I can also, incidentally, recite every telephone number I have ever had, the licence plate on every car we parked in every driveway. In 1964 I spent $28 on a long floral skirt that I wore only once — to a party at which I ate some very suspect oysters (eight of them) and got very ill. I would like to forget both the skirt and the eternal day I spent hooked over the toilet bowl, but it is not to be; it is the way I am wired: I cannot forget figures or betrayals.

Mrs. Williams was the only patient likely to die on ward that day, but there was also a girl of sixteen with improbable ulcers that made her writhe beneath her sheets, and three men were awaiting heart surgery. There were advanced cases of asthma and dermatitis. One woman probably had tuberculosis and would have to be moved. There was the Italian with his broken leg, and a Brazilian (whom no one understood) had broken six ribs and his collarbone in a horse riding accident. He had been taped together and was propped up in his bed smoking. Two women had breast cancer, another had a burn down her right side where her husband had pushed her into a too-hot bath. An epileptic had gone blind mysteriously and wouldn't stop crying until she was sedated, and there was a tough woman from Wellington who had fallen from an apple tree and dislocated a hip and punctured a lung. At the far end of the room, near the picture window that afforded a lovely view over Lake Ontario, was a woman who had presented four days ago with abdominal pain. But that pain had resolved without a firm diagnosis, and I suspected her of developing an unhelpful attachment to the room. Before the day was out, I intended to either find serious blood on the woman's sheets or to discharge her.

As charge nurse I was responsible for administering medications to all thirty-two of the patients. The rest of the duties I divided most days with Ellen Morgan, a strict, matronly woman of twenty-seven, with a prematurely thick waist and a permanently knitted brow. The two of us were unlikely friends, but there was something in Ellen's gruff manner that I found humorous, and to her credit the patients seemed to appreciate her as much as I did.

When rounds were over I excused myself and telephoned St. Michael's from the main lobby. I leaned into the cool cream wall and closed my eyes while I waited for a wave of nausea to pass.

"I'm positive I won't be able to find out until Monday," I began, "but I'm awaiting the result of some tests Dr. Pierce administered this past Thursday." I remember cringing at "awaiting." Why do we become so weirdly formal when we're nervous?

"Your name, please."

I gave the information and waited.

The next voice was familiar, but attaching a name was momentarily impossible. A relative? Someone from the hospital here? My brother, I wondered, but he was in Australia, shearing sheep or guarding murderers, it depended on the week. Frank then, from next door?

"Mary, are you still there? Mary Townes?"

It was Michael Pierce, the doctor, and I just know I turned scarlet. I had naturally assumed he would have weekends off. It was always my advice to anyone who asked: Don't get sick until Monday. "Sorry, yes. I'm here. I just hadn't expected to get you."

"You thought you were in for a couple more sleepless nights."

"It never crossed my mind until this morning. I think we both forgot."

"We did, you're right," he said. "But I came in this morning and woke up the lad in the laboratory. I put a rush on it. A professional courtesy."

There was a spot where the flat of the wall met the ceiling that the muddy brown paint hadn't taken and last year's pale yellow peeked through. I stared at that. "So you know the result?"

"I just picked it up, Mary. I'm trying to find it again." I could hear him fumbling. "I'm not being deliberately cruel. It's in here somewhere."

I heard him waving my file in the air, just as he had in the office.

"It's okay," I said, nauseated again.

"Here it is. Yes. I just stuck it in there, you see."

His way of apologizing for the suspense.

"What does it say?" I said.

"It says . . . here we go . . . that you're pregnant, Mary. Completely pregnant, as I remember you said you felt. Woman's intuition and all that. Congratulations."

Someone on crutches was being helped through the door and the tiled floor beneath him gleamed. Its intricately patterned edge seemed a maze I might lose myself in.

"Mary?"

"I'm fine. More than fine. Thank you, doctor."

"I'm so pleased for you," he said. "I trust your husband will be too."

"Yes," I said. The connection between us was startlingly clear. None of the hiss and warble I was used to. Sometimes when I called Ray there was so much static I thought it represented a threat to public safety.

"As I said before, you can see me again, or . . . well I'm sure you don't need me to make a referral for you."

I thought I sensed something in his tone. Had he wished, however slightly, for another result? We had got along well. And I had let there be some minuscule doubt about my relationship with Ray. I felt guilty about that. Our conversation had poked its head into rooms not usually included on the tour. And not just because I was a nurse.

Such idle thoughts. And they felt so irresponsible now. I was feverish, damp beneath my uniform. I rang off, thanking him effusively and promising to let him know, one way or another, and then allowed the lobby to swim a second while I leaned into the wall and wept.

Ray has never heard that story. It has never occurred to him to ask where I was when I found out, or how it felt. Which isn't intended as another criticism, it's just the way he is, the way most men are, I think — they are not as selfless as women, not as easily interested in the world outside. I talked once to Jenny about it. And she agreed with me, albeit mildly. Ten minutes in, I recalled that she was, is, gay, or lesbian (with a slight jolt — because it doesn't matter how ingrained this information becomes, it shocks me each time it rises to the surface). That would have to affect the way she views the sexes, wouldn't it? I felt suddenly ashamed, as if I had been insensitive or thoughtless, which I hadn't.

Jenny had lived with her partner (Sharon, a delightful woman it turns out) for nearly a year before she came to us with her secret. The terrific nerve that must have taken. The poor girl, she must have been exhausted. I certainly remember the way she shook, especially afterwards, when it was over (even though it had gone quite well. She must have thought so, I mean no one rushed away from the table or disowned her).

Later she told me she had known since she was eleven or twelve, and never doubted it for a second once she became a teenager. So she lived with us for six years with that secret, a fact that saddens me intensely. I suspect that hoarding that sort of news about oneself must cause bleeding of one sort or another, by which I suppose I must actually mean a psychic sort of damage. I also worry that it means we were inadequate as parents, unapproachable, possessed of a vague politics that didn't reassure her. How much better it would have been if we had talked earlier (you see — the same pattern repeats itself over and over in a life). I wonder if she might have settled closer to us if she didn't feel there was something to hide. She lives now in Seattle, as far from Toronto as you can get. That's how it feels anyway, and there is the border to negotiate too. But again, Sharon; we are glad to know her. Even Ray seems quite taken with her, in his grudging, intolerant way. I suspect that deep in his reptilian brain he imagines "converting" her, for she is attractive, and Ray is . . . well Ray is Ray. And, as his distasteful remarks about that young reporter attest he will remain that way until he is dead in the ground. God help whatever woman is buried next to him. If it is to be me I will insist that an electrified fence be installed around my plot, or one of those sonic barriers I have seen advertised that promise to restrict the movements of outdoor dogs.

I know that Jenny wants to leave. I have heard her whispering on the telephone. I can never quite make out the words, but she is furtive and that is enough; it's not hard to imagine the rest. Somewhere out there Sharon is waiting for the word, and when it comes she will descend lightly on us and whisk our daughter away. Jenny said repeatedly when she arrived that she would only be here for a day or two. And there must be a contract, a date by which they are supposed to begin work (they work together — Sharon does needs assessment while Jenny allocates funds and also provides counselling): what must she have said about Ray's condition to buy these extra days with us?

His condition is progressively worse. I have been trying to decide whether it is dire yet. I think not, but at any hour that could change. He will need to use his oxygen more and more constantly, and then a day will dawn when even that pure breeze at full force is not enough to feed his blood. That is the day, or very close to the day, that he will die and I have been told to prepare myself for it, whatever that means. Should I get my hair done or stock up on Kleenex? Tonight Jenny and I sat at the kitchen table for a while listening to the asthmatic hiss of his tank in the next room (both of us aghast at the lingering, vile stink of the kippers he had insisted on for his dinner). I timed his use of the machine at nearly two hours, uninterrupted. That is too long. Tomorrow I must have them deliver more. How awful it would be if my negligence caused him to turn blue; if his death became a matter of poor inventory control. I can readily imagine plunging a knife into him, actively deciding it is time, but I could not bear to have it happen through my neglect.

That would turn me into someone too much like him.

I don't know where his notebook is. All I know is it's not under the mattress, or in the drawer of his bedside table, or in his desk, or lined up with his encyclopedias and the numerous novels he insists he will read before he dies (one of his lamest but most often-repeated jokes). This absence tells me he is still adding to it. If he had stopped, as I requested, it would be discarded somewhere. I have checked the neat little aluminum garbage can I bought for that room when we needed a place to dispose of the needles he is regularly prodded with (they call them sharps nowadays, a new term that makes me feel very old). No, he is scribbling away in there. Perhaps that is the real source of his laboured panting — he is getting too caught up in his own fictions. His last words.

RAY

Summon the trumpeters, for here is my greatest secret.

It has nothing to do with Alice or that goddamn storm. With sex or infidelity, heroes or goats. To my mind it is this: I am high a lot of the time, stoned, half out of my mind. For I smuggle drugs into the house and ingest them nearly obsessively, like a rat being offered a choice of bourbon or water. I am not myself.

Which is not much of a secret, not in these liberal days, but that is my point. So much has leaked out over the years. More than Mary realizes. She thinks there are still vast warehouses of fact to be plundered, and the more I argue against that notion the more convinced she becomes.

I have help with the drugs, and it is provided by another woman, a widowed neighbour, and that too would send Mary into paroxysms the likes of which I almost certainly would not survive.

She brings me hashish, this woman does, or else I visit her and collect it. She will accept no payment and I have never asked where she finds the stuff. She read somewhere that it might help me, and so I repeated her research and was convinced enough that one September evening when she offered to bake a few granules into a chocolate confection, I accepted. Half an hour later I felt the narcotic creep of it in my legs and arms, and then in my stomach. The chest and the lungs seem more resistant to its approach but they do succumb eventually. She (I dare not speak her name) watched me with some amusement that first day. I tried to persuade her to join me, and though she did on a few rare subsequent occasions, that first night she said, "No. What if you were to have an adverse reaction? What if I needed to call an ambulance?"

Will it make it impossible for you to use the telephone, I asked her, rather archly. Is it that potent? But she was not to be moved and so I sat before her feeling rather foolish that early fall evening, but also rather delightful too. I had smoked before, but had always found the experience disappointing. The drug's effects always seemed confined to my head rather than my whole body. The trick, it would seem, is in the method of delivery.

Why it works to ease my breathing is still a mystery to me. Perhaps it doesn't at all and I just don't care while I am high. (I hate that word, *high*, it is so false in its description — I ride at a lower altitude, not a higher one; there is a subterranean murkiness to the experience; a mushroomy, soft-edged feel). Perhaps it relaxes me so much that I need less breath, less oxygen. I have mentioned it to my doctor, in confidence, and in the vain hope that there is some great discovery to be made here, one that will secure him the Nobel and me a few more years of this middling suburban grind that I have become mysteriously attached too. But he says gravely that he is sure the effect is all in my head (No, no! I tell him idiotically) and may well be dangerous; if I ingest too much, he warns, a sort of paralysis could fell me. He snapped his fingers in irritated demonstration, and that was the last time we spoke of it.

Because I felt better that first time, and then a second, I allowed my neighbour to become my dealer, if you will. She bakes me an eight-inch-by-eight-inch square of these brownies every three weeks and I keep them in a decorated tin on my desk. Mary is allergic to chocolate and won't go near them. My worry this week is that Jenny will stumble upon them. But I am careful and keep a strict inventory. I am also fairly positive that the sensation would not be an entirely new one for my daughter and once she sensed its approach she would lie on her bed giggling, and would stare quite happily at the small black-and-white television we have installed up there so she can watch Conan O'Brien last thing at night without worrying that she will wake me.

I eat them usually in the evenings, when I am tired and feel I can most benefit from the effect. I also want to remain in control of my faculties when Mary is about. She would see this habit of mine, I am fairly confident, as a further abandonment. I am stoned right now, so the effects are obviously not that deleterious. I don't suddenly become a drooling idiot. And my lungs feel positively expansive. Admittedly, the bathroom does seem a mile away, but at my age there is a price to be paid for every sort of relief.

I mentioned to you that I took Alice north that night. The night of nights, the rain filling the avenues and alleys. It was nearly brilliant, this plan of mine. I would do whatever needed to be done above the Humber River and then I would drive her home again. This would be the adventure she craved: a hurricane bearing down on us, a bridge at risk of collapse, me barking orders, sending good men scurrying from their warm vehicles.

The drive home afterwards would provide me with the time I needed to explain that this truly was the end. No, I would say, I couldn't go upstairs with her. And I was sorry she was so upset.

Yes, it upset me too. But I had made my decision; she had to understand. I would keep my hands firmly on the steering wheel and then drive home and pack a few clothes for my trip with Mary to Niagara Falls. I would be, for the rest of my days, the perfect husband. I had it planned to the smallest detail, ways of rebuffing every advance, every argument. I was convinced, I had convinced myself, that I would be successful. The sensation I had was similar to the feeling I awoke with that morning many, many years later when I finally quit smoking: I was filled to the brim with certainty. I had tried to quit before and had always wondered how long it would last. The time I was successful it was as if a switch had been thrown. It was the same with Alice, I *knew* it was over.

When I arrived outside her building Alice was huddled with a man in the doorway. They were under an umbrella that the man was holding, even though I recognised from its familiar grey-and-blue stripes that it belonged to Alice. I watched them. I was a snoop, a private dick hunting for signs of intimacy between them, and the irony had me grunting with embarrassment.

The man handed Alice her umbrella and dipped his head twice, then a third time, as if girding himself, before charging headfirst into the storm. Alice yelled something and he lifted an arm in acknowledgement. Alice laughed and searched in her purse for a key. I yelled for her. When she saw me her face lit up brilliantly and she yanked open the passenger door and collapsed beside me. Her perfume was on me fractionally before she was. She had her lips on my cheek and then on my ear and her breath was hot and her hand wet on my shirt and she was laughing almost uncontrollably at the joy she felt at having me sit in the rain waiting for her to get home. My protests that I had only just arrived did nothing to dissuade her from the position that she was "a wanted woman, and no woman wants more than that, Ray," and it was all I could do to stop her from climbing into my lap. The windows fogged up and Alice said she liked that and breathed repeatedly on the glass so that a white bouquet of her breaths collected there and not even the most inquisitive of passersby could see in. All of my deliberations and resolutions were in danger of dissolving. I wanted nothing to do with her, but at the same time I wanted to feel her crawling over me and even taking me into her mouth so that I could give up entirely any thought of control.

I fumbled over her lap with the knob for the glove box and extracted a chamois I kept in there because the condensation was awful at the best of times. Alice opened her houndstooth coat and where that coat had gaped around the buttons her blouse was wet. There were four circles the size of plums bisecting her left half from her right. Above the top button, her skin was wet and there was gooseflesh in there, like a thousand pearls poking through sand. She pulled the blouse away from her skin delicately, with a thumb and finger. I was aroused instantly by the curve of her breast. I squeezed the chamois onto the floor between my feet and threw the cloth into the back.

I said, "That adventure you wanted. Still interested?"

All the way north the radio lit up with squawks and interruptions. The approach to a bridge over the Don River was washed out. People were on the move to higher ground. The station man sounded harried and I picture him at his switchboard, tangled up in his coloured plugs. Hazel, he said. Hurricane Goddamn Hazel's what they're saying. So all shifts are extended through the night. And no complaining.

Smith, he muttered, was to stay where he was;

Harrington and Brooks should hie to the transit barn;

Walker, Thomson, Jeffries, get yourself down to Lakeshore.

I crawled along Lawrence Avenue, the water knee-deep in places, to where the road crossed the Humber. The river had risen markedly. Trees planted along the banks fifty years ago were being swallowed up. The road resembled an aqueduct. Along the rail two young women in white stockings and black shoes, floral kerchiefs tied tight around their chins, clung to the edge and marvelled at the animal that seethed beneath them.

Alice said, "Look at that, the sky is green. It feels like the end of the world."

I told her to wait for me, and wrestled with the door. She was already lighting a cigarette, something I'd told her never to do inside the squad car. She didn't listen. "Come on, then," I said, "out."

A fire engine blared past, and we ducked behind the car to avoid its wake. Alice kissed me, ludicrously, on the end of my nose. One of the women screamed and Alice gripped my sleeve. I didn't want that but the wind was so fierce I didn't see much choice but to allow it. The woman screamed again and was bouncing up and down. Her friend was pointing into the water. "There! There!"

I couldn't see what it was, but Alice gasped and added her own directions: "Against the willow. My God, is it a deer?"

"A dog," one of the women cried. "A yellow dog. It was on the bank a minute ago. The current has pinned it against the rock there. Oh, the poor thing."

Alice clutched at my wrist. "Ray!" she implored. But what could we do? If it had been a boy we would have launched a rope. "By the time we get down there," I began.

"We can't just leave it."

"It'll drown."

"Do something."

I didn't know who was saying what. "I don't think . . ." I began, but Alice had already broken away, was making for the end of the bridge. There were rough concrete steps down to a path that ran along the bank. Much of that path had vanished below the water, but near the start, where earth had been piled to support the bridge, it was still visible — a dark etching against frantic thrashings of sumac.

I yelled at her to come back. The two women glowered as though I was the most despicable man they had ever encountered. It was stupid. I wanted to tell them, *This is the stupidest idea.* I had at that moment a vision of the whole city being ripped apart. If this bridge was at risk then other, less formidable structures might already have collapsed. I saw in my head other stretches of the river chock-full of people swept from the banks. I thought it quite possible that streets had been inundated and then overrun with floodwater, and that uprooted trees were flattening families in their sodden gardens. These three women had no idea how bad it might be elsewhere. I should do a visual inspection of the bridge supports and then radio in. I should make myself available.

I caught her elbow just as she made the first step. Her foot slipped and I found myself supporting most of her weight. To someone driving by it would have looked as if I was fighting with her. I remembered then Mary saying that she had seen me arrest someone once, that she had been watching from Gina's eye-in-the-sky office. She would have shot me had she known it was Alice, and where I was really taking her. And here I was doing it again, before more witnesses who would remember my face.

I looked back and saw the wind rip the scarves from the girls' heads. For a moment the floral squares soared smoothly and then they were compressed into wretched little shapes and plummeted, before opening again like parachutes. They hit the water at nearly the same instant and the two women clutched at each other and the wind carried their words to me: "No no no. Oh shit!"

Alice had broken away again and was one flight below me.

"Wait," I ordered, and she did pause, as if waiting for a promise that I would help her. "Let me go ahead," I pleaded, and I was relieved when she stood back to let me pass. She tried to kiss me again as I approached and I was incensed by that and knew that I would be glad when this was over between us. I can't believe, now, that I humoured her this way. I should have simply insisted that she come with me back to the car, taken her away by force if I had to. Lives could have been saved, I'm positive of it.

But instead I slithered along the path, grasping at tree trunks amd jutting bedrock. The water frightened me. Within its speeding body there seemed to be muscles of even stronger water that roiled and flexed. I wrapped an arm around a peeling birch and shouted that Alice should turn back, but she shook her head.

"I'm going!" I insisted. "Just wait here, damn it," but she was already looking for her next handhold, using my skidding foot-prints as a guide. Through the white sheets of rain and the rocking branches I saw that the two women were still up there, pointing at us.

The dog was still in the same place, so whoever had said that it looked to be pinned, was right. I found reasonable footing on flat rock. I edged delicately into the water. The dog, a young Lab, was fifteen feet away, yipping. I cursed the two women for their eyesight. Without them . . . I let the thought die. My hands were cold, my feet soaked. Alice was closing on me and I warned her once more to stay back. "We don't need to be slipping into each other," I said, meaning that I didn't want her pushing me in. She grimaced and that expression changed smoothly into something harder, a displeasure with me, despite my being out here now, which was what she had wanted.

She slapped at the tree she had wrapped her arms around. Indicated that it joined above our heads with the yellow willow the dog was trapped against.

"No way," I yelled, stepping gingerly out of the shallows and scrabbling on all-fours up to her.

"But it's willow," she said. "Both of them are willows."

"It's just a dog. It's not even my dog." Whenever I spoke, the rain got into my mouth.

"It can't move."

"And I can't haul it up the goddamn tree with me, either."

"I'll do it," she said.

"Don't be stupid." It was the first time I had really sniped at her. It killed some of the energy in her.

"Then let's throw something."

"Like what?" I had had fights like this with Mary. I wasn't looking for a solution anymore. Part of me just wanted her to say things I could mock.

"A long branch. Something he might bite at."

"He'll be swept away." My heart punched frantically at my ribs: *Get away from here*, it telegraphed; *Do your job!*

It's a fucking dog. That was what I thought. There must be *people* in similar situations. The whole fucking bridge might come down. This was such a lousy way for us to help. I climbed into the low crotch of the tree and stepped along the first of the massive limbs. I tried to dislocate a smaller branch but wasn't strong enough. I put some weight on it and saw that it would hold me. I moved out tentatively, feeling the sway of it in my legs. It didn't seem much of a risk, not yet, but Alice's look was disconcerting. I inched along until I reached a smaller artery. I stamped down with one foot and heard it crack. After repeated stampings the branch splintered and ripped along its length. I smacked down more desperately, out of breath, and Alice pulled on it from below until finally it came free.

The dog snapped at the branch as soon as I lowered it over its head. With Alice holding my arm I extended myself over the water. The dog took hold and wriggled like a salmon. I felt the wrenching weight of it in my shoulder (*wrenching* — there, I am stealing from Katie; the history she has imagined is now the history I remember). A second longer and I would have had to let go, but then the dog swung in a sharp arc shorewards and scampered, before I could even fully comprehend what we had just accomplished, onto the collapsing bank.

It dropped, winded, onto its side. Alice kneeled and whispered something into its ear. But its eyes were open and I could see that all it needed was a few seconds. Then it would trot away and, who knows, maybe slide back into the river around the next bend.

"It's fine," I said.

"You can tell that from over there?"

"It was scared and now it's tired," I said.

"It nearly drowned."

"I don't think so."

The two women had gone. They knew better than Alice did when an adventure had run its course. And that's what it was, I decided — this was precisely the adventure I had promised. I owed her nothing more. A ride home was the extent of it.

"We have to go," I said.

"You go. Or else help me carry him."

"Alice." I stood up. "You're coming with me." I tried for her arm but she snatched it away and in the process fell onto her backside. The two of them, her and the dog, made a sad pair. As far as I was concerned, the hurricane could have them both.

"I got a telephone call from Tom," Alice spat. It was meant as an accusation or a threat. A way of saying I wasn't attentive enough. I was fast coming to the opinion I wouldn't have to end things with Alice in any formal way; this storm would do all the work for me. My plan now was to return to the car alone. I could report in on the radio. By that time Alice would have come to her senses and the dog would have abandoned her. I predicted a moody silent drive, the car thick with the smell of us drying out.

And when she was gone, an hour from now, if I could summon the nerve, I would climb onto the roof of my car. Between the jagged rooftops I would be able to see the northernmost wing of St. Joseph's Hospital set against the seething steel of Lake Ontario. And behind those brick walls I would know that Mary, lovely Mary, was toiling to save real, human lives.

I wanted to say something along these lines but Alice wouldn't have understood. This was her moment to stand up for all the meek creatures of the world. In years to come she wanted to be able to say that she was here and this is what she did; she refused to let an animal die. She was with a cruel man at the time and he wanted her to leave with him, but she had refused.

And I was okay with that. She could say whatever she wanted. "I'm going up," I said. "Two minutes after that I'm driving away."

"Didn't you hear me?"

"Tom telephoned. Right. Marvellous. Bully for him."

"He wants to move to Toronto. Wants me to put him up until he finds a place."

I shook my head. I could barely hear her, and she was as good as unrecognizable, glued to the slope. "Alice. Look at you."

And she did look, at her bottom half coated entirely in mud. The dog was beside her, waiting for a command. "Tom would never be like this with me."

"Then for Christ's sake, tell him to come."

I had no idea whether she was crying. She sniffed, certainly, and her eyes were full of water.

"You can't mean that."

"I'm going," I told her.

"Ray!" She was on her feet. "Tell me to refuse him."

"I don't think I should do that."

So there would be words after all. In the worst of spots and at the worst of moments. The dog shook itself. How odd the animal looked on its spindly legs. It was as if I had never seen a dog before. Even the river made no sense. Or the bridge. I felt divorced from everything around me.

She grabbed at my arm.

I motioned to the bridge above us, the feeble black dash of it against the green sky. "The car," I said roughly.

But she shook her head. "You're lying."

"I'm not lying, Alice. We've reached a point. I need to go."

"No!" Now she really was crying, but the dog was trotting away, oblivious. The world was neither improved nor diminished by its survival. Which was why we should have left it to chance and looked for more important crises.

She pulled at me, yanked my arm harder than the river had when I swung the dog towards shore. "For fuck's sake!" I shouted, and lost my footing. I slid into her and she fell on top of me. She tried to laugh, to turn the tide between us, but there was nothing there, and I pushed her off and tried to stand up. She grabbed at my ankle and I kicked free, perhaps I even caught her jaw. She rolled down the slope away from me, disconsolate, sobbing, and I yelled for her not to be so stupid.

But she had no sense of how close she was to the water. Before I could warn her or reach her, she tipped into the rushing brown stream as easily as a log being sent to the mill. She bobbed to the surface and gasped, astonishment and cold and fear written on her face, and then she vanished again. I saw her twenty feet downstream. She had righted herself and was trying for the shore. But it was dark and I was utterly convinced she hadn't a hope. The river carried her away.

MARY

I found a letter this morning that I thought was gone forever. The last time I set eyes on it would have been in 1961. Back then we were packing up for a move away from Aldringham and away, sadly, from Gina, who stuck it out there, after Frank died, until she passed away herself in 1980. We saw each other regularly, me and Gina, and laughed at the way gravity was having its way with us, and drank gin and pink lemonade in her garden. She remarried, an accountant named Doug, who bored her slightly but loved her immensely and even wrote her these awful poems that reduced her to laughing fits and tears whenever she read them, at least in my presence.

But the letter.

I thought I threw it away, was positive I had dismissed it as a sentimental self-pitying lament, a girlish aberration that I was better off without. How it ended up here and why I found it today, is a mystery, though not a very large mystery, I suppose. And to be honest, it appalls me to face written proof of just how immature I still was, how ill-equipped to match wits with Ray Townes, the great man about town.

Ray and I had been fighting. We had survived the

hurricane but I felt strongly in the following days that he was drifting from me. I knew something had happened to him, and I was scared of what it meant. It was as if he didn't see me anymore, as if we didn't ever look at each other. I worried that we would separate before the baby arrived, that I would have to support myself in a mildewed apartment near the hospital, that our child would never witness a pure love. That was my state of mind.

So I hid that night, whatever night it was, in the bathroom. I slid the bolt across the door. I couldn't remember ever doing that before. And it was doubly strange because I had thought that when the baby was older Ray and I might hide in there together, that it might become our sanctuary. *Mum and dad*, I had heard my future self pronounce, *are going to have a nice bath*.

I ran it deep and hot, with a capful of foaming orange blossom held under the stream. I had brought in with me a letter-writing pad from the drawer in the bedside table, and a breakfast tray that was wide enough to rest on both sides of the bath.

I began a letter to my mother. *Dear Ruth*, and then knocked the pen against my teeth. What on earth could I say that my mother would understand, or even want to hear? I tore the sheet away — not frustrated, just surprised at myself for even trying — and lay it on top of the bubblecloud floating above my legs, watched the blue ink blur and soon run into nothing at all.

A while later, I registered that the television had been turned on downstairs, a blur of unrecognizable chatter twisted under the door. I was tired, a bit dreamy, or drifty, but I tried again:

Dear Marilyn,
   I read in the newspaper that you and Mr. DiMaggio had separated. How awful it must be. You have my sympathies, dear.

But perhaps I am too presumptuous. Perhaps you have a
thousand wonderful secrets to balance this bad news. I hope so.

My own husband is being proclaimed a hero. He cannot
swing a bat to save his life, but there has been a terrible storm
here and the newspapers say he has saved many lives. These
should be the happiest of days.

My, what sorrow and regret lurks in those last few words.

I have no idea, of course, why you and Joe —

I paused — I distinctly remember pausing — to think about
that. It should really be "Mr. DiMaggio" again, I decided. This
familiar tone I was striking — you and Joe — would cause upset.
I crossed out the name and then, before I could repeat the more
formal appellation I laughed at myself. I ran a hand through the
diminishing bubbles, scooped an insulating layer over my
breasts. As if I could ever drop such a girlish confession into the
mailbox!

A confession, is that what it was? Was I about to list my
innermost thoughts? Or was it really a complaint? Or a simple
list of pluses and minuses from which I hoped to craft an elegant equation, an unequivocal solution to our problems, mine
and Ray's.

I left a space:

why you and Joe filed for divorce. Was he having
an affair, Marilyn? Because Ray did, once. This was before we
were married, but I thought we had an understanding. I thought
we had reached a stage.

Damn it, we did have an understanding, though he main-
tained afterwards that he didn't know. Well, if my mother had
known she would have insisted I break off the engagement. And
my father? My father might have shot Ray with his rabbit gun.

It is an ugly ugly time for me. The fear that he will do it again is always uppermost. I remember the way he acted before I caught him. The irritability, the flickering attention. The odd-seeming gifts. And now I see those things again, even when there is evidence that this time the root is entirely different. The television roars its proof. The newspapers that blow along every gutter in the city all proclaim his deeds. But just the same. He is cruel and there is no room in our lives for cruelty. I am expecting a child. He is here with me now.

I was losing the thread even as I wrote. I felt it from the start, but in the last lines I had forsaken any pretence that this was a real letter. I reread it immediately, hoping to glean something from its indulgences. My stomach poked through the collapsing foam. The taut round of it was immensely satisfying. Whatever else happened there was this, this slick orb, full of life.

I heard Ray on the stairs, climbing towards me. The television was still alive so he wasn't on his way to bed. He tapped lightly on the door and I tensed, lowered my knees below the surface. I eyed the bolt, then the immense shadow of his feet, like a bear's, beneath the door.

"Mare," he pleaded. "Mare, you alive in there?"

I tried silence. I might reasonably have fallen asleep.

"Mare?"

"I'm fine, Ray."

"Are you coming to bed?"

"Eventually."

"All right if I'm in there when you do?"

There was no perfect answer. My hesitation came closest, I thought, to getting it right. But Ray had been drinking. A general buzzy remorse was all he was capable of. Nuanced perception would have to wait until morning. I said, "But I don't want to talk any more tonight, Ray. I'm tired."

"That's fine, love. I'll leave you alone. Fresh start tomorrow, eh?" He was so relieved. He could barely contain himself. This was the best of all outcomes for him — he wouldn't have to defend the indefensible. He hovered there a beat longer and then crept away, murmuring. Soon he turned off the television and then I heard the rattle in the pipes that meant he was running the cold tap in the kitchen. I waited for him to come back up the stairs, heavily, puffing a bit, and then I gave him a generous half-hour to fall asleep.

I don't know why I wrote it. The root was that film I saw, *Niagara*. And a youthful willingness to believe that all women suffer in the same way at the hands of straying men. But it must have had something to do with the storm too. I am not now, nor was I then, a superstitious person, but I couldn't escape the feeling that there was a potent symbolism at work. It wasn't that the hurricane had been sent expressly to deliver a message to me — I'm not that mad — it was more that there might be ways of interpreting world events in a helpful, significant way. But listen to me. Next it'll be tealeaves, or the pattern of rose petals as they drop to the dining room table. All I know for sure is that I was scared, panicked, and looking for help. And I really didn't care whether that help came to me as an obtuse message from God, or a pick-me-up telephone call from Marilyn Monroe.

Because Ray's behaviour really had changed dramatically. I understood that the hurricane had caused all sorts of stress for him. There was the newspaper story proclaiming him a hero (yes, they have written about him before, that's how Katie found out about him; shouldn't once be enough for any man?) and I knew it had made him uncomfortable. But there was something else. He spent his days combing the riverbanks, or the morgues. Tracking down survivors etc, and he must have seen some horrible things (as had I!) but he had become suddenly hard, cruel. Like a glue that has, after a long curing stage, gone diamond-hard overnight. He was impatient with me, and every night, I shivered alone at the far edge of the bed.

It was logical for me to wonder whether he was having another affair. His first dalliance (such a jolly word) came very early in our relationship and had brought out in him a similar, nearly snarling sort of animal. I caught them eventually and Ray broke it off with her immediately (at least I think he did). She was Chinese (does that explain the attraction to Katie; is there an aesthetic preference being demonstrated here?) and worked behind a steamy pane of glass on Spadina Avenue, ladling dumplings from a boiling cauldron. I watched her one morning. I leaned against the iron railing that divides one side of the avenue from the other. I made as if I was waiting for a streetcar. I understood the attraction. She laboured beautifully. The way the sweat glistened on her face. Even the way she stirred that dull pot. She was one of those people whose every move and gesture seems made for the camera. And yet she was totally artless. The sensation was of spying on her through a keyhole instead of through that rivered acre of glass. Ray said he had seen her and been "bewitched." Watching her, I thought it might be true. And I immediately resented her beauty, hated Ray for that rare honesty about his feelings. Even though by this point Ray had ended things, if there had been a brick at my feet I might have reached for it. But there wasn't. I would like to think that was because Toronto was an immaculate city fifty years ago, the streets swept obsessively by armies of the civic-minded, the sidewalks polished as lustily as a dining table, but it wasn't like that at all. Cities have always been dirty. Deliveries in Chinatown were still made sometimes by horse-drawn cart, and the smells of dung and rotting fruit thickened the air. The gutters ran with the torn-away outer leaves of bok choy and the casings of lychee fruit, the translucent tails of shrimp. A mounded heap of boulders would have surprised no one, would have attracted no attention. But his girl was obviously meant to slave on oblivious. Perhaps she is still out there somewhere, believing that she remained anonymous, that she escaped detection. I wonder if that makes it any easier for her. I wonder if it makes any difference at all.

He says their relationship lasted nearly three months. It cannot have been much longer than that. He claims they saw each other a total of six times. He felt awful about it; he was a man divided, ripped apart. That's what he says. I am nearly positive that he would have let it dwindle into nothing, or build into something more, over a period of years if I had been less sensitive to the subtle, and then not-so-subtle, diminishments of our life together at home. His grumbling, his tardiness, the unfamiliar scents on his clothes, the tighter budget — all the routine giveaways and signs. Most notable, though, were the constant distraction and faraway gaze that he revived so eerily in Hazel's wake; the myriad unthinking and minor cruelties that were dismayingly familiar. There was, though, (and I knew this even then) nothing extraordinary about his adultery. We were a regular couple, and I accepted that. I was a nurse and Ray was a cop. We wouldn't rule the world, or change the way it rotated about the sun. But in our earliest moments I hoped, and trusted even, that we could share an extraordinary love, and that would set us apart. It would certainly set me apart from my parents who grumbled at each other in Hamilton, and who had worn separate evasive routes in the wall-to-wall broadloom. "I didn't speak to your father at all yesterday," my mother told me once, "and it was *marvellous!*" I didn't want to hear that, and I certainly didn't want a life like that. But Ray seriously lengthened the odds of us living purely when he set to dazzling that woman with his crisp uniform and his white skin.

And so when it looked to be happening again, I wrote idly, stupidly, to a woman, a film star, who would never know of my existence, but who might be wrestling with the same issues in her own life. The most remarkable thing in all this is that, even though I had no intention of ever slotting that confessional page into an envelope, one day I received a handwritten reply.

RAY

For two days I have thought, this is it: the day I die. Mary thought so, too; I saw the diving crease on her forehead, like the silhouette of a gull, and the way she wrung her hands. Jenny leaned, as she has always leaned since she was a child, in the doorway, with her head tipped so it rests against the painted jamb. I forbade them to call the doctors. There was little anyone could do. The valve on the tank was fully open; one doesn't need a medical degree to manage that. Mary sat with me, or rather she sat in the room while I gulped for breath, just one breath that might rescue me, might signal yet another reprieve. I never felt that we were sharing anything (why should I; she wasn't going to leave the planet with me), but it might have been nice not to feel so . . . so solitary.

It is laughably redundant of me to say that I didn't die either time, but the fact still astonishes me. I have been examining, in the hours since, the way I managed to relinquish all control over my life. I have always thought that I would rage, as they say, against the dying of the light. That I would thrash and writhe and rail, a foul-mouthed fish atop the soiled sheets. But there was none of that. I fought only for air, not for life. And that struggle was purely reflexive. I was detached from it, was a mind divided. The fact is, I was prepared for the darkness, found a comfort in it that in hindsight is inexplicable. I would love another year. Another six months even. Would sentence entire populations to (a preferably painless) death if it might spare me. But when the moment seemed to be upon me I was ready to succumb. So very strange.

Alice must have known with a similar degree of certainty that she was about to die. When she disappeared into the river I smashed along the shore, moving at half the speed of the water. I was a man trying to escape a nightmare. My face was scratched, the back of my hands. I stumbled recklessly over rock and root (I don't recall which moment she was referring to, but Katie used that exact phrase at one point in her article: *he stumbled recklessly over rock and root*), spotting logs and barrels out there, and even a green balloon bobbing gaily along. The water bit ravenously into the trees and the limestone embankment. Somewhere up there were houses and gardens, families looking down with awe and astonishment. I made it a quarter mile downstream. I knew I should turn back, that running this obstacle course was useless, and worse than that it was irresponsible. Already I had the strong sense that this was one of the great avoidable incidents in my life. I had let the argument between us escalate precisely so there would be an irrevocable break. I had gone out of my way to create this tragedy. If it really was a tragedy. If she hadn't actually been thrown ashore just beyond the next thick mess of willow suckers and black muck. If she wasn't already ensconced in one of the yellow kitchens up there, wrapped in a blanket and telling her story.

I took a number of petulant tearful swings at the rain, screamed into skies the colour of avocado. My clothes stuck to me and when I wiped a muddy cuff across my stinging cheek it came away red. I felt bizarrely victimized, as if this were a personal battle, the hurricane chugging north expressly to meet me.

Finally I turned. And my entire life since then has felt like a hinge nailed to that moment, the moment I stopped and stared fiercely, desperately, downstream and then decided . . . to give up. I believe it must say unspeakable things about who I am that I abandoned her. But I was so torn. She was dead, had to be, so wasn't it a hopeless, even selfish pursuit I had embarked on? There were so many people elsewhere that night who needed me. And I had been trained, hadn't I, for crises like this one? I owed it to the good people of Toronto who paid my salary, to check on them, to protect them. None of which I consciously processed at the time, of course. What I thought then, all I thought, was: *She's gone; I have killed her. My God.*

I began the uphill slog back to the bridge. The route I had taken was under water now so I scrambled further up the slope and slithered along, grabbing at whatever looked solid. Soon this level would disappear too.

The stairs leading onto the bridge were collapsing, great cracks running longitudinally through them. I gained a foothold on the right edge of one and as I pushed off for the one above it, it crumbled. The same thing happened again and again. At the top I felt a shift in the road itself and felt in that vibration the possibility that the whole bridge might collapse.

I started the car and pushed the lever across so that the heater would throw its hot, oily air at me. I reported in on the radio. The bridge had to be closed, I said, and I needed a few uniforms to make that happen. The station man snapped that everyone was tied up and I should stay where I was. There were other bridges down, he said, and two helicopters had been dispatched to look for people carried away. I didn't mention Alice.

It would make no difference to the search effort, I thought. She could be anywhere.

I wonder now, from my own deathbed, if self-pity had anything to do with me being so positive that she was already dead. After all, those choppers were looking for survivors in the water, not for corpses. This was very much a rescue effort, not a cleanup. But that never occurred to me. Now, so very far after the fact, I can clearly imagine young women, even Alice, swinging safely from harnesses lowered in their paths. But then, clinging to the railing directly above the river, all I saw and felt was Alice's passing and my own imminent disintegration.

I was reversing the car off the bridge when a patrol wagon sloshed to a stop. The driver might have been twenty years old and his hair stuck up in all the wrong places. He said he had been in bed when the call came for him to return to work. He was used to walking the beat in the east end, he said, and this was the first time he had been allowed behind the wheel. "I just hope I don't put it in a ditch," he said. He leaned over the railing. "Seen anything good down there?"

"A dog was trapped against a tree," I told him gruffly.

"You get it out?"

"With a woman's help. She went off the other way."

He slapped at the railing. "You'll be wanting me to stay here, I suppose."

I told him to set up a barricade at both ends of the bridge. "You're in for a long night," I told the boy.

"Unless the bridge goes out." He sounded excited. He had no sense yet of consequences.

"The bridge goes down, you make sure you're on the same side as the wagon," I advised him.

The kid nodded but his enthusiasm had dimmed. He was less impressed with me already; he didn't find me funny. He was turning his attention to the road, deciding what he needed to do when I was gone. "I'll do that. Thanks, then, detective. You off, are you?"

I cast one more look at the river. It gave the impression of being constant, but that was untrue. The river water that had been here when I arrived had reached Lake Ontario by now. Nothing was what it seemed.

The station man told me a footbridge off Raymore Drive was being overrun. I needed to check there was no one hung up there. It was nearby. When I was looking for Alice I must have nearly reached it. "So the water's up above it?" I asked, not wanting to sound dim, but needing to dispel an unpleasant visual that had set up behind my eyes.

But the radio was all static now. The storm was playing havoc with the signal. Men were trying to talk over each other.

I imagined Alice clinging to the bridge's iron frame, screaming my name.

I turned south on Scarlett and leaned in close to the windshield, hunting for Raymore Drive. Water chased alongside and laid waste to the grass verge and the parking lot around the Bank of Montreal. A panting, low surf tumbled into front yards and against the glass storefronts on the western side of the street. The traffic lights were out and the lifeless, stacked eyes rocked on their cables. A man clung to a lamppost and the air was full of dark leaves. There were roofing tiles everywhere, like tiny rafts, and empty bottles that had escaped their wooden crates at the back of the Bull and Chatter.

The sign for Raymore rattled against its post. I slowed going down the hill. I may as well have been in a stream. I would have to be careful just opening the door. Further down, there were lights from the houses that curved along the river. A swing set had tipped into the trees, and a garden shed lay on its side, collecting water like a wooden cup. The footbridge was just visible through the shaking oaks, a black frame fringed with white. I pulled off the road onto a flat spot at the end of a lane leading down to a row of cottages already abandoned. I prayed for a concrete pad but discovered only mud. The car flattened out, which I wanted, but the wheels sank at the same time. I tried to reverse and nothing happened. Perhaps there was enough room for me to continue forwards and arc back onto the road. I tried that and the nose of the car tipped so suddenly that I thought for a second I might capsize. I climbed out and leaned on the trunk; the car tipped like a seesaw. Without help from a police truck, or the fire department, or at least half a dozen locals, who surely had more pressing tasks, I was stranded.

I radioed in. I was going on foot; I'd report back when I could. I wondered whether I might get a change of clothes somewhere, but what was the point? The heater had done a little work on my overcoat and the wool smelled awful. I hitched up the collar, tugged hard at the brim of my fedora, and slammed the door behind me. Then I began the walk that fifty years later would bring the lovely Katie into my home, nibbling so seductively at the end of her pencil.

I felt an unusual determination. The faintest echo in me of an arctic explorer. Tomorrow, early, I would have to go to Alice's apartment. Knock on the door as casually as if I was inviting her out for coffee. How many people who lived in that building could pick me out of a crowd and say, *That's the man. He was visiting there all the time. And noisy they were too.* Not very many. And the mother was dead, of course — drowned in a ditch. I shivered at that, wondered how many would join her in that corner of heaven by night's end. And the father was not only a drunk but a stranger to his daughter. There would have been no mention of me. Tom, the boatbuilder, he might have been told a few details, I supposed. And it was only reasonable to think that Alice confided in one or more of the women she worked with. Perhaps they all knew, and when she stopped arriving at

work, my name would come up. So there would be a few com-
plications arising from this. I didn't think they were
insurmountable, or damning, but there would certainly be
things that needed explaining.

As well as being terribly anxious, I was sad, hollow in a way
I couldn't remember feeling before. I wanted to believe that Alice
had fought ashore somewhere and made her way to safety. I didn't
want to see anyone dead. I could still imagine the two of us drying off later, consoling each other before a blazing fire. But even
that engaging fantasy was subordinate to the need I felt for an
alibi. An airtight way of disengaging myself from her disappearance. Mrs. Beaton at Simpson's — was that her name? I forget
now — had seen Alice watching me. Alice had a way of appearing
attached to me, even from across a room. But there wouldn't be
an investigation. I was thinking too much. I needed to see if she
was down there at the footbridge, sure, but then I should concentrate on whatever new catastrophes the evening threw at me.

The power failed. The pretty curve of houses vanished. I
heard a shout and then a half-hearted laugh, someone saying he
may as well turn in. *See you in the morning, Dusty. You bet, Brian.*
And then the wind dropped too, as if it ran off the same grid as
the house lights, and an odd, black quiet enveloped me. Just the
sound of my breathing, ragged and hoarse, although I couldn't
remember shouting very much, and the wet crack of branches
underfoot. And of course the river. The roar of it was like a jet
plane. I broke into a cautious jog. There were men down at the
footbridge, and a flashlight threw its short line across the sky.
Another beam crossed the first as if they were two swords clash-
ing. There were voices:

"Get off the bridge, damn it!"

"I've got to check."

"Get the hell off, Geoff. They're empty. And listen to those
goddamn wires."

The steel cables that secured the bridge whined, as if an immense violin was being coarsely tuned. I had the strange (and apparently unforgettable) sensation of floating high above the earth and seeing the perfectly round hole at the centre of a slowly rotating cloud mass. I shook off the effect. I broke through the last wall of trees and scanned the shoreline — the same spot I would have soon reached if I had continued my search for Alice. I looked in the flotsam and the choppy foam for signs of a body twisted into a root system or folded over a granite hump.

There were two men at the near end of the bridge and a third kneeling at its centre. The water had risen to within six feet of the walkway (and then, as I approached, it was five feet, or maybe just four). A small fishing cabin, just one room probably, with a salvaged woodstove parked against the back wall, had lost its grip on the riverbank somewhere upstream and been carried here, to this impromptu dam. It had tipped nearly onto its back and the green-black roof pointed north and the front door, which was just a rusted sheet of corrugated metal with a latch riveted onto it, faced the rain. The man on the bridge was wrestling with that latch. "Fucking help me!" he screamed, but neither of the men on shore men would risk it. I pushed between them, startling them, because they hadn't heard me arrive.

"For Christ's sake," one of them began, as if my rudeness was the thing that stood out most about the evening. I peered into the water looking for her, for Alice. There were logs and a dog kennel and a metal chimney pipe and a bicycle all visible at the surface. Beneath those things it was impossible to say. Beyond the first cabin was a second, painted white with dark trim around the windows. This one was almost completely below the waterline, like an iceberg. I remember I whistled (and the memory has me pursing my lips again now, recreating that low hoot of amazement). I was impressed by the monstrous force involved here, but dizzied, too, and I reached up for the guywire to steady myself. I registered the awful hum in it, as if all the electricity in the world had retreated here.

"I'm a cop," I said, as if it made a difference.

"Geoff."

"He'll kill himself!" someone shouted, but I ignored it.

"I fucking heard something in there. I'm sure of it," Geoff said.

I ducked beneath the rail and put a foot on the door.

"Another idjut," I heard from the shore.

"Get the people out of those houses down there," I yelled at them.

"There's no worry," came the answer. "It's as good as over, I reckon."

"Fucking do it now, or I'll arrest you. We're in the goddamn eye of the storm. It's going to hit again any second." I turned to Geoff. "Do you know their names?"

"That there is Alden Seemes, and the other's his brother, Darren." Geoff grinned, amused by the thought of their arrest.

"You're both mad," Alden said.

"Then leave us be," sniped Geoff.

"Go!" I barked. "Get everyone up to Scarlett. There's a union hall up there. Break in if you have to."

Alden and his brother looked at each other warily. They didn't like being ordered around. I bet they lived somewhere along the river, probably without power, in a larger version of these two cabins, and that they paid no taxes. There were several dozen like them, men who fished for a living and sold their pickerel and, in season, their salmon and trout, at the downtown markets. In winter they tended to stills welded out of copper plumbing and water tanks picked from the dump, and then they sold their see-through hooch to the bars that stayed open through the night, to the restaurateurs along the Ukrainian stretch of Dundas, and in Chinatown. I felt a mix of resentment and pity and anger and even jealousy for anyone who could carve out a life so different from my own.

"If you don't do as I say," I bellowed, "I'm going to shoot you!" They turned away, waved dismissively.

"High ground," I bellowed. "Get everyone to high ground."

I stamped down again on the corrugated door. In the windows dangled tired lace curtains, and piled against the back wall I saw there were some bundled clothes and a handmade quilt that showed men aboard a fleet of tractors set against a backdrop of mountains.

"Looks like they came from out west, don't it?" Geoff said.

"There's no one in here," I said. "We'd be able to see them. Or they'd be yelling."

"If they could," Geoff said, and did it so ominously that I thought I had heard a similar voice on the television recently, during a horror show about ghosts in a country mansion.

Water was sliding in great sheets over the house now, and when the door gave in the river slipped smoothly inside and filled up a barnboard cupboard a dozen feet below us. Torn rags and a brown dustpan floated to the surface. The walls were papered in red, and at the back a small iron stove lay on its side like a black eye in a battered face. A saucepan cavorted in the froth and there were jars of homemade jam and a stack of yellowed newspapers tied together with string.

"Anyone in there?" I crouched on the door's frame. Water was up to my ankles, the footbridge becoming just a ghost, visible only because the handrails gave it away.

"It's going under soon," Geoff warned. "All of it. Watch yourself."

He was right. Another degree or two of rotation and the room would fill completely. It would sink just as its neighbour had. There was a humbling sense here that we were just going through the motions. Doing everything possible, yes, but with no real expectation of success.

"Don't do it," Geoff said, thinking I suppose that I might drop inside, ferret about beneath the rags and chimney pipe for the body of a child, an old man. He held out a hand I was supposed to take; he wanted me back on the bridge. I screamed once more into the gurgling black hole and then let Geoff grab my arm between the wrist and the elbow and reel me in.

The two of us splashed back to the shore, where the skeptical brothers had been. Within seconds the cabin sank enough that only the tarpaper chimney was visible. A wire somewhere snapped. I couldn't fathom where it had been attached but I saw its ripped end slice the air. If we had been in its path, it would have cut us both in two as cleanly as a horse butcher's knife.

Geoff nodded. "It's gonna go. There ain't no doubt about that."

I pointed. "That way. Up the slope as fast as we can."

"Yeah, okay, then. I guess you're right." There was almost a drawl to the way he spoke, as if he was used to having all the time in the world to get through a sentence.

Another wire screamed its intention to unravel and I launched myself at the slope, trusting that Geoff would follow. My eyes felt pressurized, as if they might burst from their sockets. Fear, I suppose. The effects of adrenalin that Mary had coached me in. I managed a thought of her, swamped down at St. Joseph's by now, and wished there was a way to talk to her. I knocked my knee hard against a rock and buckled; I thought I would throw up from the pain. Geoff loomed over me.

"I'm okay." I got the words out, and then I was up again. The bridge tipping behind us.

We made the road, but even there the water was up over our shins. "How many houses down there?"

"Twenty, thirty maybe," Geoff said.

"They have any idea what's going on?"

Geoff shrugged, squinted as if a bright light had been focused on him. I wondered what he did for a living, thought it must be something simple and repetitive, something that would reduce an ordinary man to this sort of dumbness.

I led the way, each step on my bad knee causing a blinding whiteness behind my eyes. At the bottom of the slope, where the road turned sharply right, the water continued straight and met up with the river beyond a stand of birch. "Maybe they'll be okay," I said.

Geoff shook his head. "Normally that's a hundred feet further away. Look at that fucker move." He pointed at a bottle zipping through the trees like a pinball.

We hammered on doors, one of us working each side of the street. The wind thrashed at us again. At the first house a woman appeared behind the glass in her nightgown. She had a flashlight and she shone it in my face. I instructed her to open the door, but she was afraid of me. I had smeared blood across her window. I told her I was a police officer but still she shook her head. She tried to walk away but I rattled the door handle. Look, here's my badge. She appeared again, opened the door a crack, and blearily examined the shield I held up.

"The footbridge, ma'am, it's giving out. There'll be an awful rush of water when that happens."

The woman regarded me doubtfully. "I thought it was just the power knocked out by the storm," she said. "Me and my husband thought we'd get some extra sleep."

"You'd be wise to evacuate for a few hours."

"But our car —"

"You'll have to walk, ma'am. The road's washed out."

She leaned out and looked down to the corner, where the water rushed headlong into the river. "Oh my."

"Really, ma'am," I took a step away from her, "I need to tell everyone. Is your neighbour home?"

"Well yes. But they did the same thing we did. And, well, Davies likes his whisky. You'll not wake him up as easy."

"So you'll leave?"

She nodded, checked again the water cascading down the hill, then hitched a thumb over her shoulder at the staircase, its neat runner in blue-and-yellow irises. "I'll wake him now," she said. "Just like him to sleep through something like this." And then, "Thanks, detective. Awfully nice of you," as if I'd returned a stray cat, or warned her of an unlocked garage.

I roused Davies next door from his alcoholic slumber, and even rifled with him through the bedroom closet for a coat and hat. His wife grew teary in a corner. She gathered two toddlers into her skirt. She was a small woman and I felt sorry for her, having to live with such a husband. He grumbled something about resenting the intrusion, but it was obvious he would accept any help I wanted to offer. And so I pulled a few things together for them and even locked the door when we left. Davies grew wide-eyed as he stumbled down the short front walk. "Never seen that before," he muttered. "Damnedest thing," and his wife looked up at me apologetically. I pointed them towards Scarlett, as if they might not know the way, and mentioned the union hall.

"There's a church up there, too," the woman said. "We'll go there. I'll say a prayer for you, detective."

"I'd appreciate that," I said, and although I've never been a religious man, never felt the need to resort to that, I think I meant it.

The third house was locked, and at the fourth a belligerent woman told me that unless I was arresting her she was staying right where she was. "You telling me I'm going to die if I do that?" she said, wondering if she had taken a stupid position.

"There's a good chance," I said.

She considered this for a moment. Then she gazed up at the sky, the low skidding clouds and the waves of rain that were pelting the wooden floor inside her front door. I thought I had her, but eventually she said, "Nah, it don't look too-too bad to me," and slammed the door in my face.

Katie, when I recounted this long-ago door-to-door for her, wanted to know, "Which of them lived, Ray? Which of them lived?" Her cloying tone was like that of a mother trying to coax the first words from a toddler. I glared at her, genuinely angry, and she recoiled. "What?" She had no idea what she was asking. These peoples' lives were no more important to her than sticks of chewing gum. Another death just meant another couple of sentences to her, perhaps a grateful nod from her editor.

I was on the next porch when I heard the bridge move. Geoff was across the street and for some reason he was dragging a child's bicycle across a lawn. There was a roar as if the plane that had been thundering along its runway for the last hours was finally leaving the ground and would pass over our heads any second. In quick succession I heard three cables snapping and then a terrible grating as the bridge scraped over rock, and finally the roar of water being unleashed. I stared into the black trees. I felt like a child waiting for a monster to appear. And it did appear. But not as the wall of water I had expected. Just a foot of it moving up the slope towards me. Swallowing the groundcover, then the road and the lawns, ransacking the houses I had already woken. A Ford parked down near the corner shifted on its asphalt drive, then began to float away towards an opening in the trees. Like a boat being launched. A scream came from one of the houses and a candle's light disappeared from a window. The Ford barged between two birch and a willow, denting its side panels. I thumped at the door in front of me. I began to yell. Nothing. I retreated to the street. Water to my knees, then my thighs. Any second, I thought, Alice could float up beside me.

"Wake up! Wake up!" I screamed as I waded along the street. Geoff splashed through front lawns rapping at windows. Men and women and children were appearing from the houses. Women were crying and children, taking their mothers' cue, were beginning to do the same. "Up the hill," I bellowed. "Everyone up the hill." A woman tried to gather up a pile of books. "Leave it. Leave it!" I commanded.

I heard someone moving in a house. I saw the dimmest of lights in there. I ploughed up the walk to the door and put my shoulder to it. When the door gave, muddied water poured in. The red sofa moved away from the wall and knocked between the walls. A pine table in the dining room kissed a hanging light set low above it. In the kitchen an uncut loaf of bread nosed at the window. While I watched, the sink filled up with the water and it was suddenly above my waist, and I thought this might be the room where I perished. There were voices above me and I gave up all hope of wading anymore. I swam into the hallway and to the bottom of the stairs. I climbed them, as if out of a public pool. I ripped away my overcoat.

On the landing a man was standing on an old ladderback chair, trying to remove the hatch to the attic. He swung a hammer at the corners. There were candles spaced along a windowsill and a flashlight stood on its end at his feet, shining at the white hatch above him. He continued to thump at it with the side of his fist. Clutching each other in the doorway to one of the bedrooms were two boys and a girl. The girl was eleven or twelve, and shivering. She had long blond hair that was perfectly straight and her face was freckled. She stood between her brothers, who might have been twins, and were eight or nine and also blond. Their mother appeared. She had the same wide-eyed stare I was seeing everywhere now. The disbelief and the fear. She bent over the railing to see where the water had reached. "It's halfway, Al," she said. Trying to sound calm.

I wanted them to go out one of the windows. "Wait for it to reach us, and then we'll swim away," I said. Trying to make it sound easy.

"Mary doesn't swim," Al said and I looked at the wife. She was shaking her head but wouldn't hold my gaze. And then I heard her name again: Mary.

"And we haven't taught the kids either," Al said. "That's why I figure the attic. If it comes to that."

Al got one edge of the hatch loosened and he put his shoulder against it, then tried to straighten up. Getting his legs involved. The plywood square tipped into the space above them and I glimpsed the pale yellow rafters up there, spaced around the black hollow like ribs. Al said, "Okay, one at a time," and held out his arms for the boys.

"Already?" Mary wondered. She saw more clearly than her husband how much it looked like a tomb up there. Or a whale that would eat them alive.

Al motioned at the water, which was almost at the landing. "That's twelve feet in five minutes," he said. His eyes implored her to see that. The last thing they needed was to fight. "There's no time."

"Joshua," she said. "You first," and she pulled the little boy away from his brother. There were tears in his eyes and he was shaking and it was clear he had recognised he would be up there alone, at least for a few seconds. His lower lip trembled and he bit at it. He sniffed and his father picked him up and whispered something I couldn't hear. Al then lifted the boy higher — as if there was nothing to him, as if I was only seeing the ghost impressions of their last moments. But then the boy rapped his head sharply against the ceiling and cried out. I held the boy's feet steady and together we eased him into the attic. A second later his face appeared and he said, "It's okay," and his mother smiled and put a hand proudly over her mouth. Her little boy, she had to be thinking; how brave and how small.

We got Joshua's brother up there next and then the girl. Al passed up the hammer and looked next at Mary. The water was at the last stair. There were leaves and mauve petals floating in it, and a wooden spatula stirring it all up. File cards with recipes handwritten on them in a blue ink that had begun to run. *Cherry cake with Frosting. My Mother's Roast. Almond Blueberry Slices.*

"Your turn," Al said.

"I'm scared," she whispered.

Al nodded and glanced quickly at me. "All of us are. But it'll be okay."

"It will," I said. "It's a good plan."

"I should have learned," Mary said, blaming herself already for things that hadn't happened yet.

"Next year," Al said, and held out a hand. He stepped down from the ladderback so that she could step up. Joshua grabbed at her head and kissed the top of it and then Al wrapped his arms around her legs and lifted her up through the hatch.

We passed up some of the candles and then the flashlight, which Mary held while Al and I climbed up. The beam wriggled on the landing. I wondered whether I shouldn't be trying to get out the way I had come. Up here I was just trapped with them. This wasn't my family and I had been stupid to let the water push me up into this dark, nearly airless corner. I thought of the war and the people who had secreted themselves behind fake walls and in crawl spaces and attics. How they had listened for months for some sign that the enemy had left. We would have the same sort of night here. Al was pushing the hatch back into place. I wondered about the wisdom of barricading us in, the utility of it — surely the water would bust through any wall it wanted to — but this wasn't my house and this wasn't my wife and children. So I let Al reverse the hatch, so that the nails were pointing down and hammer away.

I paced the attic, balancing on the joists and putting a hand up to feel for airflow. The wind was getting in at the northern corners and around the chimney. The candle flames leapt around, hid behind each other. Mary had the children sit in a row with a blanket stretched over their laps. She told them that they would hear the water on the ceiling of their bedroom and that that noise would last for a while. But then it would stop and the water would leave them alone and they would be able to go downstairs and begin to clean up. "Grace, you can help me in the kitchen, and Joshua, you and your brother will help Dad. There will be lots of work for all of us and I don't suppose there'll be any school for a few days."

She hoped, I guessed, that the prospect of no school would distract them, but the children just stared at her, waited for her to tell them something else, something more grand, or more believable.

The water carried with it all manner of furniture that thumped against the ceiling. Sometimes it sounded as if there might be someone down there, methodically working across the room, hunting the same escape we had found. So convincing was this effect that I saw Mary look questioningly at her husband, but he shook his head and said, "It's a doll or something. A bottle," and we would sit listening to it again, until it was joined by something even more convincing and they would repeat their exchange with minor variations.

When the river started to seep around the hatch and also through the holes where the light fixtures were, and where there was a duct from the bathroom, I said, We need to make another hole."

The children regarded me warily. I was a stranger and trusting me to come up with answers that had evaded their father was difficult for them. Mary stood up and touched the rafter above her head, then remained like that, as if impersonating

Atlas, the weight of the world on her shoulders.

"We might have to go up on the roof," I explained.

Mary nodded fervently. It was dark out there, around midnight, but she seemed oppressed by the woody blackness in here. She was like a miner trapped underground and the thought of seeing the sky again seemed to give her another wind.

I knocked at the roof with the dull end of the flashlight. This was an old house and the nails had square shafts. Joshua came over and presented me with the hammer. I pried up boards and heard shingles slide away and then the rain swooped in, looking like snow in the light. I worked at making the hole bigger and when I looked over at the family they were standing in line along one of the joists, like ravens on a telephone wire. The space between the two joists that bracketed the hatch was almost full, and when that space overflowed, the next two, left and right, would fill, and then the next. It was like holding an ice cube tray under the tap.

I made the hole in the roof big enough to get my head out, and then my shoulders. I had Al come over and I stepped into the stirrup Al made of his hands and put my head outside and saw that the world had changed entirely.

One of the houses opposite, the one where I had seen Geoff, moving that bicycle across the lawn, had vanished. We were in a field of rushing brown water, and either the house across the way was beneath the surface or it had been lifted clear off its foundations and swept away. There was no delineating anymore the edge of the river. The river was everywhere. I could see houses still, and trees, but they were all midstream. The ground floor of every house on the street had vanished. I could make out bedroom furniture swimming in one room because a light shone from beneath the surface, like a submarine. One house was tipping and bobbing in the current. People were up on their roof. I yelled but the wind lassoed my voice and dumped it in the water. To the south the sky was a dull yellow and I thought that must mean there was still power in that direction. Then there was a brighter light and a gathering roar and a helicopter passed somewhere west of us, heading north.

I didn't want to tell the family what was happening. I wanted to say I had made a mistake, that we should seal the roof again and wait for the storm and the waters to subside. I wanted to pretend it wasn't happening. When I ducked inside they looked up at me expectantly and the impression that they were like birds came to me again. If only they could fly.

Not since the war had I known in advance that people were going to die. And those uniformed boys were bleeding. There were limbs mangled or gone altogether. There were portholes into the stomach. In Italy, orders had been given that I considered suicidal. *We will attack from our open field the well-armed men hidden in that forest.* That came to mind. Or, *We need to cross these mountains tonight.* Good men had died needlessly. And this situation was closest to those. If they couldn't swim, Al's wife and their three kids were going to die. Al would probably die trying to save them, and maybe I would too.

"How bad is it?" Al wanted to know.

I tried to communicate with my eyes that I'd rather not say, but Mary had me figured out and said, "Tell us."

I said we should make the hole big enough at least that we could climb through it quickly when we needed to, but that for now we should stay inside. We'll get blown off, I thought. Someone will start screaming.

I hammered at the shingles. The water gurgled up around the hatch and as it slithered over each successive joist it seemed almost to sigh with relief.

A large section of the roof came away in one piece and then it was as if I was standing under a showerhead. I lurched away. The house seemed to move with me. I regained my balance and opened my eyes. The house shifted again. The floor no longer level. The boys were petrified and clinging to their mother, who in turn had reached above her head and clutched with a white hand to the angled rafter.

"We're sliding," Al announced. "The whole house is going."

"We've got to get out!" Mary looked up at the sky and then at me. "Before we tip."

I said. "Al, you go first. I'll pass them up to you. Get to the chimney if you can."

Al hesitated, and I understood that this otherwise sensible man wanted some control over the situation. But finally he said, "Okay."

I crouched down and Al stepped up onto my level thigh and then, with a grunt, pushed himself outside. He stomped around the perimeter of the hole I had made, checking for weak spots, and when he was satisfied none of his family would crash back into the attic, he sat down, like a bather at the edge of a pool. Joshua went first, then Mary said, "You go, Luke," and she sounded almost keen, as if this was a treat, a ride at the fairground. When Luke disappeared Mary hugged her daughter. "It'll be okay," she said.

"Don't worry, Mum," the girl said. "I know it will."

The house groaned and slid again. Wood tore over rock. I hauled myself outside last and saw that we might as well have been aboard a ship.

"My God, Al," Mary said, and moved an arm mutely through the air in front of her.

Al indicated a birch tree. "That's at the edge of the road. We've moved twenty feet."

"You think we'll stay upright?"

I saw in my head the two cabins capsized at the footbridge but said nothing.

But then the house rushed forwards, like a surfboard atop

a wave, and we all grabbed at the roof and the chimney's brick-work and each other.

Another house had become snagged in trees that Mary said were normally at the very edge of the river. A family of three shivered on its roof.

As we glided and rocked closer Mary began to yell and wave frantically, as if she wanted them to fire up the motor and steer their house out of the way so there would be no collision.

Grace lost her footing and slid away from us. It seemed that she would ride the shingles all the way down to the water. The house would storm over her. But then it teetered the other way, like a drunk trying to regain his balance after tripping up a kerb, and Al was able to seize his daughter just as the collision occurred.

Al wanted us to abandon ship and join the other family, but I said we should stay where we were. Someone from the other family — a teenager, a rough-looking kid who would surely glower and spit once he found out I was a cop — said, "The Ramseys have gone already." He indicated a rougher patch of water between the trees. "That was the last place we saw them," he said. "And the Cooks from the corner too."

Somewhere a siren bawled, and then another, more distant. The dull sounds of the world trying to respond.

A wardrobe floated past on its back; in the middle of the current yet another house. There was a light in one of the bed-rooms, and on the roof a man and a woman were rushing from side to side, trying to stop the house from rolling. The man yelled something at us, and he sounded panicked, enraged, indignant that we would let this happen to them. Within seconds they were gone, swept around the curve.

There were uprooted trees longer than buses. A great litter of tin roofing and sheets, sweaters and dresses. There were chil-dren's gloves in front of us and just below the surface was a pair of men's pants, legs flailing. I had already seen a grey dog with its eyes gone milky, and then a litter of drowned ginger kittens swirling around each other as if in play.

The teenager yelled: "You're going — you're fucking going!" and before we could decide where we wanted to be, the connection between our two houses was eliminated.

Branches slashed my face. Mary said there was blood. She ran a finger over her own cheek. And then I lost my footing and was sliding, exactly the way the girl had. I couldn't see anything except the blur of shingles. As I hit the water I heard another siren.

I was pulled under immediately, pinned against the outside front wall as we surged downstream. I opened my eyes and the world was entirely brown, full of grit. I fought for the surface but the pressure was too great. I managed to extend one arm and claw at the edge of a window frame. I dragged a foot across to the sill. The glass had gone and I had no idea what else to do, so I allowed myself to be pushed inside. I thrashed upwards — I hoped it was upwards — but my head hit a wall or a ceiling and there was no layer of air. I found myself again at the window. Only it wasn't the window, it was a doorway and I kicked through it and thought that I saw the vaguest lightening of the air above me and I began to let the air out of my lungs. The oxygen streamed towards the lighter water and I followed it. I reached the surface and sputtered, gasped, and sank again. I kicked against something and discovered I could stand up. I was standing on the wall of one of the bedrooms. I coughed and the pain alarmed me, was like a knife at my heart.

The light I had seen seemed to have no origin. To escape I would have to go under again. I tried to remember the layout of the house. The wall was a pale green but I thought that was true of the entire second floor. I needed to make it to the landing and from there up into the attic. Or escape through a window at the back of the house, where the pressure wasn't so great.

I took a few testing breaths and the air felt thinner than I needed. I thought I might well die there. I took a final gulping mouthful and dived.

I was blind and smashed into a cupboard. I swung myself around it, performed a clumsy dance with its swinging door and thrust off again. Another closed door resisted my efforts, as though there was a bigger man on the other side. I went deeper, wriggled into a shifting crevice I found and then, through it, I broke upwards. If I hit more ceiling I was dead. I had so little air left. Something punched my ribs and I lashed out as though it might have been a shark. I burst explosively into air.

I was in another bedroom. Some of the ceiling had gone and I could see into the attic's ribcage. The hole I had hammered into the roof was twenty feet away, like the opening of a cave. I had made it almost full circle. And, I realize now, I had stopped thinking about Alice.

Most of the roof was under water. The chimney lay parallel to the surface, like a brick diving board. I half-swam and half-crawled outside. I took it for granted someone would take my arm, help me up. But it didn't happen. When I crawled into the outside world, I was alone.

MARY

He has been delirious for more than a day, babbling, fevered. He has a cough that threatens to turn him inside out. The doctor came accompanied by a nurse and when they left they wanted to send an ambulance for Ray. "This isn't a hospital," the doctor pointed out, as if we had been living under some grand illusion. If we admitted him, he said, there were machines that could breathe for my husband, put oxygen into his blood.

"He won't go," I said. "He's being obstinate."

"Then he'll die here," the doctor said.

He was an obvious man, unsubtle and, so far as I could tell, without a sense of humour. He was fat, and on some visits it was hard to tell whose breath was most laboured, his or Ray's. Whenever he leaned over Ray to listen to his heart, or fiddle with a needle, I envisioned him falling onto Ray's chest, crushing it, and destroying the bed. He wore the same white shirt for every visit, like a starving waiter, with a tiny identifying blood stain (he is a doctor, so I won't allow that it might be chocolate or ketchup, or any of the million other possibilities) near the waistband. Shank is the doctor's awful name — what must his forebears have done to deserve such a thing?

I shrugged. "He has to die somewhere." It was a trite answer, barely worth uttering, but I hadn't the energy to point out more comprehensively the doctor's idiocy. Ray, had he been conscious, would have laughed in his face, tried to rouse himself enough to boot the man physically from his house, I know he would.

"Given that he's not going anywhere," Jenny said, striving for a more diplomatic tone, "what can we do?"

It turned out there was nothing really. We agreed, though, that the nurse could stop in each morning. Blood oxygen levels could be closely monitored. There were mysterious minor adjustments, apparently, and subtle milky administrations that might, if Ray was fortunate ("If you've been good," the doctor said moronically), buy him a little time.

"How long?" Saying it, I felt like a very poor actor on the television, as if that box in the corner had robbed me of the possibility of having any spontaneous reaction to my husband's impending death.

But Shank was not to be pinned down. He puffed up his chest (as well as his cheeks and the considerable flaps under his chin) and advanced on us. Peripherally I saw Jenny retreat into the doorway, where there was no room for him, and I took a similar step between the two old wingbacks. Shank wobbled to a stop, perhaps thinking us squeamish, or emotionally fragile. He attempted a smile (a consoling gesture is what he was after, I suppose) and offered us a view of his upturned palms. "It's hard to say," he said.

"Ballpark it for us," Jenny tried, producing a much harder version of Shank's smile, "will you, please?"

But nothing we could say prompted a prognosis. "How about you?" Jenny said, nodding at the nurse. "Want to take a shot: how long?"

It was exasperating, but I knew the protocols involved. I had mumbled these same vague answers myself, for decades. It is more important to those in the medical profession that they not be wrong than it is to provide full disclosure. The conceit is that the general public, and the patient in particular, is to be protected from any truth that might frighten them literally to death. But there is a transparent arrogance in this assumption and it robs families of the chance to prepare properly. It leaves them in the dark and it serves only to mystify the practice of medicine and the processes of the human body. It is a methodology that strikes me as pagan, primitive somehow, but also as one unlikely to change in my lifetime. What I said to him was, "Have you done everything you can?"

"Of course." He was offended by my bluntness, the suggestion that was contained within it.

"Then please leave."

Jenny and I sat in the kitchen with the door to the parlour wedged open. I put some music on to cover the awful in and out of Ray's breathing. I could see his head in profile, the clear mask over his nose like a monstrous teardrop. Jenny put her hand on mine and I let it stay there a while simply because we touched each other so rarely. It was the appropriate time for us to touch each other, of course, but I felt I was receiving her sympathies under false pretences. I worried too that she needed my support more than I needed hers; she was losing a father, and perhaps that was worse than losing a husband — she didn't know him quite the way I did. I was about to be released while she, I worried, would feel abandoned.

Later, Jenny left the house. For a woman who lives thousands of miles away she has maintained an impressive number of friendships, or claims to have done so. I stood in front of Ray for a while. He was asleep and he was grey. He still is. Grey shading to purple around his eyes and his ears. I have noticed too that his gums when he smiles are blue. Experimentally I took his hand in mine. Could I do this when the end came?

Should I do it anyway, if only for the sake of appearance? It has been twenty years, at least, since we have held hands. If Ray were to try it now, if he fumbled around the end of my sleeve in a public mall, for instance, I would have to laugh. His hand is light, a small plucked bird, a quail. I let it go and went to his desk and rifled through the drawers.

I found nothing I hadn't expected. An inch of subscription notices he knows there is no point responding to but cannot bring himself to throw away, which I understand completely. The Swiss Army knife he found on King Street one morning when he was out for a walk. The silver flask he bought himself at a booth in the Eaton Centre. It is half-full of something or other, but is just a decoy to distract from the bottle of Dewar's he keeps in here. Some paper clips and his driver's licence, now useless to him, as well as his caa card. There are no pictures, no letters or cards. It is a man's desk, and a cold man at that. There isn't much in there that sums up a life, or suggests it's a life worth clinging to. Which is cold of me, too, I know, but here, look at it.

I ran a hand under the mattress. It occurred to me that with him being increasingly bedridden he might hide his notebook there again, close to hand, but it wasn't there. So perhaps he has stopped, as I asked him to.

I also checked his pitiful little tray of brownies. I wanted to know how many there were left. The woman two doors down makes them for him and I know damn well what she bakes into them. Smell them, it doesn't take a genius. But I talked to some friends and the consensus seems to be that so long as I monitor his consumption, and don't mind his drifting off (are you kidding?) then there is probably no harm in it. He has eaten half of them, which works out to one a day; he treats them as if they are vitamin supplements, or laxatives.

There is a moment I have been returning to obsessively the last few days, a short scene. I was with Gina in her office. I had telephoned her from one of the department stores. It was nearly four in the afternoon. I was shopping for the baby. If she was nearly done, I said, then I thought I might stop by; we could ride home together on the streetcar. Gina told me to come up.

When I arrived she held open the door to the palatial suite of rooms.

"I still can't believe you're not assigned to the basement," I told her. There had always seemed to be something slightly scandalous about Gina's work. The mayor spoke through her, she wrote all his letters and bits of his speeches. How in the world was that allowed to happen so openly?

I don't remember all of what we spoke about. But as the light faded we found ourselves at the window. I was admitting to a certain uneasiness at being there with her. In the spring I had seen and heard some of what Senator McCarthy had to say, and it had scared me, given me nightmares and made me wary of all government. I could all too easily imagine men from the mayor's staff hauling me into some dank basement cell where I would be forced to admit to all sorts of unsavoury connections and memberships.

I was staring out blindly, talking at the glass. I remember a ring of condensation appeared in front of my mouth. I'd love to know why my brain thought it important to store that small round of fog, and yet has casually lost so many names and faces I would dearly love to reacquaint myself with. Gina was behind me, rubbing the small of my back. Cars out there were turning on their headlights, and clouds had piled up over the lake, like an army setting siege to the city. At the corner of Queen Street and University two men were sharing a bottle of wine. Gina pointed them out, said they were always there. "And then one day they won't be," she added, "because they'll be dead, or one of them will die and the other one will drift off." She stabbed urgently at the glass with a finger. "Hey, that looks like Ray down there."

I peered into the gloom. There were hundreds of people. Most of the men wore hats, and the women were in knee-length coats. Headlights threw a yellow ring around a few faces. But there, below Queen Street, hustling a woman into the back seat of his cruiser, was my husband. It was certainly his car, anyway. And the coat he liked to wear over his grey suit. The same brown band around his hat. I never caught his face, but the way the man hurried around to the driver's seat, and checked the seat before ducking inside, all were typical Ray. "I think you're right," I said. "I wonder what he's doing over here. I always feel slightly sorry for the people he arrests. I don't know why."

"That's because you want everyone to be happy," Gina told me. "Happy and healthy. There's way too much of the Florence Nightingale in you."

I felt the sting of that. I considered myself a pragmatist, and on some days even a cynic. I was happier out of the hospital than I was in it. I felt more pure, even more helpful, in my oldest dress and scruffiest sweater than I did in my starched uniform and pin cap.

Ray was driving away. I watched his lights swing around onto Richmond. Another nearly identical car following him. A streetcar carried a hundred people west, sparks flashing from the overhead cables.

Later, at home, Ray came back in from the patio where he'd been smoking a cigarette. I was washing the plates from his dinner. He wrapped his arms around my waist and kissed the base of my neck. "I love this dress," he told me. I reached up and touched the side of his face, depositing a smear of foam.

"I saw you today," I said. I leaned back into him, encouraged his hand up over my breast. I tipped my head so he would have better access to my neck, the lobe of my ear.

"I don't think so," Ray said. He had his nose against my shoulder.

"You were arresting someone. On University Avenue. We saw you from Gina's office." I ran the cloth around the inside of the saucepan. Needles of rosemary and shrivelled pork bits swam over my hand (again, why does one retain this sort of thing?). I dropped the cloth and pushed back against him, made it as plain as I could. Pushed his hand across my chest, keeping pressure on it.

He nuzzled absently at my neck. "I'm thinking. I took in a winehound from that corner. Could that be it? I thought he was going to throw up all over the seat."

"No this was a woman. About five o'clock."

"A woman."

I could almost hear the gears turning in his head. I shook the foam and water from my hands and turned, placed my open hands against the seat of his pants. I tilted my head and kissed the tip of his chin, felt his beard poking through the skin, and then I moved to his bottom lip, held it a second between my lips. There was the smell on his breath of cigarettes. But I didn't mind. My body was prepared to ignore the obstacles. I had read that when the birth drew nearer I "might be wise to cease intimate relations." Which meant, didn't it, storing up some memories in the next few months?

When I disengaged my mouth from his, he said, "That must have been the nutcase from Oshawa. She was walking around all day saying to everyone who'd listen that she needed to pick up pork chops for her boys. I just dropped her off for a psychiatric."

"That must have been her," I said, not caring anymore. I kissed him again. Then, curiously, "You were rough with her, we thought. I'd hate to see what you were like with the drunk."

"She slipped on something at the kerb there," he said. "I

thought she was going to fall. The wind was something awful by then. I was just giving her a hand. But I guess I'll have to watch myself if you got a different impression. I'll get a reputation."

Ray had pulled up the back of my dress, gathering it in his fist an inch at a time. His hand climbed my back and undid, with a dexterity that always impressed me, the clip of my bra. I felt the soft, relinquishing snap of the straps, and his hands moving around my rib cage and under the steel wiring. He bent at the waist away from me, performed a shaky sort of limbo manoeuvre as he took my nipples lightly between his thumbs and fingers.

He dropped his head to my breast, his breath coming faster now, matching my own. I let my hands fall to my side. A moan escaped me, like steam from a vent, and I couldn't quite decide whether it was involuntary or whether I was offering encouragement. After a minute I slumped over him, and he ducked lower, hoisted me over his shoulder. As he navigated around furniture and into the hall, I remembered that this was the fireman's lift. Gina said once that Frank would sometimes burst in to the house and carry her to the bedroom this way. Still in his firefighting gear. Would Frank have shared the same story with Ray? And had Ray decided to try it out at home, with me? Far from disturbing me, I found the notion exciting. It had nothing to do with Frank. It was about my husband still wanting to try new things. He dropped me onto the bed. I looked up at him. If I was braver I would have liked to command him to be still. Just long enough for me to get up and complete a rotation or two of him. Feel through his pants for the erection I knew must be there by now. Whisper things in his ear. Run my hand inside his shirt. But instead I concentrated on the sensation of his thigh against mine as he kneeled over me. And the way, when he lay on top of me (with the too-cheap mattress trying to fold comically around us) and whispered into my mouth that he loved me, I could feel the cold steel of his belt against my stomach.

So. I have two questions. First, why in the world am I revisiting so avidly a sex scene with this man? And secondly, that was her, wasn't it? It has taken me half of the twentieth century and a little of the twenty-first to twig to the obvious: that it was her in the car with him. While I shopped for cribs he was bundling her away to some lurid den. And I saw her. I saw them. I just didn't know what I was looking at.

RAY

I have been granted a reprieve. It is easier for me to breathe again, a belt has been loosened one notch. All are a little mystified, and the good doctor and I might be the only ones who are not a little disappointed. The young man from the oxygen supply outfit was here this morning. "The usual?" he asked Mary, as if she might not want to splurge this time on a full order. I would have staggered over and cuffed him were it not for the thought that I would be robbing myself of some minutes. Because there are only so many inhalations left. True enough for everyone, I know, but the number may as well be infinite for most of you, whereas I am like the condemned man who is counting down the final minutes before he is leather-strapped to the upright chair.

It has occurred to me, never fear, that there are better ways for me to spend whatever seconds I have. In reconciliation, for example. Or in dialogue with my long-suffering wife and daughter rather than spitting out this blasted soliloquy. Even having them wheel me to the edge of the Scarborough Bluffs so I can watch for a while the whitecaps steaming north and the gulls wheeling and tipping in a Wedgwood-blue sky. Rereading the classics or ordering in my favourite foods, now inexplicably verboten. I could be paying rhapsodic attention to Beethoven or weeping uncontrollably to one of Bach's cello suites. Begging forgiveness or plotting my own sudden and dramatic end. The list is endless, and therein, I think, lies the problem. I am an indecisive man. I have spent months of my life wondering which new socket wrench set to buy from Canadian Tire; years more on whether buying a new car or a new house is wise. And yet I have, somewhat miraculously, settled on a course here, and dare not question it, or cast about for another route out of this world. At least this way I will leave something behind. If I am lucky I might even discover something about myself. And (have I said this before?) Mary will have all the evidence she needs to write me off and take up with the mailman. It is enough. And it might well be all I am capable of.

Frank, our neighbour back then; Frank Chiarelli I think it was. Mary said something about him last night; how sad it was he had died so young. Anyway. He fought fires. There were citations for bravery and he was a good man, decent, though a bit of a drunk when he got the chance (aren't we all?). He didn't make it through that night, was one of a half-dozen to perish. A *real* hero. And while I was saddened by his death, I was relieved too, because Frank knew about me. It was as if God was granting me a little grace.

It was mad of me to tell him anything. I don't know why I did.

I was with him in his garage. It was attached to the house but cold, our breath mixed in the air between us like a phantom, but Frank had dug out two scratchy blankets from a pine chest tucked under the workbench and there were two broken-down armchairs arranged on an oily scrap of orange carpet. The sight of his tools gave him energy, he said. And sometimes it was the memory of everything he'd done with them. He had worked on the car most weekends, and also fashioned passable end tables, and even the bed he and Gina slept in.

A plastic ashtray was balanced, like a pirate's hat, on top of the vise, and on the concrete floor were six beer bottles, four of them empty. A little earlier Frank had pointed out a hole near the foot of my chair and said there were mice in there. Every time I shifted my weight I imagined I could hear the animals scurrying into an air pocket.

Gina was inside, Frank said, writing to her mother, who had recently moved to Victoria in British Columbia. She had had enough of Ontario's weather, and if Victoria wasn't at least half as beautiful as she had read, then she was going home to Italy and she expected Gina to come with her. Twice already Gina had stuck her head around the side door to see if she could get us anything, and both times, as soon as she had retreated — for more beer, for a pair of boots — Frank had said the same thing: she's checking to see if I'm still alive.

We were talking about his cancer. That's right. You know, I had entirely forgotten until now that he was sick before he died. They had all those plans to buy a cottage on Toronto Island and then he was struck with a terminal disease. It's another explanation for why I have been seeing his face all day. Frank said he didn't want me coming around for regular updates, okay? But yes, he was in pain. And the pace was frightening him. "It's like being chased by a horse," he said.

I asked him, indelicately: "What does it feel like?"

"For a while it felt like a stitch in my side. As if I was sprinting uphill all the time. And then it was heartburn." He said he thought it was funny how cancer disguised itself in the early going. "It's as if it knows we won't want to believe it. If it can approximate some common problem, then we won't go to the doctor. Not early enough to do any good, anyhow."

"So do you think you acted too slowly?"

"They don't know what to do when it's in the gut," shrugged Frank. "If they do something that works they scurry back to their labs and go over the paperwork — maybe it was this; maybe it was that. I'm a goddamn guinea pig. They want to open me up now, take a look-see. I said, what are you going to do once you're in there?"

"And what did they say?"

"They said if it wasn't attached too fiercely they'd cut it out. Well, I said, if it wasn't attached too *fiercely*, then I'd just shit it out, wouldn't I? They don't appreciate someone who talks back, Ray, I can tell you that much. How's Mary that way? Seems to me she'd actually listen to her patients, which is more than I can say for this lot."

His questions ran together, but then I supposed there were no good answers anymore and the solution, to Frank's mind, was just to keep talking. He must have thought that as soon as he stopped sliding one sentence into the next, he was a goner. I waited to see if he wanted to start again, but Frank was nodding absently and pushing off the orange rug with his feet so that his old armchair creaked and groaned.

"I've been seeing a woman," I blurted. It was that easy, like a belch.

The next morning, sitting at breakfast with Mary, I would wonder at my motive. Was my confession intended as a gift (because everyone liked to be privy to a great secret)? Or did I want Frank to take this secret to the grave, and quickly? Was I perhaps trying to distract him from his predicament? The only solid conclusion I could come to was that it was a monumental gaffe, and moreover a total cock-up. Because now, more than anything, I wanted my friend to die.

"How do you mean?" Frank asked, playing dumb, deciding

the obvious answer couldn't be the right one.

I saw, though, the fresh fizz in his eyes. I thought about retreating, about lying: *Nothing's come of it. We just talk.* Or a half-truth: *She wants more from me, but, well, there's Mary to think of. And the child.* But what I said was:

"Her name's Alice. She works in a pastry shop."

"How long?"

"Have I been seeing her? A few months."

Frank whistled, grabbed his beer again. He scratched absentmindedly at the label a bit, all the while shaking his head gently. Then he whistled again and looked up. "She better than Mary, is she?"

"No, of course not."

"Then you're crazy. Out of your head."

"I . . ."

Frank held up his bottle and interrupted. "I don't want to hear it." He was still shaking his head.

"I've been trying to end it," I said.

"So you should."

"That's it? The sum of your thoughts on the matter."

"From where I sit, I reckon it is, yeah. Christ, Mary will keel over and die if she finds out."

It wasn't the reaction I was expecting. If Frank was healthy it would have been different. Curiosity would have won out and then he would have lost the right to judge. But this wasn't the old Frank. *Piece of shit*, I thought. *To not even hear me out. Piece of shit.* "That's it, then," I said again, except this time it wasn't so much a question as it was a way of acknowledging that this was the moment we parted ways. Wanting to make sure.

"I can't believe you're telling me this," Frank said.

I reminded him angrily of the woman we had seen at the steak house in the summer. How Frank had whistled and drooled. "Remember her? If she had so much as winked at you,

you would have gone with her."

"I wouldn't, actually," Frank said coolly. "That was just cheap talk. And you know it. So I resent the accusation. You don't get to sit with me in my garage, claiming I'm the same as you. Hell, we can call Gina out here right now and tell her both our stories, see what she thinks. Gina!"

"She has to forgive you now," I said moodily. I struggled up from my chair. I collected the empties piled beside it and put them on the workbench. In the house Gina was moving towards us. Her quick footsteps on the carpet were like a pillow being smacked over and over against a wall. Frank slumped in his chair, legs spread wide. I was pretty sure Frank was thinking the same thing I was — that we had travelled a vast distance from each other in only a couple of minutes.

Gina tugged on the door and when it shuddered free of its frame the whole house vibrated. She was winded and must have been upstairs. She had no makeup on and I thought she was prettier that way. Her face was flushed from being washed and the redness extended down into the vee at the neck of her dress. She smiled — bravely, I thought. Every summons from Frank must bring to her mind a vision of him on all fours, clutching his gut. "Everything okay?" she said.

"Fine," Frank said. He put out a hand solicitously and I overcame enough of my surprise at the trusting gesture to pull him to his feet. It was as if we were shaking hands, saying goodbye for the last time. "Ray was just leaving. He's got to clean up for his wife. I thought you were in the next room, Genie. I was calling to say, Wait for me; I'll come up with you. If I'd known you were all the way upstairs I would never have bothered you."

"I was just sorting myself out. Mary not back yet, Ray?"

"Unless I missed her," I said. "I should check."

"I would," Frank said. "Maybe she's left you."

"Oh, Frank! What a terrible thing to say."

I moved to the garage door and made a great show of surveying the street. "The leaves are just about gone," I said.

"Night, Ray," Frank said gruffly.

"You boys fighting out here, were you?" Gina wanted to know.

"Ray's trying to entrust a dying man with secrets, that's all. And since I don't feel like dying just yet, I oughtn't to hear such things, is my way of looking at it."

"And what secrets are those?" Gina asked, moving off the wooden step and onto the concrete floor.

"Just some foolishness at work," I told her.

Gina turned to her husband. "So how much did he tell you?"

Frank stuck a finger into each of the empties and let them bash against each other. "Nothing worth talking about, Genie. Like I said, I don't want anybody's secrets."

"Sure you do, honey." She winked at me and then laughed. Frank, though, was moving past her to go inside.

"Damn cold," he said. "Goes right through you." He left Gina alone with me. I heard him climb the three stairs to the kitchen and deposit the empties on the counter.

"He okay?" Gina said. "Was he in pain?"

I said I didn't think so. "It must be awful, though. For both of you."

She tried to summon another smile but she looked suddenly older. A gust of wind had her wrapping her arms around her ribs. Old cigarette ash plumed over the lip of the ashtray like a wave over a harbour wall. Gina's face settled into an expression of pleading. Don't ask me anything, her face seemed to say. Let me be.

"Well if there's anything," I said, aware nonetheless that Gina would go to Mary, not me.

And Frank? I had no idea if I would get to talk to him normally again. I would try an apology in the morning, that was my

panicked plan. If Frank would hear it, I would say I was breaking it off with Alice. That I was grateful for Frank helping me
to see the light. Could I count on his discretion? I reached up
for the garage door. "You want this closed?"

"That'd be nice, thanks. Say hello to Mary for me. And don't
be too hard on her for staying out."

"I won't."

I pulled hard, too hard, and the hinged steel door clattered
over its oiled rollers and fell like a blade between us. A mere
three days later Frank was drowned and I felt like the seediest
of gods. I had no idea what he had told Gina.

Much of the last couple of days, while the doctor fretted over
me, Mary paced, and Jenny leaned soulfully in the doorway,
picking at her nails, I drifted again in that ravenous windblasted
river. And you know, while I floated downriver on top of that
abandoned house it's entirely likely that Frank was being
dragged under not even a mile away. In subsequent days, during
the cleanup efforts, as I trudged from makeshift morgue to
makeshift morgue, I had visions of the bodies of him and Alice
trapped together under the same rock, or against the same
bridge buttress. Every time I pulled back a shroud I wondered
if it would be his face or hers that stared up at me.

I woke up in my own bed the morning after the hurricane
and for half a second that's all there was: the familiar weight of
the blankets and a comforting (though brighter than usual) light
filtering through the net curtains. I recognized a vague sense of
fatigue, and an ache in both my legs. I had no idea what time it
was, or what day. And where in the world, I wondered, sliding
an arm across the sheet to find her, was Mary?

It was realizing she wasn't there that did it. A jolt of something like electricity straightened my legs and opened my eyes.

I felt immediately nostalgic for that moment just past. I peered furtively from behind the lip of the blanket, as if I might be ringed now by accusers, or police. I felt like an animal, cornered, hungry, and then that feeling passed and I simply felt sick.

I bathed and dressed, forced myself to make tea in a teapot. I sat at the counter in the kitchen, angling my chair so that I could see into the garden. The gusting wind threw a sharp grit against the glass, and the last ruby leaves had been torn from the grape vines and lay like a bedraggled velvet rope along the bottom of the fence. The trellis had somehow withstood last night's winds, and the chairs were still stacked against the property line. Mostly it was impossible to tell anything had happened. To be safe, I ought to have gone across the street, checked from there that the roof still had all its tiles. But there were a lot of things I needed to do that morning, and it was vital I do them in the right order. The worst thing would be to rush. And so I sat a while longer, filtering gingerly through the last sixteen hours. It was ten o'clock in the morning (I couldn't recall ever getting up so late). The newspaper slammed into the front door.

The page one headline read GREAT STORM HITS AFTER FOUR-INCH RAIN (I have a yellowed, brittle copy on the shelf over the bed here) which struck me as inaccurate — the rain and the storm had seemed pretty synchronous to me; there was nothing sequential about it. There was a photograph of a car, mostly submerged, and I assumed it had been swept into the river. The caption, though, described it as being found beside Dufferin Street.

I scanned for a general impression: Air traffic halted. Fifteen cottages washed into Highland Creek. Motorists take to trees on Pottery Road. Motorists rescued from the Don. Yachts beached. Train rolls over. All police on duty. Nothing on the front page, though, about deaths. Or about Raymore Drive. I felt the way I sometimes did immediately after a significant arrest: as if I could see into the future, in so far as I knew how the *next* day's newspaper would read. It was like knowing the winner of a horse race before the race was even run. It was hard to figure out how to profit from the information I had, but there were these windows, these brief periods of time when I moved around the city hoarding secrets.

There would have been many deaths, I thought. Only an abundance of caution must be holding the editors back. No one who had been out there could doubt that people had perished. It was all about deadlines, I supposed. "By 3 a.m.," the story said. That must have been the *Globe*'s cut off. Had it been five, or six, the front page would have looked entirely different.

I paced, lightheaded. The reality of what I'd done created a great pressure between my temples. I stopped, grunted, began to pace again. I felt snot on my lip and left it there. I closed my eyes and groaned. Nothing helped. I threw up in the bathroom sink.

The floating house, my ship, had finally run aground. And then, later, in dawn's first glimmering, I was plucked from the roof by an ancient man in a wooden skiff. The man's name was Cy, and his wife had been waiting on shore with dry clothes. These two had been rescuing both the living and the dead all night. A row of three bodies under green sheets lay off to one side. One woman and two men. Their faces pummelled by the river bottom. I thought my heart would explode pulling back the sheet from the woman's face. I sent the old man and his boat to Raymore Drive. "Forget the dead ones," I said. "Go around them. Just get up there."

I worked my way downstream. I should have gone back in the boat with Cy, but instead I beat my way south along the shoreline, the ever-shifting shoreline, expecting at any moment to trip over the bloated limb of a corpse, or the leg of a dog, the door of a house. I stamped through a half-acre of bullrushes. There is a story somewhere of a baby — Moses, I think

— getting hung up in bullrushes and it makes sense to me. They were a net across the shallows. In the late summer I have seen carp rolling lazily through patches just like this one. In those days Chinese men would come down and spear them; the next day they would appear on display in a stall on Spadina Avenue, their fresh wounds a selling point, a proof.

A boat skimmed past without seeing me. Helicopters hovered behind me, their light sweeping left and right. I imagined children being lifted in wicker baskets from the roofs of houses.

After an hour I saw a woman clinging mid-stream to the tail end of a black car. She was wailing for someone to help her and there was a small group of people on the more distant opposite shore trying to calm her down until they could find a boat, or have someone who might control the chopper's movements answer their telephone calls. No one seemed inclined to risk a swim.

I didn't see that I had much choice. I found a piece of driftwood that must have weighed fifty pounds and dropped it in the water. It was twenty feet away from the woman when it passed her. If the same happened to me, I was wasting my time. Maybe my life. I found another log. This one was heavier and had rudimentary arms where smaller branches had broken off. I struggled to get it into the water. It curved gracefully into the trunk of the car, nuzzled the licence plate before twisting away.

It was the wrong weight, of course, and its buoyancy would be different. But this was as close to figuring it out as I was going to get and so I shrugged out of my borrowed overcoat and shoes and I waded into the river and was pulled away from land before I could even make the decision to fall forward and swim for her.

It felt as if I was being squeezed in a fist. But the trajectory was good. In seconds I was spluttering at the back of the car. My sudden arrival frightened the woman, and she flailed backwards shrieking, as if I was a rat.

There was no possibility of climbing aboard. I told the woman she had to trust me and she shook her head so violently I thought the only way I would get her into the water was to fight her, and if I did that and then lost her, lost another woman, two in a single night, I might as well open my mouth right now and let the river water pour in.

"Is there anyone inside?"

"It's not my car," she wept. "I went in further up." She nodded, shivering, at trees that might have been the ones I had just left.

I told her, "We can do this. We'll just ride the current. We'll kick out slowly."

"Okay."

"Just let me take you."

She squinted, not understanding.

"Don't fight me. If you can, put your head back. Let the water carry you."

I felt her breath on my face. I told her to face away from me, to turn around. I put an arm over her shoulder, slotted it between her breasts, and held her side. I let the river push me into her and then said, "Let go."

We left the dead car behind. We were facing upstream and when I risked a look over my shoulder my head went under and so did hers. There were long black seconds when I thought I would have to let her go. I felt drained of all energy, like a man fallen into bed after too many whiskies. The sky was suddenly black, an expanse so broad I might have been blind. But then, just as abruptly, there were faces, including that of a panting dog, its thick curling tongue lolling like a seahorse. Surprising loops of red and yellow fattened and stretched in the sky. The clouds were there again, the spitting rain. Smacks and splashes all around us. I realized we had just floated under a bridge, and the coloured loops were rescue ropes. I reached for one and quite wonderfully felt its rough braid in my fist. I tied us up in it.

Voices broke into the air like flares and above the river's rumble I made out the flat slap of men's shoes on wet tarmac. Others slid excitedly down the bank and the rope tightened; we were dragged across the current. It was harder to breathe like this, the water cresting over our heads, but then the bottom rose to meet us and men in black waders separated us. We flopped gasping to the ground. Someone began working my limbs to get the circulation going, another was unhooking buttons, offering towels. I yelled hoarsely who I was, and why they had to leave me alone. "Take her," I said, and struggled to my feet, ready to fight if I had to.

The woman said I had saved her life, repeated that to anyone who would listen as she was coaxed up the slope. I denied everything, climbing into yet another man's clothes. It was like a stage play, I thought, all these costume changes.

There were houses untouched by the flooding and I talked my way into one of those so I could call headquarters.

"We hear reports you saved people on Raymore, Ray."

"Reports are exaggerated," I said.

I accepted some gloves from the owner of the house. They were a bright yellow and might have been deerskin. Their owner, a sprightly man, bald with green eyes and luminous white eyebrows said they were his driving gloves. "But take them," he insisted. "Rescue me from my vanities."

(The next day I skulked back into the hallway of my own home and removed these gloves from the pocket of the coat I had been given. There was a tear in the thumb of the right hand, and a stuttering graze across the knuckles of the left. They were more grey than yellow now, with green streaks across both palms, and they were still wet. They smelled of wood and of motor oil and deer. There was no point trying to find the owner again, he wouldn't want them like this, and so I carried them into the kitchen and tossed them away.)

I found nothing else in the night. Saved no one. Killed no one. Just wasted hours wading south, towards the lake. Whenever I came to a bridge (they were all flooded) I would talk to whoever was in charge. Have you pulled anyone out? Is the bridge still stable. Am I okay to keep going?

Once, I had sunk to my thighs in mud. There was no light anywhere. It took me twenty minutes to move ten feet.

I ran too, like a madman, through streets long abandoned. A young police officer pointed his gun at me, chewed nervously at the corner of my badge, testing its hardness.

"You think it's made of chocolate, son?" I asked him.

The officer apologized. "You the one they're talking about?"

"I don't know. What are they saying?"

"That you're a man possessed. Jumping from rooftops, swinging from trees."

"Sounds like Tarzan," I said.

"That's what I thought."

"So am I free to go?"

The officer stepped backwards. "Of course. Sorry."

I loped away. At the end of the street, though, I stopped. I slumped on the chipped front step of a bungalow with a spider plant centred in the window. I put my head in my hands and I listened to the world, the mash of distant sirens, and closer, waves. There was a stronger light in the east and below it somewhere, I figured, must be the sun. It was past five. The rain had stopped. The trees shivered and dripped. It was over. I wasn't going to find her. And so I went home.

It must have been six before I made it to bed, and when I awoke to face the future I had slept for maybe three hours. Not long enough to think clearly, but that was all I'd get for now.

After throwing up, I decided I would call the hospital. It was what husbands did. They checked that their wives were okay. That they had made it through the night.

"Thank Christ," Mary said when she heard my voice. "Where are you?"

I told her I was at home. But I didn't say that I was looking at a photograph of her with her mother. The two of them in front of a stable somewhere. I seem to think it was in America, on Martha's Vineyard perhaps, and that the trip was a birthday present to Mary from her parents. In the gloom of a red barn there loiter the silhouettes of two horses. The photograph made me sad. It was as if I was looking at uncorrupted youth; Mary before I tainted her.

"You know what I thought, Ray?"

"That I was dead."

"That's exactly it."

"I'm sorry. You can imagine how it was."

"I did, Ray, that's the problem. It turns out I'm very good at imagining."

"You haven't been home," I said, trying to give the conversation time to straighten itself out.

"No. When did you get there?" she asked me. "I called."

"It was getting light. Whatever time that is."

"Around six. I was looking outside about then. Thinking of you. Hoping you were okay. Praying. I'm so relieved, Ray."

"I'm sorry, Mary. Are you feeling all right? Were you on duty all night?"

"Until you got home, it sounds like. Then I found a cot in the basement. It was wonderful. I just this minute woke up."

She told me how it had been. She had never seen the hospital so dirty. Or the morgue so full. "All those people, whole families. It's terrible." She paused. "Are you completely okay, Ray? Did you get hurt?"

"A bit wet," I said. "Nothing to worry about."

It was difficult for me to talk to her and I hoped she didn't feel that way about me too. Mary would attribute everything to the storm and to the fatigue. She had no reason yet not to do that.

"I have to check charts," she said.

"I'll let you go."

"It's not that. I'm just saying, that's what I have to do. Check that the right chart got sent to the right ward. Match patients with their records. Then I can come home. By lunchtime, I'm sure. You don't think we'll see more patients from this, do you?"

"Some cuts and bruises, you will. As they go through the wreckage. But I'm sure the rush is over."

She said, "I suppose our trip to Niagara Falls is out."

"Haven't you seen enough water?" I was trying to be kind, but her silence suggested she wanted me to be more serious. "We can go next weekend," I said. "But all police are on duty today. I just haven't called in yet."

"They must think the same thing I did — that you were a goner." She was cheering up.

"I hadn't thought of that," I said. And I hadn't; it was a blunder. I was surprised no one had rapped on the door while I slept. My car was still up there, top end of Raymore. It had been a long time since I reported in. But wouldn't there be dozens like me, who worked until they dropped? That seemed reasonable too, and I told Mary that.

"I suppose so. So you're going in again? I won't see you?"

"Not until tonight, at least."

"God this is awful. The things I saw," she said.

"The baby's okay?"

"The baby's fine, Ray. I was careful."

"You're a nurse," I reminded her. "You know what to do."

"How's the house?"

"It's fine too. Nothing a rake won't sort out."

I was talking now just to hear her voice. We had said all we could. The stories, Mary must have realized, would wait until we saw each other. I ran a finger along her jawline in the photograph. I hadn't moved, just continued to stare at her without registering that I was doing it. She was alive and I was glad. She was coming home to me and I was glad for that too.

When she let me go I dialed Alice's number and just let the phone ring. I put the receiver down still ringing and went to open a few curtains. Frank's car was in his driveway and I cursed the decision I had made to confess to him. Every time I looked at the inscrutable facade of their house, I imagined my life unravelling.

When I came back to it, the telephone was still ringing. Soon the food would begin to rot in her refrigerator. Winter flies would buzz at the windows. Eventually those rooms would be emptied — her father would do it, perhaps — and someone else would move in.

MARY

What he has never fully realized is that I was in absolute hell that night, too, just as he was.

As a young nurse I had always thought fire represented a worse fate than water. An explosion at the Ford plant, perhaps, sending rough-cut door panels shearing into men's bodies. Or a grease fire in the cramped kitchen of an apartment in one of the new towers next to Yonge Street. Hallways filling with smoke, the elevators — their cables burning like candle wicks — free-wheeling into the basement. One particularly gruesome night I dreamt of a fire that began in the stomach of a pig hung on a hook at the slaughterhouse on Tecumseth. Its ribs exploded away from the carcass like two dozen knives. Men and women arrived at the hospital splattered in pig grease and pig blood. I had to claw it away from their faces.

Water surprised me. How dirty everyone was. If I had been asked in advance to describe a drowning victim I would have said: pale, immaculate. But these people weren't like that. They were broken and they were blackened and bloody. A boy had been thrust into the crotch of a tree and held there until the water had made one bruise of his back. His legs were identically broken at mid-thigh, and something had happened to his insides so that the whites of his eyes blazed red. He spoke lucidly, though, and asked after his sister and a cat named Snow. His parents, he claimed, had made it to shore and they would arrive for him any minute.

With a hooked finger, I fished mud from inside the cheeks of an old, frightened woman who had been pinned under her upturned bed for an hour before firemen had appeared at her window, clinging to a ladder that reached so far into the distance the woman thought angels had come to reunite her with her dead husband.

Another woman arrived covered in lacerations. It looked as if she had been chained up somewhere and whipped. She threw herself about and screamed. The doctor prescribed tranquilizers, and stitches for a deep cut on the woman's right forearm. Ten minutes later she died.

There were whole families brought in together. One had been stranded in an unheated car. The water had poured in around the door seams and from the trunk. They had been carried downstream until they collided with a concrete pylon. A helicopter had trained a light on them and one by one they had been lifted clear. The mother couldn't believe they had made it, and she kept counting her children — *one two three, one two three* — as if the number must surely be wrong.

A distraught man arrived on foot with his infant daughter in his arms. Her lips were blue and she had stopped breathing on the way in. Her tiny bare arm flopped over the sleeve of his jacket and as soon as I saw it I knew I would never forget it, pricked with gooseflesh and with a greasy zigzagging swipe just below the elbow, as if she had been marked by Zorro.

During one awful hour, between two and three in the morning, five people were pronounced dead. Two of them were children, dead on arrival, and they should have been delivered straight to the morgue, but the ambulance driver had been afraid to trust his own judgment.

At four o'clock there had been no new arrivals for twenty minutes. The staff were bracing themselves for the next round. Ambulances were sailing through the washed-out streets. We knew that soon enough they would return. A young man was trying to clean the floors, wiping great red-brown smears across the tiles. A woman was slumped against the wall, crying. An intern knelt in front of her. "My father hit me," the woman bawled.

On every seat and every bed were people in shock, waiting for the Valium to take effect. Every time a doctor walked past they eyed him hopefully. Perhaps he would prescribe something extra, something to clear their memory.

I sipped at a bottle of apple juice. The chill of it hit my stomach like a white flower blooming. I stood at a window, the rain lashing the glass. I tried to breathe deeply. Ray was out there somewhere. I wanted him to telephone again, hear him say he was okay. It was selfish of me, but I didn't care. We were a family now, and he needed to let us know.

The juice made me feel better. It had been several hours since I had eaten, and for a while my nausea had returned. But now I thought I had simply been hungry. I moved through Emergency as lightly as I could. If no doctor stopped me, and if I saw nothing that required my attention, I would escape to my own ward for a few minutes. Some of the arrivals were being moved there and I wanted to see how many beds were available, as well as check on the student nurse. Slowly, more staff were arriving. Some grumbled at the imposition this storm consti-tuted, but most were simply thankful they lived on high ground.

I stopped to comfort a young girl. Her mother was being tended to further back. The girl, though, was more concerned with a lost doll. "She couldn't breathe!" she cried, thumping the arms of her chair. "She couldn't breathe!"

In the hallways it was quieter. A nurse I knew passed with a cart piled with fresh towels. A man in a filthy coat was wringing his hands and pacing between two wall lights.

My ward was quiet. Everyone not working was asleep. A radio at the desk provided an updated list of calamities, and the two nurses had gathered around it. When they saw me they straightened, brushed out the creases in their aprons, but I shook my head and told them to relax. To prove I was serious I leaned against the counter with them, and while we listened to the news I scanned through the patients' charts.

A temporary morgue had been established in an Etobicoke church, and another in a fire station. Crews from CBC Television were using their lights to help police and firemen spot anyone caught in the flow. The rain was lightening, but the river had risen some twenty feet already. It was astonishing, it was tragic, and it was apparently "*beyond* anything in memory." I snorted with exasperation as the announcer tried to shake up his listeners. I twisted the volume down to zero but not before gathering that it was "biblical out there," and listeners should "consider prayer."

I returned to Emergency. My stamina was down; I knew I would have to find discreet ways to rest. I would have to delegate. A doctor was straightening the arm of a man who had broken it badly when he fell from a tree. Nothing to do with the rain, he said. He had been trying to place an antenna in the highest branches. He'd been a radio operator in the war and hearing men talk in Iceland and Greenland, even if the language was completely unintelligible, kept him alive. He claimed Canada was too small for him, he needed to be connected to everyone else. Over the doctor's shoulder, I could see the smooth white knob of the man's humerus where it had broken the skin. He had been sedated with morphine and with the doctor's manipulation the bone retreated beneath the skin like a tortoise gliding back into its shell.

I said, "Can I help, doctor?"

When he turned and I realised that it was Michael Pierce I blushed and scratched nervously at the small of my back.

He had me wrap the man's arm and motioned for an orderly. "You'll be right as rain, Mr. Thomas."

"The rain, that's right." Thomas shook a fist at the ceiling. "The goddamn rain."

"I was at home," the doctor told me later. "Just sitting in the window watching it come down. So I didn't mind getting the call to come in. I was waiting for it, actually. How long have you been here, Mary? How many hours?"

I looked to see who might be watching. Normal protocol dictated that a nurse not even talk to a doctor unless she was spoken to, let alone exchange personal details. Dr. Pierce, though, seemed not to care.

Another doctor rushed past — "Nice to see you, Michael. Mad, isn't it?" — and Pierce agreed cheerfully. He told me he had heard that the Don River had breached its banks, too, and so St. Michael's was also busy. But nothing like this. Along the Don there were so few houses.

A woman was delivered to us unconscious but alive. There was no circulation in her legs or her arms and Dr. Pierce said we had to warm her, but slowly. I remember that he said her heart was only beating eight times a minute. "We'll put her in a bath," he said. "Could you sit with her; do you mind doing that? You'll save her life." He said this as if it was a consolation of some sort.

"I'd like to be sitting down anyway."

"You will be," he said. "I did wonder how you were holding up."

He was protecting me, I realized. Getting me out of the fast water.

I liked him, even found him attractive now. The sum of the parts, I guess; that old sawhorse. But there was a childlike side to him. He would be unreliable in a crisis, I thought. Not at the hospital, where our responses were so legislated, but out there — in the wind and the rain and the flooding — I would want to be with Ray. Every time. Because he would save me. The doctor's mouth, though. That long thin line. There was something about the way it was framed, or rather contained, by his jaw, the perfection of the angles involved, that diminished all the criticisms for me, mysteriously reduced them to minor quibbles.

I got the woman into a bath. An orderly helped me, and then I sent him away. It was a very small room in the centre of the hospital. There were no windows and no sound other than a regular drip from the old faucet. I had set up an intravenous and propped a thermometer between the woman's lips. I placed a thermal wrap on the surface of the water and took her pulse every two minutes. For a while I let my index finger rest across the woman's wrist. The easiest thing in the world would have been to sleep.

Half an hour of this and I knew I was wasting my time. I opened the door and waited for footsteps. I flagged the porter down and said I needed someone to stand in for me. "Find a student who's had enough of Emerg.," I said. While I waited I scribbled down what I wanted to see in the way of improvement, how the woman's temperature should continue to climb.

A girl showed up ten minutes later, apologizing. "I couldn't find you," she said. "He told me where you were, but it's more like a cupboard than a room, isn't it?"

I told her what to do. "Do you understand? I won't leave you here if you're not sure what to do."

"Is she going to be okay?"

"We think so."

"So, I'm not looking after someone who's going to die anyway?"

"We're not wasting your time, no," I said, pausing in the doorway. "Is that what you mean?"

"It's just so I can prepare myself," the girl said. She must have been eighteen or nineteen. "It's not a callous thing, nurse."

"I hope not."

The girl shook her head. "I've just never seen anyone die yet."

"Where have you been all night?" I asked her.

The girl shrugged. "I'm just lucky, I guess."

"How long have you been at St. Joseph's?"

"Nearly a month. Most of it with the depressed people. I cheer them up."

"That's quite a skill," I said. "Perhaps we could loan you out to other hospitals. You could make everyone happy."

"I'd like that." The girl smiled innocently.

I left her anyway. There was less risk leaving her here than assigning her anywhere else. The woman was getting warmer; that was all that mattered.

Emergency was buzzing, a hive. I should never have left. It was odd, the way I behaved: escaping repeatedly but always returning. Knowing this is where I should be. I thought of how the child inside me was a magnet too. I thought of its hands forming, and its toes. I wanted this child more than I had ever wanted anything. Which seems so obvious. But did I want it more than I wanted to do the job I was capable of? More than saving lives? All I knew was that I wanted to protect this little one inside me, and that instinct was driving my decisions. I would have to talk to Ray. Explain this to him.

Michael Pierce was still there, slumped over the reception desk. A nurse stood behind her chair watching him. It took a second or two but then I realized he was studying his own reflection in a panel of chrome that framed the doorway. Tilting his head slightly to provide a profile and then teasing the silly curls above his ears. It was nothing really, just a small sign of vanity, of self-consciousness. I felt strangely like I had discovered a great secret, when all that was really happening was that preconceptions were being replaced with knowledge. I had no idea why it was so important for me to decipher him.

He registered my presence and turned. "How is she?"

"Coming back to us, I think."

"Wonderful."

He indicated towards the doors, and beyond them to the outside, to the ambulances. The rain had eased. The sky over Lake Ontario was brighter and the upper edges of clouds were tipped with white.

"It's over," he said. "It's blown itself out."

"We made it," I said, meaning only that the hospital had coped. There were no more stretchers lined up outside, no one waiting for treatment.

"Most of us did," Pierce said. "I'm hearing thirty or forty dead. There are still bodies in the trees."

I asked him how he knew that. It sounded so dramatic, more something that might have come from the horrible man on the radio.

"A reporter," he said defensively, and looked around, as if the man might still be here to corroborate his story. "If it's true it's just awful."

"Did any police die?"

"I didn't hear that," he said. "So I don't think so. I'm sure he's fine."

I couldn't remember telling him what Ray did for a living. "I'm sure he is, too."

We watched the light expand across the water. After a minute an ambulance drifted to a stop beyond the glass and the driver emerged as casually as if he was delivering the morning newspaper. He swung open the rear doors and his partner climbed out. Together they carried a body inside. A blanket over the head. The two men passed silently through the ward and into the long hallway that led to the elevator and from there down to the morgue.

The day I saw Ray from the window, hustling her into the squad car, was the same day Gina told me Frank was sick. Once Gina had locked up we sat in Bowles' Diner pushing sausages through a sea of gravy, both of us crying. I am sure the waitress thought us both mad, or lovers, from the way we clutched at each other (a truly shocking sight that would have been; Jenny is very lucky to have come of age later in the century). We went home together and I made us a drink. I remember Ray arriving. I heard him in the bathroom and then skulking wolfishly upstairs. Stupidly I thought he was just avoiding the bad news, but he didn't know yet. He had no idea what we were talking about. No, he was removing the smell of her from his clothes, his hands. And to think I was so glad to see him, had ached for him all afternoon, had thanked God — as I did every day — that he was alive and well. I remember perfectly the sensation of his thigh against mine (hot, like a log that has just rolled from the fire) when he finally appeared and sat beside me because I had asked him to. I remember how uncomfortable he seemed, and how I attrib-uted that to his not possessing the right words. Everything seems so obvious now; the man of my dreams seems such a see-through cad.

RAY

It feels as if I am tuned presently to the finest frequencies. It would not surprise me to open a door and find you there, Mare, twenty-five years old and in your uniform (yes, I found it erotic); or else Alice, in one of her sugared blouses. Whether this clarity of imagination is a result of the energy I am devoting to the exploration of these ancient spaces, or a common near-death experience, I cannot say. But it is as if I have been sipping from a flute of the finest champagne, the memories fairly explode, pop with colour for me. Translating them, getting them down, is proving trickier than I had thought it might, but I soldier on.

The day after the storm, when I reported in (so very nervously), I heard my name being scratched off a list.

"Townes, Ray. Got you. Let me put you through."

Stiff plugs were pulled from the board and others inserted, then a voice. "There were sightings of you all night." It was Albert Beckett, the English desk sergeant. "Trying to do everything on your own, were you?" he said. "We got a call from Calgary just now, detective. They want you for the rodeo. Say if you can ride a house the way you did, a horse is going to be a piece of cake."

"I wasn't trying to be conspicuous. Who saw me?"

"Consensus seems to be you're some kind of hero. Pulling a woman from certain death."

I laughed uncertainly.

"Some fella from the *Telegraph* has been badgering me for your address."

"Christ."

"That's what I said. But you never know, Ray. Times like this, complaints always surface, too, and we might need to set you against some of the less distinguished moments. Lot of tired officers out there last night."

He told me they had pulled my car out of the muck and, miraculously, it was running too. "I'll get someone to take you up there. There's a car up on the Lawrence Bridge we'd like you to take a look at."

"There must be cars all over the city," I said. The last place I wanted to go was that stretch of the river.

"Yes, but this one has blood all over the steering wheel and it's registered to someone with a prior for assault. It's probably nothing, but all the same."

He sent over a constable for me, a red-haired boy who drove as if we were involved in a chase. I told him, jovially I thought, to slow the hell down before we got ourselves pulled over, and he was never quite the same after that; the criticism took all the life out of him.

We sped along the eastern edge of High Park and there were trees down and water ran in brilliant rivulets over the grass. We planed through reflective pools and the sky was a wasted sort of blue. On the sidewalks everyone was pointing and muttering and shaking their heads. There was misery, but there was also the knowledge that in ten years they would still be talking about this, and I think that was already a consolation of sorts.

My car looked just as I expected it to. When I opened the door, filthy water drizzled out. The constable said he would wait while I got it warmed up, just in case, and I slid into the drenched driver's seat. Sure enough, the car turned over, first try. I thumped the steering wheel excitedly.

"I'm okay," I called out, beaming. "Would you believe it?"

The boy, taking me literally, shook his head. "Not from the sight of her, no sir, I wouldn't. I thought you and me were going to be a team."

"Sorry to disappoint you."

"I ain't disappointed as much as I am amazed, sir."

I asked him if he knew his next move.

"Down the hill, sir. See how I can help. You coming down too?"

I climbed out of the car but left it running. Men were working with chainsaws to clear a route so that a fire engine could make it a little further. There were five, six houses still on their foundations. Yesterday there must have been twenty, thirty. A small boat buzzed between them, tying up to fence posts so that divers could tip into the water and look for bodies. Across the river, so swollen still that it might have been a hundred yards to the other bank, there were bonfires and teams of soldiers dredging the shallows with green nets. There was the intermittent flash of a camera and a smoke that smelled of leather, which puzzled me, and made me think of tanneries and of men and women and children being found thousands of years from now, perfectly mummified in the wet soil.

"Sir, you coming?" the young constable called again.

"Afraid not," I said.

"I understand, sir." The lad sounded so reverential that I wondered if I was being teased. But he was quite serious.

"I mean it," he said. "I'm not sure I would want to go back

down there either. If I was you."

So, he had heard things already. Stories. A mythology was coalescing around the facts. I offered my hand. "Thanks for the ride."

At the bridge (the bridge where a little more than twelve hours ago I had stood with Alice, staring down at the pinned dog) a blue rope had been strung loosely between wooden bollards. Behind this rope was a black Cadillac, this year's model, parked at an angle to the sidewalk, as if someone had pulled over in a hurry. The passenger door was open, giving the impression of someone diving out of the car and then over the railing.

I identified myself to the cop working the barricade. Someone took my photograph and asked for my name. Christ, I thought, is this where it begins: my unravelling? I walked around the Cadillac and crouched down next to the passenger door. The steering wheel and the gauges around it were stained, though I was hard pressed to confirm it was blood. The floor — like the floor in every other car in the city — was muddy. That mud thick enough that both driver and passenger must have been in and out more than once. The back seat was spotless. No kids in this family. Probably those springs had never even been tested.

I popped the glovebox and found a lipstick, which I pocketed, as well as a heavy brass lighter, scratched up but still working, and a receipt for a GE refrigerator and a steak dinner at Morton's. I went around and climbed in behind the wheel.

I wished first of all that my salary made a Cadillac possible. I could have slipped easily into the skin of a man who woke up on a weekend morning and looked forward to cleaning his mile-long car, taking it for a powerful cruise. What I really wanted, though, and I felt this as a ravenous vibration in my head, was for last night never to have happened.

In Italy, in the mountains one night during the war, a man I knew quite well stumbled on a crumbly white path at the edge of a cliff. For several yards he fought to regain his balance. He threw his arms out, assumed the pose of a man on a tightrope. His rifle bounced around on his back, slapping dustily against his greatcoat. The sergeant had bellowed for MacNiece, that was his name, Doug MacNiece, to quit fooling. The column of men staggered to a halt. I assumed Doug would fall comically to his knees, then onto his chest. Graze his hands maybe. But his ankle had turned, I think. Afterwards I picked up the rock that I assumed had caused this to happen. An unremarkable piece of chalk about the size of a tennis ball. So soft it was rendered smaller simply by picking it up. I stuffed it in my jacket. I still have it, on a shelf in the garage next to assorted drill bits and a tobacco tin full of one-inch screws. And every time I look at it I remember how that rock spun out from MacNiece's foot as my friend twisted sideways, grunting. There was the startled cry of a man who is astonished to find himself falling, and then still falling.

It took three days to recover the body. Almost a quarter mile straight down. I volunteered for the recovery. It was reluctantly agreed I would catch up when I had buried him. The sergeant wanted to leave MacNiece where he was. He made chilly speeches that were supposed to sound noble. Terse sentences about the mountains making their own graves, and how there was a muted dignity in being lost forever. I wanted to push him over the brink myself and I saw the same look on several other faces.

I thought of that winding descent as I peered through the smeared windshield of a luxury automobile I didn't own. I remembered the knife-like pains in my knees during the descent, and saw flashes of the granite rockfield I had buried MacNiece in. I don't know, though, why that episode came back to me then. Did I see myself as the man who had fallen over a precipice?

The blood — I had no doubt now that it was blood — had dripped onto the steering wheel from above. I had seen the pattern before. When a man hits his head on the wheel after a collision it drops like that. Just hitting the kerb might have been enough. I felt sure I would find the owner at home with a bandage wrapped around his head.

I told the officer guarding the bridge to give me a couple of hours to confirm my theory, and then to have the car towed.

"Doubt that'll happen today, sir."

"Why's that?"

"They say a hurricane went through these parts. Folks is kinda busy."

"Well put the order in anyway."

"Yes sir."

He was a punk, one of an identical hundred working the force in those days, but likeable enough. I drove past the Islington Avenue fire station, which had been converted into a temporary morgue. Like everyone else I slowed down as I passed to eye the gaggle of head-down mourners. But then I pulled a U-turn and swung onto the forecourt. A man in a black suit was circling a pile of muddy clothes. He was shaking out a can of lighter fluid over the coats and pants, shoes and scarves. There were worries that cholera or malaria might already lurk in suit pockets and dress linings. After two revolutions he patted himself down for a box of wooden matches. He struck one and its flame flared and died. A woman in a brown fur coat put a hand over her face and began to sob. The man lit another match and tossed it onto the pile. Blue and green flames raced over the surface of the clothes. A fur caught and sparks spat from the coat. In seconds the heat had reached me, fifty feet away, and the bawling woman had to turn away. She bent double, coughing, and another woman led her inside the firehall. I followed her in.

A clothesline had been strung through the centre of the main space, dividing it in two. Grey blankets had been folded over that line to provide some privacy for both sides. To the left was a neat line of covered bodies. It looked like an art installation, something to do with pattern and repetition. There was something obscene to me about trying to impose an order on death, as if it could be controlled or denied. But there was no choice really — a random pile of bodies would have been even worse.

To the right of the divide a half-dozen folding tables had been pushed together. A spread of coffee mugs and aspirin bottles. I saw a Bible, all twenty pounds of it wrapped in black leather and gold type. A wan minister with scuffed shoes spoke in hushed tones to a young boy with a wind-up balsa airplane. There was a stack of folded handkerchiefs and a plate of pastries with white icing and a strawberry filling that spilled rudely from the ends. A maze of muddy tracks and a dozen wooden chairs folded against the far wall. Three middle-aged men loitered near the pastries, apparently wondering whether decorum prevented them from eating their fill. Two women clung together. One sobbed nearly soundlessly while the other rested a hand on a table for support. Directly in front of me a small battered desk had been established, as well as a very efficient-seeming woman with her long hair tied back severely. She eyed me suspiciously and struggled to cross her legs under the low desktop; she tapped with her pen at a list of names typed on a sheet of paper. Finally she cleared her throat. Everything about her seemed wound a fraction too tightly.

"Those the deceased?" I asked her. I unfolded my shield for her, and saw how that changed what she was going to say.

"It is," the woman said. She had a Scottish accent, so the steely straightness of her back made more sense. The grey stare. There was something attractive about her, now that her voice had been added to the mix. Perhaps it was the extraordinary lengths a man would have to go to just to have her melt even a little. The thought of her dissolution aroused me slightly, as well as the way she squirmed in her chair. But monumental efforts were far beyond me this morning. All the same, I smiled and thought I saw, deep in her gaze somewhere, the infinitesimally slight sign of a thaw.

"May I see?"

She handed me the sheet of paper and I snapped it rigid. She watched me read, and that made it harder to concentrate. I was looking for three names. The owner of the car and his wife, and Alice. None of them appeared.

"There are only seven names here."

She nodded. "Aye."

"I thought I saw at least ten bodies."

"Eleven."

"Who are the other four?"

"We don't know yet." Her O's were extraordinary, the purest I'd ever heard.

"They had no identification," I said.

"You're quick."

"You mean I'm slow." I smiled again.

"I'll show you which they are." She scraped her chair away from the desk and marched me smartly before the bodies. She indicated three in the middle of the line and the one at the far end. "Two men, two women. Those there are children," she said, indicating smaller bodies. "Found together, if you can believe it. A girl holding onto her little brother."

"Where are the parents?" I asked.

"They just left. They've gone to the church. Bereaved doesn't begin to describe them."

"I don't suppose it does."

"Well." She paused. Then decided that to say more would be

to diminish the way these two children had disappeared from the planet. Eventually she reddened slightly and said, "I'll be letting you get to your business, then, whatever that is."

I hadn't seen a lot of bodies in recent years. I bet Frank saw a lot more corpses in his work than I did. And Mary too. The awful last minutes she must have witnessed every day. And yet she knew that I didn't want to talk much about death and so she kept quiet. That made her life more difficult, I knew it did, made her more lonely, but she never said a word. She respected me more than I did her.

You listening, Mare? You were better than me.

I lifted the blanket away from the first body. A man of fifty perhaps, his features frozen in that expression of horror and surprise I used to imagine MacNiece wore as he fell, before a shrink told me that was the most unproductive thing I could possibly do. A smear of mud across the forehead obscured slightly a gash that at its centre was bone. The jaw on one side was broken so badly it reminded me of a bag of marbles. This could be the Cadillac's driver, of course. I hadn't seen a photograph, but the age matched near enough. I went through the man's pockets in case something had been missed. They were full of grit and when I reached into the bottom of them I felt his cold and wet and hard skin and had to check that the man hadn't opened his eyes disapprovingly.

The second body was less battered and the man was younger, late twenties maybe; still someone's son. His left hand was bent at an impossible angle and the crystal on his wristwatch was smashed, freezing time at seven minutes past one. His nostrils were full of mud but someone had washed this man's face, perhaps wanting to restore him for viewing.

The third and fourth were women, sisters from how similar they were. The red hair blunt cut at the shoulders, freckles on the face and showering into the neck of the matching silk blouses. A wedding ring on one and not the other. Red lips that were similar but not identical, and something blue painted onto the eyelids. It was as if they had fallen asleep after a long formal dinner. Women from a fairy tale. I checked them against the lipstick in my pocket but it wasn't close.

I covered them up again. Christ I hated it: the possibility of Alice under every cover.

I thanked the Scottish woman, who was back at her desk. She asked me if I'd found what I was looking for.

"I hope not."

She nodded as if she understood. "The minister says he can talk to you if you like."

I said I didn't think so, no, and something in my tone caused her to look down at her list of names as if to save me embarrassment. "It's not for everyone," she said.

"Words would ring a bit hollow," I said.

"I think he knows that," she said.

"He's feeling the pressure, is he?"

"He is, aye."

I turned to leave but then stopped. "So what does he say?"

"The minister?"

"Yes. Why did God do this? Can you boil it down for me?"

"I haven't really asked him."

"You're not curious?"

She admitted to me, "I've listened a little. Enough to get the gist of it."

"The *gist*?" I smiled. "That's a good word." I was flirting with her, yes. Exploiting even this fleeting connection.

"He says that God didn't do it," she said. "He just *allowed it* to happen. He seems to think there is some solace to be found in the distinction."

"Negligence is better than cruelty, is it?"

"Aye. Well, then. That's why you're as well not to talk to

him." Her smile was hard again. She shifted her backside. She wouldn't mind at all if I left, that was what I decided. And so I bowed, probably awkwardly, and thanked her. I had known her less than half an hour and there was already an arc to our relationship. She had met me and warmed slightly to me. But then I had said something, or more than one thing, and she had formed an irrevocable negative opinion. Other couples took years to work through that sequence — Mary and I certainly did — and driving away, past the bonfire of clothes and the crying women, the man with his can of lighter fluid and his stony glare, I thought that she and I should consider ourselves fortunate.

MARY

We managed a dinner together last night, the three of us gathered knock-kneed around the kitchen table. The dining room would have felt too formal, too conciliatory, and so I said to Jenny, "I'll do it, fine, but here, next to the fridge, and we order in, pizza preferably; I'm not slaving away for hours, and neither are you."

Ray tottered in as soon as he heard the delivery boy at the door. His appetite remains undiminished, though the sight of him eating with his mouth so wide open, trying to get as much air as he does meat, is a foul sight indeed and I think the world would be a better place if he realized that.

Jenny helped him to sit down. "Did you want your oxygen, Dad? Shall I get it for you?" Fawning horribly. But she has to leave soon, her employers have called more than once, and I know she wanted us together so that she could break the news to her father. I am convinced she envisioned this as some sort of last supper. But there are surely more dying over there than there are here, and so I think it is right she leave. One must help where help is most needed. I am proud of her. It proves to me that she knows the word *family* cannot be allowed to imprison us, to make us lose perspective or, worst of all, individual freedom. She has already done what she can here.

But dinner. Those awful rounds of dough. One — Ray's — was acned with bacon and sausage and . . . God, was it ground beef too? Upon the other, a pound of congealed mozzarella had trapped assorted withered vegetables. (He takes a perverse delight, a nearly sexual glee, I think, in the revulsion he knows I feel at the sight of meat, the sight of him putting it in his mouth. When I converted, nearly two decades ago, at Jenny's instigation, it was also a way, I have come to believe, of separating myself from him, of establishing that we were entirely different animals, my husband and I, irreconcilably different, without actually having to take the logical step of packing a suitcase and leaving him in his own gristly stink. My cowardice, even as it has doomed me to this ethered gloom, has also, ironically, saved at least a barnyard's worth of animals.)

The wine made it all bearable, I suppose. For several months now Ray has been opening, whenever he gets the chance, one of the bottles he has laid down over the years. He has bought well, I must say, and one of our very few shared enthusiasms is for a fine bottle of wine.

Jenny finally broached the subject of her departure. "Christmas," she said. "I'll come back at Christmas."

Ray shook his head. "Too damned expensive. When's your contract up?"

"May, or June." She looked so pained I could have wept.

"Wait until then. You can wheel me up to the bluffs."

I looked for the corkscrew, anything so we didn't have to look at each other.

Jenny nodded. There were tears in her eyes. But what could she say?

"That woman coming, is she?" said Ray. "To take you away? Are you working together on this one?"

| 161 |

"Sharon, yes."

"Good."

"Good?" I asked him.

He dabbed imperiously at his lips with a cotton napkin. I saw the sauce appear on it like blood. "Sure, of course, why not?" And then we were all very quiet.

Every few minutes one of us would tear another slice from the wheels in front of us. The other two would watch. Ray's breath ebbed and flowed. There were long silences and we drank nearly three bottles of wine before it was over. When I stood up to make coffee I put a hand against the refrigerator, felt its subtle vibration against my palm. It was more alive than any of us; we were all so consumed with picturing, and then denying, the inevitable near future. What Ray saw I'll never know. How does one envision the world after one's departure? How can it possibly go on — the world, I mean? I know that's going to be my question when I arrive at that point of departure. To my mind, if I have to get off the ride, you may as well pack up the whole fair and leave town with it. He must feel like that too, mustn't he? Jenny suggested to me this morning that perhaps he feels like a guest who has been asked to leave the party early. He knows all too well that the music will get turned up after he leaves, and the booze will have its effect; the real fun will begin then. He is the interloper, the hanger-on, the outsider. She put a string of loose ideas together and I saw that if she stopped doing it she would collapse.

How depressing it all is. Mostly for him, though. I do know that. When dinner was over and we had cleaned up together, and I said I was going upstairs, could I get him anything, and Jenny said, yes, it was late, she should turn in too, and I had turned off the light over the stove so that the kitchen lost half its light, I saw the panic in him, the frantic little jerk of his arm along the back of the chair. We were going to leave him alone.

The moment had for him, I think, the quality of a premonition, a reflection of the instant when he had to leave us forever and the lights would be totally extinguished. I felt for him. My heart went out to him; I couldn't stop it. You never can, can you? I have seen the worst sorts of men die in the hospital wards. Abusive monsters. And I have wept for them too, as if they were saints, as if they were children.

Gina hammering at the door. I remember that. The thin glass rattling in its frame. It was the morning after and I hadn't been home for very long. I didn't make it home by noon as I had hoped, as I had promised Ray, but it wasn't so much later that I felt I had lost a day. I got home and I dropped my coat in the front hall and stepped out of my shoes. Virginia Woolf wouldn't have needed to stuff her pockets with rocks if she'd owned a pair of shoes like those we nurses were forced to wear. I limped into the kitchen hoping there would be a note from Ray, but aside from a dirty cup in the sink and a plate with an unidentifiable grease stain, it was as if he had never been there. The bed would be unmade too, I knew, and there would be something irritating about the state of the bathroom. I would have to be careful not to say anything. With luck I would have time to sleep before he came back and I would bathe and eat something, and maybe treat myself to a glass of wine (such an old friend), and then none of it would matter.

I sat and I breathed and I tried to only do those two things for twenty minutes. But I have never been very good at shutting everything down. I have read of men in India who go without food for days. Well I'm not that disciplined, or even that interested. My mind drifts laterally more than it probes deeply, but I don't mind that. A mind stilled altogether is a mind doing no one any good.

And so I sat and I breathed and I thought.

I thought of how tired I was and of the odd sensation in my stomach, as if my muscles had hardened into a ball around the baby so as to block out the hospital screams and the barked nervous orders.

I registered the sunlight that came and went from the room and the ache in my feet and my hands when I flexed them.

The fact that I was hungry and would, when I was done, check to see what havoc Ray had wrought in the refrigerator.

I remember shifting to a mild contemplation of the general sadness in Toronto that day. Insurance agents were packing the trunks of their cars with the weight of unheard-of numbers of claim forms. Families were gathering whatever they could from the wreckage of their houses. Ray was out there too. Sweating, I bet. Rushing from one scene to another, trying to set everything right. I thought Ray would do better to concentrate on one thing at a time. He divided his attentions too much. That would have been my advice to him back then, if he ever asked. Which he wouldn't.

But someone was knocking at the front door. I had heard it a few seconds earlier, but convinced myself it must be something else — tree branches scraping the roof, a raccoon knocking over a bottle on the patio. But it became more insistent and I opened my eyes.

I recognized Gina before I got to the door. Her favourite tangerine sweater burned through the frosted glass panel like a fireball. And I was pleased. We could swap some stories, I thought, share the horror I felt at the suddenness of all this death. We could sit at the table and eat something together. A proper meal — a salad would be nice — rather than a handful of this or that before I made for bed. Frank's night must have been just as incident-filled as Ray's, I thought. Sleep would wait just a little while longer.

Gina, though, was shaking so much she might have been one of those who spent the night in frigid water. Any second she would crumble. I said, "What on earth?"

I sat her in the armchair in the living room and kneeled at her feet. Gina had no shoes on and her feet were black from the road.

"What is it? What's happened?"

Gina sniffed. She peered around as if the room was full of a thick fog and she was trying to identify landmarks. I offered to make her tea. "I was just boiling the water."

Gina nodded and smoothed out nonexistent wrinkles in her skirt. She followed me to the kitchen. When I checked on her, her eyes were closed and there were tears on her cheeks. She was rocking slightly back and forth, trying to calm herself.

And then I realized what it was.

I replaced the kettle on the stove and twisted the lid onto the teapot. I reached high into the cupboard and brought down two matching cups. Found sugar next to the breakfast cereal and poured a little milk into a jug shaped like a cow. I put all of these things onto a bamboo tray my mother said was from the Philippines, but which I had discovered — by way of a declaration burned with a small iron into the underside — had actually came from China. I waited for Gina to open her eyes. My heart thumped frantically; I wanted to run, run, run. But I touched Gina on the forearm. Her top lip began to quiver. I said meekly, "Is it Frank?"

Gina looked at me imploringly. If she were to confirm anything it would become real for her in a way it wasn't yet; that was the look. I gathered the pieces of her in my arms and for a long time we stood swaying together. I tried not to imagine how it might have happened . . . if I was right. I stared at the door frame, saw how the paint hadn't covered the pine well at all, was more of a wash, really. It seemed to me then that the whole house might as well be made of matchsticks for all the protection it offered anyone.

Finally Gina sniffed again and lifted her head from my shoulder. "He said this weekend was it," she managed. "He was going to say goodbye to everyone on Sunday." She pulled back slightly so she could focus on my face. "The chief was going to throw a party for him. I said I would keep it a secret." She broke down again and I held her until the sobs ratcheted down into shivers and then into a humid stillness.

I coaxed her to the couch. We sat beside each other with a view of the windblown garden. "How?" I said. I had visions of Frank battling smoke, then burned, blackened. There were good and bad ways to meet death. There was a spectrum along which were arrayed the infinite ways it could take you.

Gina said, "They were trying to get a car out of the river. There were boys on the roof. They extended the ladder but it wasn't long enough. So they sent it out at a flatter angle. They're not supposed to do that, Mary. They're not supposed to do that."

"Did the ladder break or did Frank fall?"

"I guess something gave way, and he fell. So both."

"Was it just him?"

She shook her head. "There were two of them. But Aidan — the other one — managed to get on the car."

"What happened to Frank?"

"He disappeared."

I saw the blackness at the centre of Gina's eyes; it was the hole Frank had vanished into. "Someone saw him grab a tree and for a minute he was okay. They were throwing ropes. And one of those made it to him. They were pulling him out."

I waited. I saw everything Gina described and I tried so hard not to have my mind elaborate, to fill in the whitecaps and the blistering rain.

"He couldn't hold on long enough."

I saw the rope go slack, flop grey within the current.

"Perhaps he's okay," I said. They were the stupidest words, but Gina had yet to say he was dead. It seemed my duty to float a meagre hope.

Gina tipped her head back and her eyes filled with tears. "No," she said. "He's not."

For a while she couldn't talk. I got her to lie down and I brought a blanket downstairs. "I know you probably can't sleep," I said.

But for a while Gina did drift. She was like an infant, crying out, restless. I tiptoed around her, cleaning the house because I had to do something. I put on the radio in the kitchen while I waited for some American cheese to melt on a piece of bread under the broiler, and then I heard it: *Five firemen perished when their pumper truck was carried away in the Humber last night. Not all the bodies have been recovered yet. In a separate incident another fireman perished trying to rescue a man from a car that plunged into the same river. That brings the total number of confirmed dead during last night's hurricane to twenty-seven. That number is expected to rise throughout the day.*

The announcer's voice was dispassionate, firm. He moved eventually on to other subjects. The strike at the Ford plant. The poisoning trial. A list of misery that hit the room like a clenched fist. I thought I might open the cupboards and find all my china in pieces, the food in the refrigerator turned to ash. I sprinkled salt and a little pepper onto my toast — I felt faint, I had to eat — but in my mouth the cheese went hard and after two bites I threw it away and simply waited for Gina to wake up.

There was no planning what I would say. But I knew I ought to find out where he was now, where Frank's body was (they had found it, hadn't they?), and whether Gina was planning to see him again. And had a funeral director been contracted? Gina and I would have to deal with these practical matters. They were awful, but perhaps they were more easily managed than the grief and the shock.

I wondered, too, about the little cottage on Toronto Island. And Frank's pension. There was a payout to the widows of firemen who lost their lives in the line of duty, and it was more generous, I knew, than that for policemen. I remembered Ray being angry at how little would be given to me if something happened to him.

I didn't have the strength it would take to weep, or more especially to stop weeping if I were to start. I watched a robin bounce around the lawn, pecking hopefully at the dirt.

When Gina stirred, I stood very still in front of the stove. There was still some residual heat coming off the broiler and I felt it along my waist. I waited for the sound of Gina lifting herself up, or else turning over and sinking again. Being awake was the worst thing for her. I had seen it at the hospital so often — doctors handing out sedatives like they were chocolates.

Gina called my name and I went to her.

"I didn't know where I was," Gina said, dragging the back of a hand sleepily across her forehead. Then, quietly, "Oh my God." She screwed up her eyes and her face went very red and after a few seconds' resistance she gave in again. I sat on the floor and it was as if the last hour had never happened. The world had opened up to swallow her.

Ray and I went to bed early that night, both of us were exhausted, and we lay side by side in silence. Shadows jumped across the ceiling, like cast members readying themselves for our dreams. When did Frank know that he was going to die? He must have been convinced to the end that his comrades would find a way to rescue him. No man who swims can conceive of a death by drowning. I found that I was holding my breath, eyeing the ceiling as if it was the surface of water. I saw it clogged with debris. The colour and the texture of it was like cake batter. Much later, months afterwards, I realized that Ray would have been lying there that night with nearly identical thoughts.

I rolled onto my side. Ray's stillness worried me. I had my head on the pillow and was watching him. He was careful not to let out his breath in one gasp. I said to him, "I'm a third of the way there."

He correctly understood me to mean I had made it through the first trimester of the pregnancy.

"And how do you feel? Are you worried?"

"No," I said, "I'm not. I feel fine."

"Will you have to work tomorrow?"

I said I didn't think so. Things were pretty much back to normal. "I'll see what Gina needs; but apart from that, nothing. You have to work, though."

"Sorry."

"I'm changing fast now," I said. "Feel." I pulled his hand over to my stomach.

It was true. There was a curve that was new. We had been so busy. Ray said he had noticed it before but then forgotten to say anything. He lifted the thin, short gown I had worn to bed and put his hand down again. The heat of it surprised him, he said. He felt higher, over my ribs, to see if it was constant, and then lower, on my thighs. I put my own hand there and said, "I've noticed that too." I had tears in my eyes and they drizzled lazily over my cheeks. He crooked a finger and wiped them away. He put that knuckle in his mouth and tasted the salt of me. I said, "We'll be okay, won't we, Ray? Tell me everything will be okay."

He kissed my shoulder, said there was nothing I should worry about.

I murmured that with his mouth so close to me every word was like a moth on my skin.

He slid his hand over the new hillock of my stomach and around the far side of me. He turned me towards him and pressed himself against me. I gasped, maybe at the suddenness of it, but then I closed my eyes and parted my lips to meet his. The heat he had felt on my stomach was also in my mouth, my tongue. Soon it was in him too, a flood in the brain.

At one point I was above him, writhing softly among the shadows, and he saw that I was still crying. He slowed, said breathlessly that we could stop, did I want to stop? But I moved more fiercely against him, clutching at his arms. "No," I said, "I don't want you to stop. Don't ever stop."

I really do hate him.

RAY

The picture of me. The one that made it into the newspaper twice — fifty years ago and then again this week. I remember it being taken. I had just reported in about the Cadillac. I had talked to the woman who was a passenger in the vehicle and she was fine. She had had an argument after dinner with the abusive husband she was estranged from; but the blood was his (he had hit the kerb, just as I suspected); and the end result was nothing more dramatic than a fierce walk home. I came out of the station and a damned shutterbug nearly fell over himself trying to back up. I put up a hand, scowled unappealingly at him. "You've got the wrong man," I barked as the flash exploded against the building behind me.

"A few words, Ray," the photographer gasped, trying to swing the camera over his shoulder and extract a notebook.

"I've nothing to say."

"People want to hear from you."

I hesitated, a dozen feet from his car. I thought of the little child growing inside Mary; what harm could it do to let them write the story? But no — what about Alice, all the hidden facts of that night? I was suddenly nauseated by this kid with his bag of cheap tricks, the telephoto lenses and the coloured filters.

"Be a sport," the photographer yelled as I hauled open my door. "Don't be such an asshole, at least."

"Now you're getting somewhere," I admitted. I dropped inside the cab. The camera went off again but I doubted it was intentional and as I pulled into traffic I saw in the rear-view the photographer struggling into the middle of the road, giving me the finger.

When accidental death seemed somehow an inadequate label to describe what had happened with Alice, I tried *misdeeds*. But I scoffed at the word immediately. How slight it seemed, how petty. As if I had thrown a ball through a window, or stolen a chocolate bar from the corner store. Others less subjective would call it a crime, mincing no words. And I knew more than a few lawyers who would happily whisper *manslaughter* to each other, their eyes glowing like coals at the prospect. Then talk themselves over a few martinis into *murder*.

I was afraid by now. There were moments of sheer panic, as if it was me rather than MacNiece who had lost his footing and was clinging to a sheer rockface. I expected the streets to fill with blood or skeletons or accusers. The insipid sunshine that appeared in the days after the hurricane was a jaundiced accusing eye. I tamped down the fear and the loathsome possibility that rose in me from time to time, that I had done it on purpose. I had killed her because I wanted her gone.

That's why I lied, Mare. I was in the darkest of spots. I really thought I might reasonably be found guilty of murder. The only answer as I saw it was to deny any knowledge of her existence, let alone her death. Ignorance was bliss, I thought. It was an idiotic plan, I acknowledge that, and a dumb conclusion for me to come to. I had reached for her, tried to stop it from happening. The evidence was clear. But in my heart I wasn't positive that was true (hadn't I kicked her away?), and somehow, in the chaos of the recovery efforts I came to believe that my heart was legible to all, that its anxious thumps formed a sort of morse code that screamed *guilty, guilty, guilty*.

There was also this worry: if you discovered the truth you would hate me. I was betraying the child, as well as you. The newspapers boxed me in. They proclaimed me a hero. If they suspected they were wrong, they would have pounced on me again, made a scandal of it. They would have made it sound as if I had sought out the attention, as if they had been duped. I was cornered. I had no choice. I wanted to save our family. You have always held that I destroyed us, and perhaps that is true, but my intentions — I can already hear your derisive laughter — were, after a fashion, rather honourable.

Alice once told me that her father shot gulls for sport. He would sit on the back step with a rifle and bring them down, sometimes dozens in a day. They would litter the road and the neighbours' yards and one of them had once blocked a chimney so that the living room had filled up with a salty grey smoke. I asked why nobody had called the police. "Because he's a maniac," Alice said. "Everybody knew it, including the police. My mother told him, but he didn't listen to her any more than he did to anyone else. Once a week a truck came around and a boy shovelled them all into the back."

"That's crazy," I said. "That wouldn't happen here."

"It happens everywhere," she told me. "People are always getting away with things they shouldn't."

I thought about her saying that as I entered her apartment building. I thought perhaps she was alive and hiding from me. I wasn't sure what I wanted to find. I certainly didn't want to acknowledge it, but if she was dead, I could be a better father. A better husband. (I was a mess of contradictions.) For months I had planned to reverse course, to disengage. I had even told her as much, while she regarded me sceptically from the molten disarray of her bed. I had hoped, I think, that by putting voice to what I knew was necessary, I would accumulate the strength to act. It is the most dissected few seconds of my entire life and I still don't comprehend how she ended up in the water. I felt her ghost hand against my shin. The mud again, and the rain. There was something sharp too, there on the riverbank, a sliver of flint that cut into my palm. And then that imploring look. But even then there should have been time.

The absence of her was like a constant insect hum. But occasionally I registered more fully Alice's death, and when that happened it was with the force of an unwired elevator slamming into the earth, my bones turning to sugar.

No one saw me knock timidly at her door; no one moved in the shadows. I put a shoulder against the door and pressured the latch through the thin strip of molding Alice had tacked there, and which I had warned would one day get her in trouble.

From her refrigerator I took a beer I remembered buying. I stood well back from the windows with the ale subsiding in my mouth. I remember these things: a blue dish half-full of change, mostly pennies, and tortoiseshell hairpins; the lid from a Coke bottle, and the dry, stained cork from a French wine we had shared. Next to it was a larger, square, wooden bowl with three oranges lost in the bottom. When I lifted one of them free it left a stain and over its bottom there was a grey-green mould that gave off a metallic smell. It was as if she had been gone forever. There was no doubt Alice hadn't been back. From the second the door swung open, I knew she was dead.

I sat on her bed and ran a hand over the wrinkled sheet. I poked through the medicine cabinet, and through a cardboard box I found on top of her wardrobe.

I turned on her radio and then turned it off again. I sat uncomfortably in the threadbare armchair that I had claimed as "my" chair, and wished I could one more time listen to her tease me about something inconsequential, something I had said hoping to impress her, or maybe deceive her, but that she found transparent and amusing. Her face would be sidelit by autumn's weak sun dropping like a firebomb over the park, and something would be warming in the oven for us because this was one of those rare visits when I said I could stay long enough to eat with her, after we had done what we always did in these cramped humid rooms.

Alice never much liked her own face. There were photographs of her, two in fact, but they were small and nearly hidden at the back of the dresser, behind an elaborate crystal perfume bottle that had been her mother's, and an African violet that seemed to harbour more aphids among its soft, furred leaves than it did violets.

In one of the photographs she was barely recognizable. Just a mass of hair (isolated from her profile it might have been water, under a haze of moonlight, or the night face of a granite cliff) and the soft blur of her right eye. Beneath the eye swung the bowl of a martini glass, and the gin in it (she hated vodka) was like a swirl of wet stars. I loved that image, had wanted her to give it to me, or at least find the negative, but early on Alice sensed its power. "It stays with me, Ray," she said, approximating its boozy pose. "Where it goes, I go."

She loved me, that was the problem. If only she hadn't told me how she felt. She was doing everything she could to entice me. It was all so sad. I considered taking the photograph but what would I do with it? Stick it in a drawer at work? What if I was shot one day and my effects were returned to Mary? I could all too easily imagine her turning the photograph in her hand, hoping a name would come to her, an explanation for this little silver frame.

I checked for letters, some communication from her father, but couldn't find any. No mention of another place, a life before she had arrived in Toronto. I finished the last of the beer and rinsed the bottle under the tap. I placed the empty in the cupboard under the sink. There was a brown paper bag of potatoes under there, and another of onions, in front of some cleaning supplies — a dish rag and some soap. The potatoes were mottled, going green, and they had sprouted eyes. Before anyone else looked in this cupboard those eyes would have sent forth feelers that wound themselves around the plumbing, worked themselves into knots hunting for daylight.

Downstairs, in the hallway, I levered open her mailbox. It was empty, but it was the weekend and there had been no delivery. I would have to come back. I pushed outside. The trail of a jet plane (still a novelty, then) crawled over the sky's blank wall, and to the south I picked out the shadow of St. Joseph's.

When I got to the car I took out my notebook. I leaned on the roof and scribbled roughly onto an empty page to bring the ink to the nib. I wanted people to see me now, to see that this was police business; I was not a man whose presence was to be doubted or questioned. I thought that was it. But perhaps even then I wanted to be caught, to lodge irritably in the coarse net of someone's memory. I didn't know what I should write down. I came up with *4:45 Nobody Home,* and then I slapped the cover down on the scratchpad. I was a fool, I thought, yanking open the door. A damn fool.

And I still think so, Mare. I was a fool.

Later the same night I was at Alice's little abandoned apartment, a call came while I was watching the CBC news (and thinking Mary would walk in the door any minute, and would she like the flowers I had spent twenty minutes trying to arrange in the vase?). A stolen car had been recovered in Kingston and the thief was in lock-up there. I had arrested the kid before and so the long drive fell to me. The car could stay a while — they couldn't spare two officers — but they needed to get the boy back and in front of a judge.

I was glad of the chance to escape my obsessive searches of Toronto's gullies and alleyways, and thought Mary would appreciate my absence too. But when she got home and I should have told her, I was already in bed and when she came up I feigned sleep.

I woke early and she was there, crowding the far edge of the bed, and she didn't stir when I slipped away. I shaved downstairs and afterwards I wiped the sink clean with a wet ball of toilet paper. I scraped a dried speck of toothpaste from the mirror. These were fragile, dangerous times. Before I left I searched all the flat surfaces but there was no note, no sign at all that she had even seen the blooms, let alone appreciated them.

I was out of the house before seven and on the highway approaching Kingston before eleven. The seasons were more advanced here. The trees were already barren, the clumpgrass in the roadside pastures was a pale wheaty colour. The clouds, if they opened their hatches, were as likely to release snow as rain. I ignored the signs for Kingston and drove on, past shot-riddled markers for Gananoque and Smiths Falls and Brockville. At Cornwall I pulled in at a gas station and bought a map. I was trembling; if she was anywhere at all she was here, she had to be; it seemed so obvious, so right. The search would end here and my life would begin again.

"You know Olympia Billiards?" I asked the attendant, a wizened man with flickering green eyes and a runny nose, axle-grease stains blackening his hands. The old man slid shut the drawer on his wooden cash register and scratched like a rat at his sparse white stubble.

"Can't say it's ringing a bell. New place, is it? Supposed to be good?"

I asked again at the grocery store, and then at The Blind Pig. Surely here they would know.

"Someone's pulling your leg, mate. There was a decent place to play stick, we'd know about it, wouldn't we, Jer?"

"What's that?" The deaf sidekick cupped a hand to his ear, a cigarette burnt to almost nothing between yellow lips.

"I said, if there was a decent place —"

I left them to it.

I found the police station on the map, went in and located a sergeant, propped up behind a counter that might have been assembled from the ruins of an outhouse.

"Never existed," he informed me. "Trust me, I'd know."

I was confused. I said, "Let me just run a name past you, then. Gordon Tanner."

The sergeant said he didn't think so but give him a minute. "Man got a record?"

I told him his wife had died in the last year. "Car went into a ditch and she drowned. Tanner was at the wheel."

"Let me look."

He came back shaking his head. "Didn't think so, but you've come a long way so I double-checked."

I tried a last line: "His daughter says he used to terrorize the neighbourhood. Shot all the birds from his back porch. Said a truck was sent around to pick them up once a week."

"You in the right city, you think?"

I bought a fried egg sandwich at a roadside diner and ate it moodily, hunched over the counter, then reversed my course. Drove too quickly along the Trans-Canada Highway, headed west, for Kingston, my mind spinning as fast as the tires. At Brockville I took the first exit, intending to make for the water, but then swerved onto the gravel. All I had in this city was a first name — Tom — and a trade — shipbuilding. That and a bread factory Alice claimed to have worked in. It didn't seem worth my time. I swore, thumped the steering wheel, and heard the chastising tick-tick of a hot engine. I checked the mirror and pulled a U-turn.

I tried not to listen much to the kid I picked up in Kingston. I had him strapped and cuffed in the back. I wanted to think. Any other day we might have shared a laugh. There was nothing in the rules that said we couldn't talk to each other, and I was of the opinion these long drives were an opportunity to build some good faith. No point sending the kid away for five years, stewing a good part of that sentence about all the pricks he'd run into on the force.

His name was Errol ("As in Flynn," he told me. "My mom was a big fan") and his sheet said he was nineteen. Two years earlier I had found him asleep in the back of a dairy truck all stocked up for the morning run, after an alarm had gone off in the main warehouse. He'd worked through three pints of milk. "I was thirsty," was all he'd said, and I talked to the manager, convinced him to settle for restitution.

But five months later he set fire to a new Buick in the parking lot at the racetrack. There were witnesses and Errol was too stupid to catch a bus out of there. He told the arresting officer, "I lost a bet," and grinned at him. With me he pretended to cry like a girl when the cuffs went on. So I had lost all sympathy. There were better places to use my pity.

"What do you want to talk about, copper?" Errol asked me. I checked the rear-view and that's where Errol was waiting for me, a grin hard as the glint in his eyes.

"You've developed a bad habit," I told him.

"Only so I can see you again." He blew me a kiss.

"You've nice teeth, I'll give you that much, kid."

Errol examined his own grin in the mirror.

"It'd be a shame to lose them so young."

Errol smiled all the more. "You're too good for that, copper," he said.

"Fuck off," I retorted.

Errol rolled around laughing, interrupting himself to yelp whenever the cuffs dug in (all I could think of was Alice when she'd been back there, the two miles of stockinged thigh). When he settled down he stared off at a foaming Lake Ontario. He didn't see me watching him, wondering whether Errol was destined for a good life or a bad one. Around Belleville he fell asleep, keeled over horizontal, and I left him like that so I could think.

It was as if Alice had never existed, was a ghost (which I supposed she was, by now). I felt betrayed by her, though knew I had no right. I was also oddly impressed. I'd swallowed every one of her lines. She had invented an entire life and I'd bought it. I had no idea who she was. Or whether she'd told a different story at the pastry shop. Her boss Tavares must have asked some questions when he took her on. There would be paperwork filed somewhere, tax information. Or at least there *should* be paperwork.

She was gone and everything I knew about her was suspect. Everything she'd said. The feelings she claimed to have for me. Her dreams for the future. She must have laughed every time I left her. *There goes gullible old Ray.*

Were there loving parents somewhere, then? I doubted it. They would have come forward by now, looking for their gone-to-ground daughter. No, she was probably an orphan. Perhaps only the names and places had changed, then. The basic facts might be true. She just didn't want me nosing into her life.

I shook my head. She was a goddamn crook.

Traffic began to build at Eglinton Avenue. Errol was upright again, peering blearily at a city he must have thought he'd left behind for a while.

"Where were you going? Was Kingston the end of the road?"

"Apparently." He was grinning again.

He was just a boy. To him these were still pranks. But he

would serve real time now and just maybe that would be enough to scare him into a different sort of life.

I motored south on Bathurst and then I dropped Errol at Headquarters ("See you in a few months," Errol chirped. "I was thinking Montreal; you fancy a night in Montreal, copper?") and then bought fish and chips from a place on Harbord. I couldn't bear the thought of sitting opposite Mary at a table. Listening to each other chew. Better to arrive late, say I wasn't hungry.

I parked between streetlamps and carried the food into High Park. I thought back on the day Marilyn Bell swam ashore. October 15th. Alice had wanted me to arrest her, to leave some bruises.

I was always revisiting this particular set of memories — her breathless requests from the back seat; her quivering, pale legs, the intense heave of her chest and disarray of her hair. I was becoming like the hobbled Portuguese man I saw nearly every morning at the bus stop opposite Headquarters, chewing on the soggy end of an unlit cigar. The man's wife had been struck down by a bus, and he came to the same place to see it happen over and over. *Could I have stopped it?* That must be what he asked himself. *Will something change if I relive it enough times?*

But the strength of my allegiance to these few scenes, with their undercurrent of violence and even death, was unfathomable to me. They were sexual scenes, I understood that much of the attraction, and they were recent. But there were all sorts of sexual memories I could have fixated on. The silk scarves I had used on her at her apartment. The way she fluttered them over my body when I finally released her. The dusting of flour she had taken in the shop's basement one night, long past closing. My disbelieving hand between her legs near the back of the Bloor bus; the look on her face as she came, surprising herself (*I can't, I can't*, she had whispered, her breath searing my cheek) and suppressing as much as she could the frantic thrust of her hips.

What frightened me was the possibility it was the water that drew me here. The quiet stream down there between the skeletons of trees. She had led me to it and suggested I restrain her. Said she was falling for me. And then, not long afterwards, she had led me to water again. And again I had tried to grab at her wrist, to restrain her. The experiences were like bookends. In one I had indulged a harmless fantasy and in the other I had let her die. Some part of me knew that: I was here because I couldn't be there. This was my nod to the process of grieving — a squalid few minutes reminiscing with a slab of haddock and a side of chips.

I was making such a mess of everything. If Mary ever discovered the truth she would leave me. A son or daughter would grow up without me. Mary would lose the house she loved so much.

I was on my feet now, trotting heavily down the runaway slope. At bottom, I leapt from one mossy rock to another, made it in four jerky strides to the far bank. I turned and skipped back more smoothly. But at any second the moss could slough away from limestone like a snake's skin and I would fall awkwardly, graze a shin, twist an ankle, suffer in some small, entirely deserved way. I was out of breath and so I stopped. I drifted a cupped palm through the water. The moon appeared to hang like a decoration from a tree limb. I drank from my hand, and then again, hoping the water would make me sick.

MARY

He didn't even tell me back then that the newspapers had written a story about him. Two or three days after the hurricane I was at the hospital, sitting with Ellen Morgan, who was a very good nurse, in the sun-filled room at the end of the ward. I had my hands across my stomach. It was the new way I held myself. A cradle, that was how I thought of it.

Ellen said, did I think about not coming back, when the baby was born, had me and Ray talked about that?

"We can't afford it," I said.

"But Ray's doing so well. He might get a promotion out of this. Don't you think? I know that's not the point of it, I'm being crass, but it's a consideration."

"Out of what?" I had no idea what she meant.

"The newspaper."

I shook my head. "The newspaper?"

We found an unread *Telegraph* on top of the locker next to a man's bed. Cito Bennett was his name. He had been brought up from surgery and after a brief period of wakefulness — when his wife and his four children had gathered around his bed and chattered at him like he had been away for months, telling him about school and the bicycle with a flat tire and what they'd had for dinner last night (*the bottom was burnt but it was still good; there's a bit left if you come home today*) — he had dismissed them gently and fallen asleep again. He would be out for most of the afternoon, and certainly wouldn't miss his newspaper for twenty minutes. The surgeon had confided to me that the man's heart had been surrounded by fat, and in cutting that away to get at the muscle, the blocked valve, they had caused more damage than they had repaired. No one else knew this, he said, but that man won't make it through the next week. *I'd wager money on it.*

And so as I looked at the picture of Ray, that awful picture, I couldn't help but feel I was robbing a grave somehow, stealing from a man before he was even cold in the bed.

"He looks terrible," I said.

We were at the main desk, the newspaper laid over still-unread charts, next to the hulking black telephone. A student nurse hovered in the background, hoping she wouldn't be sent away before she discovered what we were so excited about. "Was that the best picture they took?"

"They're trying to show that he's reluctant," Ellen said. "Read the article."

I read, with my ears and cheeks lighting up. "I had no idea," I said at last. "He didn't tell me any of this. He's been acting so strangely."

"Men," Ellen huffed, trying to be funny.

I picked up the telephone and dialed home.

"He's not there," I said. "But you know, I saw the news-paper in the kitchen, so Ray must have seen this. He should have woken me up."

"I've met Ray," Ellen argued. "He's not the type."

"Obviously not."

I wanted more copies. Would they all be sold before I

escaped the hospital? Did newspapers ever sell out? I wouldn't be surprised, not when the editors could plaster images of victims and heroes all over the front page. I felt slightly panicked. There was the one at home, but we should have extras. We needed extras. I wanted my mother to see it. I was proud of Ray. I felt it in my hands and in my knees, my toes, as if it was a substance the blood carried around. I remembered how, when Marilyn Bell came ashore after swimming from America, I had wanted to show up in the photographs, even if I was just one excited face among hundreds. I had felt deflated the next day when I proved invisible. My child would never know I was there. He or she would have to trust the stories I told, which surely wasn't asking too much. But my God, I thought, what a difference it would have made if there was some photographic proof.

And now, so soon afterwards, here was Ray, staring up at me. He was frowning, and unshaven, but I knew time would lessen my disappointment at those things. He was a hero. That was what I needed to concentrate on when I found myself noting his mud-splattered overcoat. A man with absolutely no time for the vanities.

I folded the newspaper reluctantly and replaced it next to the sleeping, dying man, and then I did my rounds.

None of the hurricane victims were on my ward. There had been a young girl whose ankle had been cut on a barbed wire fence she was swept against. She was lucky. A horse had bled to death when it was wrapped up in the same steel braids. The doctor had suspected she might have a mild concussion and so she had been admitted, but this morning she had received a bright new wrapping for her two dozen stitches and a pair of crutches she would have to return. She was gone before I arrived. There were two more still in Intensive Care, and a third in another ward. Eleven were being kept cool in the morgue. Three of those I had delivered personally.

And then there was Alice, Ray's Alice, who I had warmed in a bath as tenderly as if she was my own child.

It's true, she didn't die. But I might never have discovered her identity if Ray hadn't been so utterly stupid. I might eventually have decided that I was wrong, my suspicions unfounded. If Ray had had his way I would have apologized to him eventually, blamed the stresses of work and pregnancy perhaps. I would have let him get away with his murder.

This is how it happened. After Frank Chiarelli's funeral, a week or ten days later, all the mourners gathered at a one-storey union hall high atop the Scarborough Bluffs. Frank's father had spent nearly forty years riveting fresh panels onto the storm-bruised sides of grain haulers. His seals held like no one else's, that was the reputation he had, and it was enough to guarantee steady employment. During the war, the Department of Defence had him shipped out to Halifax and he plied his trade around the grey gunships and the limping destroyers. He had imagined himself patching torpedo wounds, long lines of tracer blasts. But those ships had mostly sunk, or been scuttled at the docks in East Anglia or Newcastle. Instead it was inspections that kept him busy, which had the bonus effect of providing the nervous men and boys about to sail with some measure of trust in their vessels. The Steelworkers union put him on their recruitment posters and he was okay with that, though it divided opinion on his character, both at the docks and on the quiet green street he and Sophia lived on. Bottom line was this: Frank Sr. called the union when his son was killed, figuring they would want to help him. The first thing they did was provide this hall, rent-free, for the day.

Frank Sr. stood at the door and greeted people like his son was getting married that afternoon, not buried. For a while

Gina stood with him. He put his arm around her and they might have been father and daughter. Frank had the same sharp nose and splendid hair (no wonder the union had wanted his face up on the wall), and any day but today he had the same laugh too. Frank's mother had intended to be brave like her husband, but she ended up in the basement cloakroom, mumbling into the trays of crustless sandwiches and deep glass pans of noodle bake that would soon be debuted upstairs.

When we arrived, Gina still had her head on her father-in-law's shoulder. They were singing something together, quietly, in Italian. Swaying smoothly within the door's frame. I wanted to stand at a respectful distance and let them finish, but Ray said it was too late for that, we'd been seen and this wasn't a pop concert.

It was a cruelly perfect day, the sky bluer than it had been in weeks. A shade that would have looked nice on a dress. Gulls wheeled over the tumbling sand cliffs, and Lake Ontario was a single heaving sheet of blued metal that Frank Sr. could have spent an ideal lifetime bolting to the shore. Across the street, the Royal Bank was offering new customers a free china place setting with every new account.

Ray was aiming for nice. Making no sudden moves, taking nothing for granted. On several occasions, I mentioned to him that he was acting strangely. "It's not just the storm, Ray," I said. Because it really felt as if he was trying to sabotage our relationship. I told myself over and again that we were on edge only because of what we were seeing at work. I tried to ride it out. After all, it was an awful time in the city and I was sure there were tensions in every home. And in a month, I thought, we would be able to take up where we had left off. We would pack our suitcases and head to Niagara Falls. But niggling doubts began to work me over; I thought Ray was selfish to let me suffer. Suddenly, he seemed stone deaf and several times each day I had to repeat myself. And he was so impatient, always checking the time. He has to damn well quit this, I fumed. He has to remember that I am pregnant; that he loves me. But as the week passed, and the city managed to gather itself, it seemed less and less likely. Worst of all was that I couldn't talk to Gina about it. So I sat alone, thinking myself into horrible dark corners where I came to believe that he must love someone else, and to make that new love possible he needed to hate me. Once I had come to that conclusion, I couldn't leave it alone. Every missed meal, every awkward telephone call or rude grunt, was another piece of evidence. By the time we made it to Frank's funeral I was in an awful state. We were bickering, talking at awkward, sharp angles.

But he had driven to the funeral at a stately pace, and when I requested that he pull over because I needed to compose myself before we arrived, he had done so without comment.

At the church he had bowed his head and even muttered along to the Lord's Prayer (though singing the hymns had proven beyond him). Graveside, he held my hand. He had also offered more eloquent sympathies to Gina than I thought him capable of, and at a particularly awkward moment he helped Frank Sr. regain some self-control when the older man's lip had begun to quiver, and then a tic had developed beneath his right eye. Ray took him firmly by the arm and marched him smartly away from the grave. He might have been placing him under arrest. They stopped some distance away, beneath a bare slim elm and I disengaged myself from the crowd enough that I could eavesdrop. The minister had said his words by then anyway, and mourners were breaking into smaller groups. Frank's mother, Sophia, eyed her husband with worry but turned away when someone touched her back to offer condolences.

Frank sniffed his thanks while staring at his shoes. Finally he squinted into the sun. "He liked that he had a cop living next door, Ray. Said he felt that between you and him, Gina would never have to be scared of anything. Same went for your wife."

"Mary."

"Mary, yes. Said you could rule the world from there. What with Gina in pretty good with the mayor."

"We had some fun with that idea one night in the summer," Ray told him.

"Glad to hear it."

And that was all it took. Frank indicated his wife. "I need to be by her side, Ray. You understand."

"Of course."

As they returned to the fold, Frank said, "Not supposed to happen, is it: them going before we do?"

"No, it isn't."

"Gina tells me your Mary's expecting."

"She's three, four months long."

"Take good care of that child, Ray, you hear?"

I thanked Ray afterwards for being so good. He was saying I could put the map away; he knew where we were going. I said, "Sophia was grateful too. People were asking who you were; if you were really the man from the newspaper."

The comment bothered him. "It seems lately like you're always trying to reinforce that I'm a good man. As if you suspect me of morbid self-doubt. And that is not how I feel," he said. "I know damn well what me strengths are, my weaknesses too. So quit mentioning that damn story."

There were children at the hall, three of them most notably, running in a tight circle inside the horseshoe of folding tables that had been covered with paper tablecloths and which were expected later to accommodate the food. For now, though, the tables bowed under the humped weight of dozens of unnecessary overcoats. The boy — he must have been eight, nine — was chasing his sisters, who screamed and skipped and weaved in their flared navy dresses. Their patent leather shoes smacked loudly, like castanets, on the salt-stained wooden floor, and a worried-looking woman who must have been their mother was trying to corral them. She stood at the centre of the hall and lunged at her son as he scampered past. The three of them were only encouraged by her participation and they somehow engaged an even higher gear.

Frank stuck his head in. Gina tried to hold him back, expecting an outburst. But Frank just bellowed, "Let them run, Doris. Let the children run, for Christ's sake."

An hour later, after the sandwiches and lasagna had made their appearance, and the crowd had thinned, I said to Ray that Gina's parents were going to drive her home and I had offered to ride with them. "So I'll make my own way," I said. Ray quite rightly took that as an invitation to leave whenever he saw fit. And within the quarter-hour I saw him making for his car.

I thought that was it, that I wouldn't see him again until late that night. He was still incredibly busy, as was every other police officer and fireman in the city. We had stopped making any plans and might as well have been anonymous roommates rather than husband and wife. I had no idea where he was going (although I suspected the worst) and, as became abundantly clear an hour later, he was just as ignorant of my schedule.

Gina and her parents invited me in but I declined. The hospital, I explained. I had taken time away for the funeral; I really should get over there. Frank Sr. offered to drive me but I declined — I think he wanted some time alone and once he'd dropped me off he would have been able to dawdle a while, at a coffee shop or simply driving the sun-splashed streets. I didn't realize this until too late, though, when I was up in my bedroom gathering my things, and however much I wanted to help I couldn't go back.

I don't know what I was thinking about as I navigated the

warren of corridors and elevators to my ward. Most often I entered a sort of daze for this task, became a rat trapped in my own maze. Whatever it was, it stopped when I saw Ellen Morgan at the desk. She saw me and I was about to say something when I realized who it was she was talking to. It was Ray.

When he saw me he looked decidedly uncomfortable. No, it was more than that, much more. He was suddenly petrified. If I had caught him screwing someone, if his pale backside had been bobbing up and down in front of me, his expression would have been exactly the same. I knew, right then, as certainly as I have known anything, that whatever he was doing at the hospital had to do with whatever had estranged him from me since the storm. It sounds dramatic, I know, but it is so much more mundane than that. I could see it in his face, that's all. I apologized to Ellen for my lateness and at the same time I raised an eyebrow to Ray. "What are you doing here?" I asked him.

"I assumed you were taking the rest of the day off," he said, or something like that. Something evasive; conclusive proof, I thought, of his guilt. "You were going home with Gina. I took that to mean —"

I walked my canvas carry-all around to Ellen's side of the counter. "No. What are you doing here?"

Ellen followed our back-and-forth as if she was at a tennis match. She had met him only a couple of times and apparently hadn't recognized him when he arrived.

"A missing-person case," Ray said. "You said there were survivors here. I was just finding out who they were."

"You didn't tell me you were looking for someone. Why didn't you tell me? I could have saved you the trouble."

"But then I wouldn't have seen you." He moved to put his hand on top of mine, to suggest an affection we both knew was false, so I drew mine back.

"Me? That's stupid. You thought I wouldn't be here."

Ellen was embarrassed now, shuffling. "Nice to see you again, Ray. I should —"

"Thank you, Ellen."

We listened to Ellen's uncomfortable hard-soled retreat. Ray fiddled nervously with the telephone receiver, tipping it back and forth in its cradle. It was suddenly so obvious. Jenny would have said, "I'm not blind, am I?" The woman, whoever she was — and I knew she existed now, was as positive of her existence as I was of my own — must have gone missing. I said, "I have to change. I'm late."

And he took a backwards step, as if I might want to use the narrow channel he was creating between himself and the desk.

"You said there were surv—"

"I know what I said." And I had said that. And I remembered how surprised he had been. We were at home, arguing blandly. Ray was telling me how hard his life was, how he spent his days trolling the morgues, looking into the faces of the dead. Forgetting completely what it was I did every day. And so I had told him. "I see them too, Ray. Every day."

"You see who?"

"The dead. And the survivors."

"There are survivors?" he had said. The news shocked him. "I thought everyone was either dead or at home again by now."

There was a spark in me of suspicion even then, but I didn't recognize it for what it was; I think I just found Ray a bit dim not to have thought about that.

And here he was, following up. But he had waited until he thought I would be elsewhere, tied up with the grieving widow. Tumblers were falling into place. The box where he kept his darkest secrets was tipping open. That's how it felt.

"Do you have their names?" Ray said. "Ellen hadn't got around to telling me that. If you have their names."

"Don't treat me like a suspect."

"I'm sorry." He showed me his hands. The discomfort was plain in his face. There was a questioning quality there too, as if he wondered if I might pretend I didn't know anything.

"Why don't you give me the name of the person you're looking for." This was so very awful. How had we let it come to this?

"Gina's okay, is she?"

"Her parents are there. She's fine."

I looked at him expectantly and I swear if he had stalled any longer I would have gleaned everything, he would have become transparent as glass.

"Alice," he told me. "The woman I'm looking for is named Alice. Alice Beauchamps. She used to walk along the river most evenings. Our thinking is —"

"Whose thinking?" I snapped. I was racking my brain. Alice. Alice.

"My thinking."

"She's not here."

He nodded slowly. "That's all I needed to know."

"Glad I could help."

"Might she be elsewhere?"

"One would assume so," I said. I was coming around the desk.

"In the hospital is what I mean."

"You should check with admissions."

"I was already down there," he said. "Their records are unreliable."

"I haven't found that."

"They recommended I check for myself. I'm not making this up."

I pretended to be looking for something inside the bag. I produced my cap and set it on the desk like a crown. I dived in again. "How did you end up with this case?"

"The information was passed to me first."

"By whom?"

"What are you looking for?" he asked. He thought, perhaps, that if we stripped away just one layer of artifice something good might happen. That his lies might stand more solidly. He was confused, I saw that. He wanted to accuse me of something, perhaps that was it. Of a falseness that might balance his own.

"I'm looking for a good reason to believe it's as simple as you say it is," I said, flustered. I left both hands inside the bag. "Can you give me that?"

"It's just a missing person, Mare."

I lowered my head. When I spoke it was as if through the fog of a narcotic. "She's not here."

"And I believe you."

"Then you can go."

"Mare. What have I done?"

Ellen was bustling towards us with a food tray.

"You tried to do this without me knowing about it."

Ellen slowed, tried to gauge whether her presence would be helpful, but I wouldn't engage her. "Dispensary," she called. "I won't be a minute."

"I explained that," Ray said. "I thought you were spending the day with Gina."

"You don't think I'd have been interested?"

"I didn't know I was coming here."

I stared at him. "Then you've done nothing wrong, have you? Go save the world, Ray."

Later, at the end of my shift, I tracked down Michael Pierce at his office. The receptionist huffed that it was almost six; the doctor was done for the day and she was just packing up. "I shouldn't really have picked up the telephone," she said.

"But he's still there? He'll want to talk to me."

"I know this must sound far too mysterious," I said to Michael. "I just don't know who else to turn to. I'm sorry."

Of course he would meet me, he said. He was delighted to hear from me. No, there was nothing important on his calendar. "Quite the opposite. All afternoon I've been hoping something would come along."

"Et voilà!" I said.

He said, "Exactly!" Where did I want to meet, then? Would his home be too threatening? "I simply have to get out of this office," he said. "And a change of clothes is definitely in order, I think. But a restaurant is fine too. A pastry somewhere, would you prefer that? Or just a walk?"

I told him his home was fine (even though I was thrown by the suggestion) and he gave me the address, explained where that was. "It's very convenient," he said, still trying to paper over any impropriety. "I could pick you up. Would that be appropriate?"

"I'll walk down to Lakeshore," I said. "There is a bench backing on to the parking lot."

He said he thought I would be quite cold, down there at the lake. "But fine, I can be there in fifteen minutes."

I should say — even though it must be so obvious — that quite quickly Michael and I had become almost friends. I had decided to retain him as my doctor for the pregnancy and I had very much enjoyed my appointments with him. The fact that I was a nurse seemed to create an instant pact between us. He had surprisingly disclosed, at our second meeting I think it was, that he had begun dating a jazz singer who was far too sociable and far too beautiful for him. I was a little unnerved by his openness. I think that, in a complicated way, he said so much so I wouldn't think he was being too forward with me. He was, I knew, a rare sort of man, and I found myself, at odd moments, extrapolating from fleeting and entirely accidental contacts: his hand brushing my arm in the emergency ward that night; his hand on my waist for a second as he helped me into my coat. Were we still flirting with each other? Of course we were. (Over the years I have tried to put my finger on what it was about Michael. The closest I have come is to accept that he was nearly the opposite of Ray. Physically, yes, of course, but he was his temperamental opposite too. I never saw Michael Pierce so much as frown, whereas Ray did little else for long periods, years even. He was funny as well as generous, and — I think I've said this before, so it must be important — he was attentive. He was also vulnerable, or possibly he was just weak, but I didn't mind that. Another thought I've had is that he was one of the very few men to ever show a physical interest in me and, sadly, that was enough for me to provide him a little permanent space.)

When he collected me from the lakeshore he was apologetic. He had forgotten a file, he explained, and had had to go back for it. He pointed to the green folder on the backseat. It was something he needed to review.

I lied that I had been late too, but he put a hand on mine. "I doubt it. Look how frozen you are."

We motored east through mild traffic, past the elegant brick chimneys of the power station and the corrugated warehouses and skybound chutes of the sugar refinery. Warm air fluttered about my ankles. Whenever I risked a look, Michael's attention was fixed deliberately on the road — a truck wanted to cross in front of him at Cherry Street; a weaving cyclist had a full paper shopping bag clasped to his stomach, and he rode one-handed. Michael was waiting for me to begin. I was still in shock that I had called him.

The front hall of his home smelled of daffodils, I was sure that was it. Michael smiled; he said he had been trying to place the scent for months and claimed not to know its origins.

Along the long deep-carpeted hall (and I mean *deep* — that

chocolate wall-to-wall put up some real resistance) I detected a more subtle scent. Violets, I thought.

"It's a proper greenhouse," Michael said. "I suppose it could be worse."

I shook my head. "No, I like it."

He led me straight to the wall of glass that comprised most of the southern wall of his ground floor. "My view," he announced. Not boasting, just doing what he could to put me at ease.

"My God," I said. "I've never seen anything like it. This house. This!" I gestured at the massive window.

"Yes, quite," murmured Michael. "A bit much isn't it?"

"Not at all. God." I was gushing. I told him that at home I could see perhaps twenty feet to the back fence. Although I supposed that if I concentrated on the gaps in that eight-foot fence I might get an idea of the next twenty feet too. "But then I'd come smack up against the neighbour's window. Probably there'd be another woman just like me, standing at her window squinting back."

"But you love that house. That's what you told me."

I said, "Yes, but I have been ruined for anything other than this now. I mean, look at it."

He claimed to barely notice it anymore. "It might as well be a painting. Very little changes out there."

"But all the weather you must see coming."

There was nothing but water between us and America. But then: a short line of lights, a hyphen, mid-way to the horizon. A cargo ship, he guessed. "From Duluth. Or maybe it's grain from the prairies, loaded on at Thunder Bay and bound for Europe."

He made me tea, in an elaborate Chinese pot with a braided wicker handle that creaked when he carried the pot to a pink-topped table he said was his "breakfast spot." Self-deprecatingly he pointed out his "dinner spot," at a low teak coffee table in a distant corner, and his "reading spot" in a leather armchair studded with ridiculous brass rivets.

I remarked that there was no television, and he said no, not yet. "I'm loyal to my radio."

I told him he was far too young to say things like that, wasn't he? He was making me feel better. If I had felt this cheerful at the end of my shift I might never have telephoned.

He was running a finger around the rim of his thin-walled cup, making it moan. Watching me. "I won't hurry you, you know. So if you're waiting for me to ask what's up, we might be in for a long night."

"Some might say that's a prod in itself," I said — demurely, over that quaint handleless cup, more something made to hold an egg than this honeyed liquid. The prospect of talking to him terrified me. He had, like a spider, lured me (a willing victim, I'll admit) into his web. Unnerving poisons had been administered. I suddenly couldn't remember making any of my own decisions in this matter. I had been transformed into the girl from a nursery rhyme.

"The very gentlest of nudges," he said. I was disarmed. Partly it was that Boston accent. And the perfect (and perfectly steady) hands he wrapped around his tea. His patients must have lain awake nights wondering how they got so lucky. "But we can also just watch the water together. I have some food. Then I would take you home. Sometimes all a person needs is a little time." He gestured at the file he had tossed aside. "I could read, leave you alone."

No one had spoken to me like this before. These moments were the closest I ever came to duplicating Ray's infidelity. I told Michael it was difficult.

"I see that." He poured more tea. There was ginger in there somewhere, I felt its heat in my chest.

I began with: "It has to do with Ray."

Michael folded his hands professionally in his lap.

I told him it also had to do with the flood. There had been so much tension since then, so much in our relationship had gone missing. A good friend had died, too, and that hadn't helped, and then Ray was in the newspapers —

Michael interrupted me to say he had seen that article. "He's a handsome man. It bodes well for the child."

"I thought he looked awful. Like he'd been mugged."

"We should all stand up so well to the elements."

I gazed out the window. It was important I not look at him for a moment. The cargo ship had crawled another half-mile towards Montreal and the Atlantic Ocean. "Anyway," I said, "now he's looking for this woman. And he just seems so furtive about it."

"A woman?"

I explained how Ray had gone to the hospital. I had been at Frank's funeral, I said, then I went home with Gina. "But I never intended not to go to the hospital. He just *assumed* that." I must have sounded crazy.

Michael ventured that perhaps Ray was just protecting me from the drudgery of his work, trying to spare me gruesome details. Was this possible?

I shook my head but contradicted the gesture: "Of course it's possible. It's probably nothing, I know. . . . But Ray has been so secretive lately. And so moody. The only other time I've seen him like this was . . . was when he was seeing another woman."

We talked about that. Michael was gentle with me, sympathetic but still uninterested in persuading me of Ray's innocence or guilt.

I said, "You could have been a psychiatrist, did you know that? A nice leather couch, rather than that horrid table you have in your office."

He laughed — I was flattering him, he said — and went to

the kitchen. He returned with bread and cheese arranged on a wooden board. There was a serrated knife designed for cheese and beside it a more blunt instrument for the butter. A bowl in the same pattern as the teacups held a vinegary mix of sweet peppers and capers, a brilliant froth of parsley. "For the baby," he said, "even if you're not hungry."

We ate, and afterwards I felt better. I excused myself and stood in front of the bathroom mirror, refusing to read anything into my blazing face. I offered my profile to the mirror and raised my blouse so that the tight swell of my stomach sat neatly on the waist of my skirt. I tensed and the ball heaved slightly higher. I relaxed again and was tickled by how smartly it dropped, like a head onto a pillow.

I dabbed cold water onto my face and neck, then patted it dry with a towel so thick it was like two towels stitched together. I was still astonished to find myself there.

Afterwards I asked him. "Do *you* have Alice Beauchamps?" There were breadcrumbs in front of me on the table and I swept them into my palm. "Among the victims," I said. "I heard you were monitoring some of the more difficult cases. Are you? I'm having trouble getting a proper list."

He raised his head and seemed to study the darkening sky for a minute. Stars were few and far between — the city was too bright — but his attention seemed to flit between very specific points, as if he was tracking a bird. "No. There's no Alice. An Alison, though. That any help?"

"How old is she?"

"I'm joking."

"There's no Alison?"

"Well yes, there is. But you distinctly said Alice. If you start thinking Alison is close enough I might have to refer you to a colleague, and he really does have one of those leather couches."

"Michael, tell me how old she is. What's her full name?"

| 200 |

"She's young, Mary. Your age. And we don't have a surname yet. Alison is all she's been able to give us."

"What's wrong with her?"

"She was under water a long time. We're having trouble bringing her all the way back." He looked forlorn. "It's the woman you looked after," he said. "The one who almost froze. We put her in a bath, remember?"

"A coma, then. Where is she?" I said stiffly.

"Mary, you know this is irrational."

"Would I be able to speak to her?"

"I don't think I could allow that."

"Is she married? What does she say?" I tried to recall her face.

"She doesn't say very much. They all tell pretty similar stories — panic, darkness, wind, water, sleep."

"Does she have family?" I was frantic for details. Something masochistic was coming awake inside me.

The doctor scraped his chair towards me. "I want you to stop this! I demand it. Do you hear me? Mary?" He had me by the arms. He wasn't shaking me, exactly, but he said, "I want you back. Do you hear me? This instant!"

I cried out and he pulled me in against his chest. He put his hand over my temple and held me there. An ivory shirt button pressed against my nose. If he had put a finger under my chin and raised my lips to his, I wouldn't have been able to stop him. After a while I realized that he was rocking me back and forth. He was whispering something too — *Hush*, I think it was. *Hushhhh*.

I pushed away. This would only make it worse. If I allowed myself to be comforted like this — even though it was what I wanted (was it what I had come for?) I would leave a weaker woman. Every time Ray looked at me the wrong way I would want to immerse myself in this botanical garden, plant myself here, in this man's arms. I tried to see him as I had at the beginning, as a weird man physically, and not my type at all.

I said (pitifully I'm sure), "What is this doing to my baby? Am I hurting my baby?" God it all sounds so incredibly melodramatic, doesn't it? As if I was experiencing my very own Marilyn Monroe moments, my sad little *Niagara*.

Michael assured me the baby was fine. "You can stay here," he said. "Call your husband. Tell him you're needed at the hospital. I'll set up a bed for you."

I knew I could say yes and he would be pleased. But I said, "He'll worry. No, I have to go."

"I'll drive you, then."

I struggled to my feet. "Thank you. You can drop me at the corner." The lake was the purest black now.

"I can drop you at the door," he said. "Don't be silly."

"Not anymore, you can't."

"Whyever not?"

"You're involved," I told him, laughing through tears.

"Well, it's not how I imagined it might be," he said ruefully. He was in the hallway, wriggling into his shoes.

He stood up straight and I wanted so much at that moment to reach out and touch him, brush his cheek, perhaps with the back of my hand. But all I could manage was, "It never is, Michael, is it? Not quite."

And then, a short while later, as we turned onto Aldringham, he told me hesitantly, but shockingly, "She says things."

"Who? What does she say?"

"She calls out. Mary, I shouldn't tell you — in fact I've been trying not to tell you for the last mile or so — but I've heard her. It's sort of horrifying. A terrific nightmare for her. We've had to tranquilize her. I think now that she might be crying out for a man."

"A man?"

He paused, grimaced, as if in pain. I thought he might still retreat from what I suppose I knew was coming. But finally he said, "For Raymond. She says it over and over. At least I think she does. To start with, I thought it was something about the rain. And then, for the last few days, I thought perhaps it was 'raiment' — do you know the word? — and that she was reciting Shakespeare at me. She's barely intelligible, Mary, and she raves about a lot of things — about the storm, and about a dog, even about a shopping list she needs to find. At least I think she does. Whenever I see her I can't help but think of King Lear wandering mad in the rain, ripping off his clothes." He looked at me. "But now I must admit, I do wonder. And Raymond, if it is Raymond she's saying, does seem to be at the centre of her thoughts, such as they are."

We were stopped in front of my black house. "You see, dear, I had no reason before now to connect the two," Michael said. He seemed confused, flustered. As if he was trying to decide not just whether he had even heard her words correctly, but also whether he had now betrayed his patient. And there was that *dear*.

"But as we drove here," he said, "I was thinking about how I'd seen his face in the newspaper, and wondering if I might possibly meet him tonight, your husband. Suddenly those two trains of thought collided. Christ, I shouldn't have said anything."

"Where is she, Michael?"

"You know this doesn't prove anything," he said very sternly. "I'm feeding into your paranoia, that's all. And we do think her name is Alison."

"You *think* her name is Alison?"

He shrugged noncommitally. "We thought so."

I waited up for Ray.

"I found her," I said. He was only half out of his coat. There was water on the hall floor. "Your dear Alice."

All of a sudden he was like a man wrestling an octopus. Finally he slapped his coat down and bypassed me and stationed himself, aquiver, in front of the liquor cabinet. He splashed whisky carelessly into a glass. He shook his head, but he wouldn't look at me. He said he was pleased. That was one more name he could cross off a long list, wasn't it? A smile then that was more of a grimace.

"She's calling your name, Ray. Look at me. Actually she calls you Raymond. Isn't that nice? Very proper of her."

He poured himself more liquor and I told him there was no escaping this, even if he poisoned himself. I may even have said to him that the game was up, I recall being a touch embarrassed by the banality of some of my words. But it didn't need to be fancy. "Ray!" I demanded. "Your reaction tells me everything I need to know. Don't do this." But he did. He built a wall, assembled it magically between us. "You're crazy," he said, paranoid. I thought the glass would be crushed in his hand. "This can't be good for the baby," he declared. "Look at yourself," he said, piling it on, "you're being illogical, Mare, you need to calm down. I've done nothing."

"That's not true," I insisted.

"Oh no, you're right," he allowed, mocking me. Mocking me! "Have you read the newspaper lately? They say I'm a hero. And yet here, in my own home, I'm a goddamn monster."

There was no talking to him. He labelled me a hysteric, said it was unbelievable what he was seeing. He didn't have to put up with this. Every denial he tried, every insult, opened the wound a little wider and a little deeper. I distinctly remember thinking as he laboured up the stairs and away from me: *This is going to leave a scar.*

So it doesn't really matter that he's sorry now. Because he must be, mustn't he? Beneath all that hard knotty veneer. That doesn't relieve him of the obligations he had to me back then, as my husband, as the father of our unborn child. And he's had fifty years to come clean, to admit fault. Any day before he got sick would have been fine. I could have found some way to deal with that, some previously unknown reserve of energy and forgiveness. But it's too late now. He's frightened, that's all it is. He just wants a clean slate, a clean conscience, when he gets to the pearly gates. He's the atheist reformed. He's also a coward, just when he thinks he's being so damned brave in the face of everything.

And one more thing. It doesn't end there. It gets worse.

RAY

I'll die soon. If not today, then within a week. If I last two weeks, I'll have a heart attack from the shock of making it that far. I feel death creeping within me like a drug, like the honey-thick formaldehyde they will pump into me once they have drained me of this dull blood. I try to imagine my body rigid, then myself as a homunculus trapped in my own skull, looking out from my casket. I am remarkably successful. Tears well up, I feel a sympathetic, fleeting paralysis. The plastic oxygen mask rarely leaves my face now and has begun to smell sourly of death. The air it funnels into my mouth tastes of plastic. And the inside of each of my lungs is a bloody concert hall. The pair of them are cavernous, and the ruined alveoli are like torn velvet curtains that hang bloodily and limp from the rafters. I'm a goner, there's no denying it. I've stood over a few bodies in my time and said those exact words — *he's a goner* — and they have always struck me as grimly humorous. And they make me laugh now, they really do. Though that may be the drugs.

I saw Jenny's suitcase this morning, half-packed in the kitchen. Did she ever really unpack, I wonder, or is she getting ready to leave now? Surely she isn't doing it because she senses the end is at hand. No one is that insensitive. And besides, she will have to help Mary. There will be things to do, and I really wish there were more than the two of them to take care of the details. If you spread grief thinly enough no one suffers too badly. It is a theory anyway.

I know she said at dinner that she had to leave, she has a contract to fulfill, but I thought she would wait. I don't want her go. I have always wished we had had more children.

The air left behind by that storm smelled thickly — of wood mostly, but there were other more cloying scents that hugged the ground and caught like spikes in the throat. The army had set alight massive bonfires by aiming flamethrowers mounted on tanks that crawled along the quaggy shoreline. Mostly these fires had been built with the remains of trees bowled down by the river, and with the debris from demolished houses. But there were sofas and chairs, lamps and carpets; there were bicycles losing their rubber tires and saddles to the flames, and there were the hideous bug-eyed dolls, and the crackling velvet pelts of cheap stuffed animals. Visibility had been reduced so much that the search parties — the groups of volunteers and boy scouts and army reservists who combed the banks for bodies — had given up and were gathered in tight circles in front of drab green trucks, hugging tin mugs of coffee or, for the young boys, a watered-down hot chocolate. Above everyone's heads swirled complicated constellations of ash and spark, and I was reminded of paintings I had seen as a boy. Those had been by Turner, and the river in them was the Thames, the city in flames was London.

When I arrived one morning (the morning after? Or was it later still? I didn't know yet that Alice was at the hospital anyway) they had just found a boy's body, a foot down in the mud that had swept across the flat grassy floodplain as easily as melted chocolate might pour over a pan of hot shortbread. Everyone had gathered around the small black form — a dog, I thought at first — as if at any moment he would spit out the mud plug that packed his mouth and yap at us for saving him. For these men, finding a body had become not much different than finding a shard of neatly painted pottery, an arrowhead; those who didn't manage it would go home disappointed. I wanted to yell at them, to curse their indifference, but they would have stared at me incomprehendingly. You have us all wrong, their looks would say.

There were navy divers at the failed footbridge just above Raymore Drive. If Alice was still in the water I thought it most probable she would be found here. Which I suppose made me a ghoul too.

There were sixty-nine of them so far — the missing and the drowned. Eighteen from Raymore Drive. *The Globe and Mail* had published a list of the deceased in alphabetical order, but after checking for Alice's name, as if the newspaper might know something the police department didn't — I had turned hurriedly to the sports pages. I didn't want to read that those children — Joshua and Lucas and Grace — had perished, or their mother, Mary. I tried unsuccessfully to dredge up the father's name. Al seemed right, but I wouldn't be confident enough to use it if I ran into the man on the street. No, I told myself, they weren't dead. They were meeting with insurance adjusters at a downtown hotel. They were cashing a handsome cheque and blowing some of it on ice cream.

There were scenes like this morning's back when I was in Italy. The fog and the smoke were the same, as were the tanks I had seen through the trees, and the knowledge that bodies would be found and that they would have to be cleaned up before they could be identified.

In Italy there were also booby-trapped bridges. All the

members of my unit had taken turns wading or swimming beneath any bridges we came to, inspecting the mossy, oiled planking for wires and tubes. When the bridge was too high above the water, or the water raged too fiercely, the designated soldier would swing, monkey-like, from support to support, while the rest of us scratched agitatedly at our armpits and hooted at him. Trying to convince ourselves it was all a game.

Some of the Italian bridges, because a bomb had already detonated, looked much like this one over the Humber. They lurched drunkenly into the water, and snowmelt boiled around their failed supports. I saw the bodies of cows rotting in the swirl, their eyes swollen to the size of tennis balls. Smoke twisted from stone farmhouses and ambushed pickup trucks. Once, we saw leaping flame at the distant horizon. The road we were on had degenerated into a muddy canal and it took a day and a half to cover the distance. Eventually we arrived at a copse of ancient oaks. Every tree had burned to its core, and now the blackened, brittle limbs pointed accusingly at the blue sky, the distant mountains. An entire population destroyed, that was how it struck me. It was sadder than anything I had seen til then, sadder than men's bodies, and for the first time I wanted to be at home, in Toronto; for the first time I felt useless and scared.

The divers in Toronto, though, those were a new detail. Ruddy-faced men in rubber who surfaced like monsters to shake their heads — no, they hadn't found anything — and then upended themselves again. Their lights were visible down there, poking nervously into pilings, and sometimes two lamps would be aimed at the same spot and a clump of swaying weed would appear in the beam; they had mistaken it, I assumed, for someone's hair. And I, trapped above them, had mistaken it for Alice.

I am part of that chaos again now. That is my reason for bringing it up: all is dense fog and bitterest smoke. The mud is in my lungs now, not that boy's. He is me. I am him.

There is another body, one I have been avoiding here quite intentionally; one I think about as little as possible. But I must face her now, I think. For in her death I believe there is much that explains my actions during the last days of this affair.

Mary knows nothing of her so I was exaggerating somewhat when I claimed earlier that hashish is my greatest remaining secret. What I do know is that Mary would leap to use the Perkins woman against me, would love to see me as the direct architect of yet another death.

She is, was, the estranged wife of the man who owned the marvelous car, the Cadillac that was abandoned atop the Humber bridge on the night of the hurricane. You might recall that I took a tube of lipstick from the glovebox and held it up to the lips of a corpse at the firehall. Her husband had a violent history record and my superiors were worried that the storm might have been used as a cover. I revealed that much. But there is more.

On the 16th, at the end of the day, I visited Mr. Perkins at his rather palatial digs in Rosedale — a twenty-year-old house masquerading as something out of the last century; bigger than three homes in any other part of town, and at the back a stream burbled through. It was probably the only stream in Toronto that hadn't burst its banks, and I wondered if money could buy an outcome like that too.

Perkins — Oscar Perkins was his full name — let me wait a good while but finally the front door opened a hair, and then that gap widened and the round face of a man was inserted into it, like a moon between hewn trees.

"You want to open a little wider and show me your hands?" I asked him. I was irritated. "I've been out here a while."

"I was hoping you'd go away," Perkins grumbled. "I suppose you want me to let you in."

"I can set you up in the back seat if you'd rather."

He opened the door all the way. Oscar and his father ran a tire factory north of the city; they were intent on building a mountain of rubber up there. "You get five minutes," he said. "Less if I decide you're wasting my time."

I followed him to a room at the back of the house. The ceilings must have been twenty feet away and the walls were at least forty from each other. A fireplace in black wood looked as if it would accommodate a full-grown pig, and the assortment of iron tools next to the grate was surely sharp enough and heavy enough to subdue the beast right there in front of guests. All that was missing was a suit of armour, although the head of a moose had been mounted on a wooden shield. The rugs looked to have been cut away from zebras and bears that very afternoon, so brightly did the hides gleam. There was a smoker's pipe resting on a stand, and an ornate cabinet showing off a dozen full decanters.

Perkins collapsed into a wingback chair facing the fire, which burned so perfectly I thought there must be an attendant, a butler, hidden somewhere nearby, a man whose only responsibility was to maintain this perfect architecture of logs. "Wherever you like," Perkins said, indicating the selection of armchairs crouched among the skins.

A bully, I thought and so I sat — disrespectfully I hoped — on the arm of a chair, crushing its padding, and stretched my legs towards the fire. "We've been trying to reach you all day."

"I'm a busy man."

"About your car." I watched for him to flinch, or blink, do something I could get worked up about. (In case you're wondering, I was fully aware of the hypocrisy involved in my getting steamed at the thought of this man causing the disappearance, the death of an innocent woman. These days they would say I was "projecting," I suppose. Or acting out. Back then, fifty years ago, I was just pissed off and panicky and not thinking straight.)

Perkins stuffed tobacco into the pipe. "Blocking traffic, is it?" He set fire to the shredded leaves and sucked gamely. "I'll send a man if you can't tow it."

"We're more concerned about the state you left it in," I said.

"Well there was a hell of a lot of water out there. Lizzie thought we'd never make it. She had visions of me driving clear over the railing. Which would be a hell of a trick, wouldn't it? But you know how women are when things get a little dicey."

"I have no idea. Explain it to me."

Perkins shook his head. "She's a little excitable, that's all."

"Is she here now? Elizabeth, isn't it?"

"God I hope she's not!"

"Why's that?"

"We don't live together, detective. I threw her out."

"Last night?"

"Months ago. Couldn't stand the sight of her a moment longer."

"But you were out together last night."

"If she needs something, she calls me."

"Where does she live now, Mr. Perkins?"

"She has a little place in Toronto."

"That narrows it down."

"Among the subway builders, the bricklayers."

"You mean the Italians?"

"Down there, yes."

"I'll need an address. And a telephone number. We were under the impression she lived here with you."

"It suits her to have people think so," Perkins snorted. "Her social aspirations rather depend on her link to me."

"Did you have a fight, then? Last night."

"What gave you that idea?"

"There's blood all over the steering wheel. The passenger door was open next to the railing."

"We discussed our options and then she left."

"Your options?"

"Like I said, I wanted to plough on and Lizzie was against it. I told her she was free to go back."

"That's not much of a discussion."

"We were under the impression there was a hurricane in the vicinity. It didn't seem the time for anything more drawn out."

"So you let her walk."

"She insisted on not coming with me."

"But then you left the car there anyway."

"It stalled and wouldn't start again. If I hadn't stopped because of her yelling at me, it would never have happened." He looked thoughtfully into the fire. His face was red from the heat of the fire and an apple-scented cloud of tobacco smoke had gathered above him. "She might have woken up in more pleasant circumstances if she'd kept quiet."

"The poor woman," I said. I brought my legs in and then extended them again. Perkins was trying to decide whether he had been insulted and could take offence. I watched the gears turning. "Explain the blood to me," I said.

"Nose bleed."

"That's it?"

"You want I should have bludgeoned her to death, detective? I sense that might have made you happy. The chance to arrest me. Odd how we make up our minds about people. Don't you think?"

"Whose nose was it?"

"Bleeding? Mine. A reaction to the weather, I think." He must have spotted my skepticism because he said, "I'm quite serious, you know. A sudden drop in barometric pressure can bring it on. Check with a doctor. Lizzie had just got out of the car; she was in a terrible state, I thought she might get blown away, and I was about to go after her when it started. Before I could staunch it, it was all over me."

"You have the clothes?"

"Excuse me?"

"It was all over you. I'd like to see your coat. Or your shirt. Whichever took the brunt of it."

Perkins placed his pipe carefully in the rack. He rose into the apple cloud and squinted down at me. It was all he could do not to cough. When he left the room I hoped he was intending to make a run for it. I would have dearly loved to tackle him on his own driveway, use him to mark up the gravel.

But he returned a minute later with a white shirt folded over one outstretched arm. Playing his own butler. I confirmed the bloodstain. "Boiling it's your best bet."

"An expert opinion?"

"Something like that. You didn't find that address up there, did you?"

A log tumbled and rolled to the front of the grate. Perkins kicked it to the back, like a football, a reckless-seeming action at odds with the meticulous order of everything else in the room. Sparks scattered and spat, and Perkins regarded them as if they were disobedient children. "Claremont. Two hundred Claremont. Tiny whitewashed place. Here's the telephone number." He fished a fold of paper from a pocket and handed it to me. "She'll be home now. The telephone's in the corner."

He reclaimed his pipe and paced with it before the fireplace, hunting any embers that might have settled on his precious rug. "You've judged me, I think we can agree on that, but you really should talk to Lizzie before you set anything in stone."

"You did check that she made it home," I said.

"Of course I did. It would have been very late. Two perhaps. She had just got in herself and had little time for me. I don't suppose she'll sing my praises when you reach her."

And that was about it. We exchanged a few primitive accusatory glances and then he said he wanted me out of his house. I said I understood that and he nearly stiff-armed me to the door and then slammed it behind me. I knew even then that I couldn't blame him.

The next morning, first thing, I drove into Little Italy and onto Claremont.

I marched smartly up the cobbled walk. Official police business, that's what this was, and I found great comfort, great distraction in the thought. I stood straighter than I'd been able to for two days, and didn't mind at all the notion that old women up and down the street were peering around dingy curtains to get a glimpse of the official young man banging on Mrs. Perkins' door.

Elizabeth was much younger than her husband, which was no surprise, but she also seemed sharper than he had, despite his aggressive, growling demeanour. She kept one hand on the door, as if she might choose without warning to slam it in my face. She had brown heels on, and a short cream coat lay along a bench behind her.

"I won't keep you," I started.

"No you won't."

"But I have a couple of questions." I identified myself, produced my badge. How many times had I done this in my career? A thousand by now? "It's about Friday evening. You were with your husband."

Mrs. Perkins stuck her head out far enough to ascertain that her neighbours weren't leaning over the fences. "What's the damn fool done now?"

I cocked an eyebrow. "What did he do before?"

She huffed at me, tucked her hair behind an ear. She stamped a foot in irritation. She was like a bull preparing to charge and I admired her immensely.

"I wanted mostly to confirm that you were with him on the bridge that night." I waited. "That it was you in the passenger seat."

"Does he say it was me?"

"That's not the point, really."

"I'm not inviting you in," she said. "So you'd better make it quick."

"I'm trying to do exactly that," I told her. "Was it you, Mrs. Perkins?"

"It was me until I left," she said. She wanted to show me, I supposed, that she was irritated with her husband; she didn't want to help him out of any jam.

"He says you wanted him to turn back."

"Didn't that bridge collapse?"

"It's suffered some damage, yes, but it's still standing, as far as I know."

"But the end of it, the end we were heading for, that's messed up, right?"

I confirmed her information.

"Then I think I was being the reasonable one, don't you?"

"I've met Mr. Perkins recently, ma'am. I had little doubt you would prove to be more reasonable."

"So he didn't kill himself? That's not why you're here?"

"A nosebleed seems to be the extent of it."

"He gets those." She released the door and let it knock into a square umbrella stand. At the end of the hall was the kitchen and on the right the door to a bathroom. The house was expensively furnished. This might be a modest part of the city, but Mrs. Perkins had clearly brought some of her husband's mansion with her. "It's too bad that's all it was," she said.

"You're no longer a fan?" I said.

"No one is a fan of my husband," she told me. "I defy you to find a man or a woman, or even a dog, willing to stand up for him."

"I won't waste my time, then. Do you mind telling me why you were with him?"

"I do, yes."

She was getting the better of me, making me run, find ways around her. Just as she wouldn't allow me into her house, she wasn't going to tell me any of her secrets.

"He owes me money, detective. Simple as that. He owes me a considerable sum and I didn't want to step foot in his house. So we had dinner. I'm sure he misinterpreted my invitation. Men tend to do that, don't they?"

"All the time."

"I thought I'd be safe driving around with him."

"You're scared of him, then?"

"Not anymore." She showed me the thick chain on the door. She checked the street again. "I should have had you in after all, shouldn't I?"

"That's fine. I can see why you'd be reluctant. You're describing a nasty setup," I said. "You must be relieved to be away from there."

"It doesn't feel like I'm away. It feels like I'm living in some lavatory at the edge of the grounds."

I indicated over her shoulder. "I wouldn't mind a toilet like this," I said.

"Yes, well."

She was a snob, then. I felt my sympathies for her diminishing. "Did you get your money? Perhaps there are legal avenues."

"He has monkeys blocking off those avenues. As we speak, I should think. Now that he knows what I want."

"So what will you do?"

It was her turn to raise an eyebrow. "I thought you only wanted to establish my presence in that hideous car of his."

"It's a weakness of mine," I said, which was true. I talked too much, and I strayed from the point. I wanted connection, Mary had said — because she had noted this trait in me (and yet failed to identify what it might lead to) — I wanted to connect with everybody. That was her word — connect — and I said that sounded so nuclear somehow, so modern. "He sounds a nasty piece of work, is all," I said to Mrs. Perkins. "I was wondering if it might be best for you not to provoke him."

She unbuttoned the cuff of her blouse and peeled back the snug sleeve as far as the elbow. On the inside of her forearm, rising three inches from just above the wrist, was a thick white scar notched at a dozen points where the stitches had gone in. It was the sort of thing I had seen on men's legs and arms after the war. Shrapnel wounds. "This is what happens when you provoke that man," she spat. "No stranger needs to come knocking at my door telling me what I'd be wise not to do."

I reached for her arm and she withdrew it sharply. "No!" she said, and tugged down the sleeve.

"How did he do that?"

"A knife," she told me. "A very dull knife as I recall."

I screwed up my face. "I didn't hear about this."

"Why would you?" she asked sharply.

"Because his nose bled all over the steering wheel. The doors were open, the car abandoned. Anything could have happened. So we checked his record. I didn't see anything about this."

"He abandoned the car?"

"He says it wouldn't start after you left."

"He had to walk?" She tipped back her head and she laughed. Her neck was long and smooth and white and I didn't want to start thinking about her that way. This was the most rewarding moment of her day, I understood that, and so I let her extend it. There were tears in her eyes. It was as if she had just won a big prize. "I love that. Oh I absolutely love it. He must have been livid."

It was an odd thing for her to say, this woman so scared of

setting her husband off.

"Oh I know what you're thinking," she said. "But he'll blame the car, not me. He's so damn literal. Trust me. If anything it'll make him forget all about our little tiff."

I found myself squinting at her, as if she emitted a sort of light that I needed to filter out. I said, "I'm glad you're okay."

"One less for you to worry about."

"Something like that."

I told her she could call me if things got rough.

"Tell me your name again."

"Ray Townes," I said. "At Headquarters. You can ask for me."

I saw that she was used to men offering help. It was just as obvious from the look on her face — not quite a smirk and not utterly dismissive, but not grateful either — that these were offers she routinely declined.

"I'll write that down," she said. "Thank you."

She was fumbling for the door edge again, even as I said, "You're welcome." The last thing I saw was the pantleg and polished black shoe of a man in the kitchen, a man who must have been leaned against the wall in there, trying to eavesdrop, and who, now that I was leaving, was turning away. I tried to engage Mrs. Perkins again, but she was shutting me out, and I couldn't think why it was any of my business who she kept in there with her.

And then I mostly forgot about her. There was the odd lustful image of that swan's neck and the haughty, blatantly erotic tone she took with me in her doorway, but I considered the case closed. But then one day, immediately after Mary and I had arranged to meet within the hour at the Royal Ontario Museum (my intention was to try to calm somewhat the fevered waters between us), Merrick, my immediate superior, summoned me into his office. There was a brown-bread chicken sandwich on his desk next to the telephone, and a half-done bottle of Coca-Cola with a fat red straw stuffed into its neck. A picture of his wife and his two children on a beach somewhere. A diminutive aspidistra squeezed into the bookshelf next to his Criminal Code, its fronds going brown at the tips. A streetcar squealing past.

"The Perkins woman," Merrick said.

I did the slight mental work necessary to bring her to mind. "Okay." I nodded.

"They found her this morning. Neighbour reported a stink and her newspapers piling up on the step. Hell of a mess inside." Merrick shuddered so violently I figured he must have been in there himself. "I just wanted to make sure we didn't miss anything."

"How do you mean?" The office was unbearably warm and smelled of that spidery plant, its decayed roots.

"We've brought the husband in. All the signs are there and he's not denying anything. Seems pleased with himself, if anything. But his lawyers are crawling up our arses already. Figure you were pretty much the last one to talk to them both. You didn't get the impression he was about to go over the edge? Nothing he said? Or her? She seem scared to you?"

"Christ." I squirmed. "She seemed like a nice woman."

"She might have been, once. Hard to tell now."

In my head I went through the conversation she had had with me. I arrived quickly at the marks on her arm. *A knife*, she had said. *A very dull knife*. The man hiding in the shadows behind her. Did she even know he was there? It must have happened later than that, mustn't it? The impression I had of him was of an ally waiting for her to return to him. Finally I managed to say, "There was nothing to raise any alarms. Sounded like a nasty breakup, that's all."

Merrick let me go. "Just covering our tail," he said, and opened the door again.

I wanted very much to telephone Mary, head her off. Rather than seeing her, I wanted to drive — east or west, I didn't care which, so long as I travelled at a crazy speed.

I had totally missed, or at least discounted Mrs Perkins' fear, the chain on the door. I was so damn preoccupied that day with getting my own story straight. Even if her guest wasn't the killer, there was basic followup I should have done. Reports I should have filed and fast-tracked. A uniform could have kept tabs on both of them; it wasn't something that would have cut into my own schedule. All it would have taken was a "We're on to you" visit to Oscar at his home. Some flashing lights on the forecourt, some dirty size-twelves on the oriental rugs.

I drove in a blistering fog to the museum. I hovered around my car for a long moment, contemplating my options before finally deciding there were none. I made it on complaining knees to the top of the worn stone steps. I turned to face the city, the colourful squalls of children who had escaped school, and the black snakes of traffic heading south towards the parliament buildings. I had the sense of putting myself up there so everyone could see me. If they knew everything I knew, they would have thrown things at me. Rotten fruit.

And then Mary arrived. I realized again and instantly that our meeting was a mistake, that I was incapable of saying the things she wanted and needed to hear. Should I have sent her away? Was that even a possibility, given how tenuous our relationship had become, how brittle? Regardless, I guided her inside and bought us tickets. I led her, nearly mute, to a display I wanted to see, hoping it would calm me. But then . . . then I said the most terrible things. I set in motion an express train of events every bit as awful as anything I've admitted so far. And I hold that we might have escaped the 1950s with only a few faint scars if I had done my job, my police job, properly, followed some simple protocols. This is the bitter kernel for me, another of the few nuts around which my wobbly world has revolved all these years. There is the affair, of course, and there is Alice's dark ride in the river, there are all the lies I employed to disguise those things. I deny nothing; I acknowledge nearly everything, at least in this half-light. But in addition to the shared knowledge, the unlocked storehouse from which we gather our spitballs, there is also this stranger's death and the thought that had it been avoided my life could have been better. And Mary's too. Especially Mary's. My shattered reaction to Elizabeth Perkins' slaughter provoked, I think, a tipping point for Mary and me, several decades before anyone even knew what a tipping point was.

MARY

Remember that letter I wrote to Marilyn Monroe? The one I would never have mailed? Well one day a reply came through the slot at such an angle that it caught the air and rather than flopping to the beige mat, it lifted its nose, actually gained altitude before pausing, diving and then straightening out. Finally it skidded over the floor some dozen feet from where it had started. A single sheet of airmail paper, folded once and sealed at its centre with a fraction of silver tape, creating a perfect wing. I had been about to pull the ironing board from its hook on the inside wall of the coat closet, and I'd watched the entire flight with the first twinklings of amusement I had felt in days.

I read standing up at the front window, watching the road, which was deserted, as if the letter had delivered itself.

Dear Mary,

There's no knowing what drew me to your letter when, as you say, there are so many. But there was something, obviously, and I was happy to receive your kind words. Thank you. I was also moved enough by your predicament, and your obvious pain, to pen this entirely inadequate response.

I don't pretend to have any special insight, Mary, and cer-
tainly any wisdom you discern here is almost certainly a mistake
on your part. All I have is experience. More than most at my age,
if I do say so. And I am more than willing to share that with you.

I wish I had been able to forgive Joe. That is all I will say
about our dissolution: I wish I had been able to forgive him. It
would have spared much misery for both of us. He is not a bad
man. Just a distractable one. Forgiveness — and I am not a reli-
gious woman — is a divine virtue. It can make angels out of the
shiftiest demons. You should do whatever you can to encourage
angels — the world is in desperate need.

The second thing I want to say, and I'm sure you know this
already, is that trust, when it has been abused once, is the hardest
thing to rekindle. It is as if oceans have risen up to swallow the
most delicate of fires. But rekindle you should. And if that fire
does spark again, then spread its light around, Mary. Trust
everyone you can and trust them to your absolute limit. It will
not always be to your benefit (trust me!) but you will sleep better,
knowing you have done everything you can.

And that is all, really. There is no point my rattling on. But
perhaps it will help.

Persist, Mary. Persist.
Affectionately, Marilyn

I knew the letter was a fake, but I set it on the windowsill
anyway, and found in *Life* magazine a picture of Marilyn I liked
very much: the actress ensconced in a leather desk chair in a
book-lined office. Sunlight from a high window settling like a
breath of lemon in her hair. I reread the letter and studied the
woman in the photograph, watched her metamorphose into an
entirely different creature.

It was Gina's work, of course, and I loved her for it. She
explained later (once I had wormed a confession from her) that

she'd found my original missive when the two of us were sorting through some of my old clothes. She was packing Frank's things up, a charity was coming to collect them, and apparently I said that I had bits and pieces that may as well hitch a ride. I must have tossed it into the drawer of mine that she snooped through, late on the night I wrote it, not thinking.

I wept when I read that note. And rereading it now, marvelling at the effort it must have taken, the altruistic spirit who made it, I still think the words have much to recommend them.

And my immediate reaction was that I would live according to its advice. Forgive, if I was capable of forgiving. I *wanted* to do that. Past tense. Because Ray made it impossible the same afternoon.

He telephoned me. Would I meet him at the Royal Ontario Museum? (In fact, Ray surprised me by alluding cryptically to this whole horror show this morning at breakfast. He is largely responsible for sparking this memory, I think. He must be musing on his mistakes, down in that stinking cave of his, adding and subtracting from his ledger. It is beyond him to express out loud any real remorse, but I assume his acknowledgement of the event's existence is supposed to constitute at least a minor act of contrition. Or perhaps he just thinks he is being heroic, manly somehow.)

I said of course I would meet him, but why there? There was an exhibition of shrunken heads — yes shrunken heads — he was keen to see. I hoped that he also intended to tell me everything, to finally come clean. Gina was there when he called and although she remained intensely protective of me, and skeptical of Ray, she suggested that perhaps he wanted a neutral space, somewhere we would have to talk with hushed, reasonable voices.

When I arrived, Ray was waiting for me on the stone steps fronting onto University Avenue. His eyes were red. He wore the same suit too many days in a row and it hung shabbily off his shoulders. "You look like a gangster," I told him, although I said it kindly. I was excited, I think, attached to the idea that we would stroll together arm-in-arm through the dim medieval halls. We would peer into arcades overflowing with polished fossils and posed suits of Welsh armor; Egyptian mummies laid out in stone sarcophagi, rough diamonds from Africa, and dinosaur bones from Alberta. I was a romantic, even then, after everything he had done. Though I suppose I was also residually suspicious of his motives. But when we entered and I looked up into the vaulted limestone distances I thought of a church, a cathedral, a blessed space we could fill with positive thoughts and conciliatory words. I wanted to be able to forgive him.

He butchered a smile for me and leaned down so that I could kiss him. "This is nice," I said, keeping my face close to his. Even with a coat on it was possible now to tell I was pregnant.

He paid for our tickets. My eyes were fixed on him as he replaced his wallet. I was apprehensive, staying a step behind, but also trying heroically to maintain the illusion that nothing unusual was going on here; just a man and wife taking in the exhibits.

He thanked me for coming, even though he looked right now as if he would have paid strangers to keep me away.

"You don't have to thank me, Ray. This is nice. This is what we're *supposed* to do."

We stood beneath the ribcage of a tyrannosaurus. Off to the right the pendulous head of a brontosaurus hung at the end of a delicate arc of bones like an absurd lampshade. The tag said the skeletons had been transported from Mongolia twenty years ago. A wall mural depicted in pastels the hissing swamp the creatures would have slogged through. Birds the size of helicopters careened through a blue-green sky. Stone platypus eggs had been arranged in a straw nest built by museum volunteers.

In the adjoining gallery Egyptian dogs and cats had been preserved in gauze. Pyramid construction was explained in simple diagrams. Hieroglyphics had been reproduced on a woven cream canvas and then pinned in a band running around all four walls.

We had still said almost nothing to each other and I was beginning to worry.

"Where are the heads you wanted to see, Ray? Can we find those?" I tugged at his arm. "Come on, let's look for a map."

I pulled him through rooms that, so far as I could tell, were lined with nothing more than shards of pottery. Another (and it made me uncomfortable) contained cabinets stuffed with crucifixes, all ridden by the same tortured figure. We flitted, murmuring niceties, through rooms of sharpened flint, then bright rooms of bronze, and long, dim hallways hung with faded tapestries.

Eventually we arrived in front of a head. A Latin soldier, said the tag. I was repulsed by it instantly. "They wrote about *this* in the newspaper?"

"Do you want to hear how they did it?" Ray said. I blinked and scratched at my arm. He knew I wouldn't like it but he told me anyway. "They take a hammer to the skull to break all the bones," he said. "Then they suck everything out through the neck with a straw. They pour hot sand in to shrink the skin. They do that five or six times."

"Ray, stop! Why are you telling me this?"

"Each time it's emptied, a sculptor puts his hand inside and molds the features some more."

"Ray!" I didn't understand. I was shaking my head slowly, disbelievingly.

"We're both in the business," he said. "I thought you might get a kick out of it."

"The *business*? A *kick*?"

I was losing my patience, it was obvious, and he should have steered us onto more relevant ground, but instead he said, "It was just a ruse, okay?" He spun away. "A con-job to get you here. I thought we needed to talk. And I needed a hook."

"You needed a hook?"

He was making things worse. He had lost all the words he needed to talk to me properly. Those words that were left were all too tough when what he needed was tender. He should have apologized, damn it, sunk to his knees. An elderly uniformed guard twitched at the door.

I turned into Ray and he saw that I was crying. My wet face next to the shriveled features of the Latin soldier. Our "reconciliation" was unfolding as a fiasco.

"Mary —" he began, trying to halt the progression from silent tears to open sobbing.

I opened my eyes wide, trying to clear my vision. "I don't understand you any more, Ray. Who *are* you?" I felt my face twist horribly, as if threads had been looped through the corners of my mouth and then pulled tight. "You brought me here for *this*?" I pointed a wobbly finger.

"Mary."

He lifted an arm but I staggered away. The guard took a step forwards and Ray caught that movement. "Stay!" he called to me.

The old man, a senior probably, maybe even an ex-cop, shot a look in my direction. Did I want him to do something? Could I give him a sign? Perhaps feeling his dignity was at stake, if not his gainful employment, the guard took another step forward.

I screamed, "Leave him alone!" and it was unclear to both men who I was talking about. Both of them stopped, then Ray spat on the old flagstones. I was afraid of him now. At the doorway I put a hand on the smooth limestone and began my turn. But then I caught the heel of one foot on the toe of the other and

| 228 |

tripped. I fell heavily and the breath thumped out of me. For several seconds I couldn't inhale. I grabbed at my side, and Ray darted for me. I waved him off. "No."

My rejection stunned him and he jerked upright. In doing so, he smacked into the guard who was close behind him. It was an accident, and Ray must have known the guard hadn't meant to apprehend or even crowd him but he shoved him away anyway. "I'm a cop," he said. "Get back to your corner."

I bleated, "Go, Ray. *You* go." I had one hand splayed on the stone and all my weight was on it; my fingers were white. "I'm fine," I said, rolling into a sitting position. "Just leave me alone."

Ray checked once more on the guard, who had closed his eyes momentarily, as if to deny this was actually happening.

"Go!" I couldn't make it any more plain. "Go *now!*"

And Ray stepped over my feet and fled.

I lost the baby.

I won't appall you (and upset myself) with the details of the next thirty-six hours (thirty-six hours during which Ray almost entirely disappeared). I have more memories of sensations, anyway, than of a comprehensible narrative. The steel bed against my backside, for instance, how cold that was, the coldest thing I could think of, until instruments forged from the same metal were inserted . . .

The hot, then cold sensation of blood on my leg.

The smell of wet dog in the taxi that honked its way south along the avenue to the hospital.

Cigarette smoke in the waiting room and on the fingers of the doctor who first examined me. The perfumed oil in his hair.

The needle in the back of my hand and the pain when I removed the bandage from that pinprick wound days later.

But enough. All I know is that to my mind all the hurricane

business is really just subplot to this personal tragedy. Which is why I began my story with that day I visited Michael for the first time, when he examined me and made a cautious prediction about my future.

There are two doctors here now. One or the other of them has been here all day long. They both want to move him but when I asked them whether it would make any difference they said, "Not to him, Mrs. Townes, but you might find it easier yourself."

And so he will die here tonight. He has spoken his last words. He is asleep or he is comatose, the assessments vary. They inject their remedies and they adjust their valves. They monitor his heart and his lungs. His blood is increasingly pale every time they remove another vial. The ride is all but over, isn't it, love?

Jenny has already pledged to stay on a few days. Sharon, her partner, arrived this afternoon and is out buying tea or something. I think she is afraid of being underfoot, of making it even a little bit worse. For my part I worry about her being thrust into such drama. So there is more than enough concern to go around. Ray is the only carefree man left alive.

RAY

She was being smart with me. It was as if she knew I was an impostor. All of eighteen years old and a mouth full of orange segment, and yet here she was, licking her fingers, egging me on. But I was in no mood. I'd just left Mary at the museum, sprawled on the floor. And I still felt as if I was being flogged with the fact of Elizabeth Perkins' death.

"I'm looking for a woman. A patient here. She survived the flood. Alice Beauchamps."

The girl at the desk drew spit through her teeth. She would die lonely, I predicted. Childless and lonely, ignored by her own parents. "She was discharged," the girl said, flipping through a list of names. "Yep, she's gone. Went real early this morning. You okay, are you?"

I leaned on the counter. Gravity wanted to flatten me. "There's no picture of her, I suppose?"

"We're not in the portrait business, no. I might be able to rustle up an X-ray if you like."

"That's very funny," I told her. "You're really brightening my day."

"So you suspect her of something, do you?"

"Only of being alive," I said grimly.

"Well doesn't that sound ominous."

"Look," I began.

She waved the folder in my face. "You need to cool down, you really do. You'll have a stroke, I swear."

I drove across town and broke into Alice's apartment. Her fridge had been emptied, and so had the garbage can under the sink. The dresser had been emptied of her clothes and the drawers left hanging.

A girl appeared behind me in the hallway. She was five or six years old. A dress so white it had to be fresh from the store. Red hair tied back into two pigtails. Freckles. Like a postcard come to life. Her mother, I thought, must be a real stunner.

"Is she coming back?" the girl said. She clutched a doll to her dress.

"Is who coming back?"

"Alice."

I knelt on one knee, reached for the doll, intending maybe to stroke its head, but the girl snatched it away. "Sorry," I said. "I shouldn't have done that, should I? Do you know Alice?"

The girl nodded. She kept her chin against her chest.

"She didn't tell you? She had to go away."

"Where?"

"Far away." I wasn't good at this. It was harder to lie to children.

"Alice said she might be back. She said it would be a long time but I thought maybe it would be this afternoon. Maybe she forgot something she needed."

"When did she tell you this?"

"This morning," she said, still looking at her feet and swinging her hips. The picture of modesty.

"You saw Alice today?"

"Uh-huh. She was packing for her holiday. I said I'd help her with her suitcase but she said it was too heavy."

I stood up. My knees were grey. I brushed them off and the little girl stepped backwards. "Well I don't think she'll be back today," I said. "I think she really will be gone for a long while. I just came to say goodbye. I'm sad that I missed her."

"I'm sad too," the girl admitted. She was sidling away now, moving onto darker portions of the landing.

"Yes it's very sad when someone leaves," I agreed. "But someone else will come along. Someone very nice." She couldn't really be falling for this, could she? I was totally unequipped. Until now I had been able to ignore how awful at it I was. There was so much for me to learn. "It's a good thing you have your doll," I said.

The awkwardness was building in me, soon she would run screaming to her mother. I looked away, embarrassed, and ran a hand once more over the door frame. Nothing too serious, I thought. Probably every door in the building had been jimmied at one point or another.

The girl had backed against the wall and was sliding along it, becoming indistinct in the murk. She was paying more attention to her doll than to me. I hadn't been able to help her and so she was abandoning me. That might be the second time, I thought ruefully, that I'd been abandoned in this building.

I spent an hour in the tunnels of Union Station. Sprinting up and down the stairs. Loitering outside the entrance to the women's bathrooms. Checking the departures board: Oshawa, Belleville, Kingston, Brockville, Smiths Falls, Montreal. Or south to Windsor, north to Sudbury. I bought cigarettes. I was turning into another man, one who leaned suspiciously against stone walls eyeing all the women, ready to pounce should the right victim appear, hobbled by the weight of her luggage.

I bought a sausage from the basement restaurant at the Royal York.

I paced again on Front Street, scanning the taxi ranks, the spinning doors, the solicitous porters.

The porters! I darted through honking traffic, fumbling already for the photograph I had finally lifted from her apartment.

"Have you seen this woman?" My hand shaking. Reaching also for my own identification to settle the black man's nerves. "I'm a cop, it's okay. Look again."

Moving to the next man, and the next. The ticket agent. The floor sweeper. Collapsing onto a bench eventually, the uncomfortable wooden arc of it like a fist in the small of my back. Closing my eyes, tipping back my head. Trying to breathe.

She was gone.

I drove home slowly, not at all sure that this was where I wanted to go. Mary must have had the same doubts every time she left the hospital recently. I cut through unfamiliar neighbourhoods and stared up driveways into garages full of cars and bicycles, coiled snakes of water hose and canvas-covered prams and gleaming lawnmowers oiled and wiped down and put away for winter. Spotless bay windows hung with opaque folds of lace, behind which I occasionally discerned the silhouettes of women moving smoothly past, as if on tracks.

Then the lazy curve of my own street. I was tired of this, but resigned too. And if I was honest with myself, there were routines I enjoyed: filling the oversized bathtub for Mary; taking a whisky onto the patio and watching the new passenger jets descend towards the airport. I had frequently enjoyed Frank's company, and the uninhibited sight of Gina moving within my orbit was also not to be discounted.

At that moment Gina, as if summoned by my inventory, burst from her house as if it was on fire. She was banging on the hood before I had the door open. I worked frantically at the latch. It was as if a drunk had leapt from an alley and I wanted a bit of room to move in.

"You asshole!" she bellowed.

Everyone was either scared of me now, or angry: Mary, of course, but also the little girl risking a dark hallway rather than stay with me a moment longer; the porter who thought I was going to arrest him or beat him up. And now Gina. I put up my hands, hoping to persuade her to hold off her attack, or at least to fend off any blows that might rain down.

"I went to bat for you. I *wrote it down*, for Christ's sake." She scrawled in the air between us: "*Forgive Ray.* That's what I basically said to her. Forgive the son of a bitch. In my own hand." She looked at her wobbling fist as if it might be someone else's.

I closed the car door so she wouldn't think I was going to run.

She leaned on my car and lifted a bare black-soled foot and pried free a pebble that had dug into her. "Jesus, Ray!"

I shook my head, opened my mouth, and when nothing came out I closed it again. I let my hands fall to my side. "Hit me," I said. "Go ahead, hit me."

She smacked the car again. It was a surrogate for me, I understood that. "I told her to forgive you. Don't you understand?"

I shook my head honestly.

"I should never have done that. You had chances to make things better and you just made them so much worse. You made Mary *suffer.*"

"I know I did."

The thing was, I wanted to argue with her. I *did* understand. That I had compounded my mistakes. That I had made Mary suffer, yes, and God knows whether we would ever fully recover. And I appreciated Gina giving me a chance to set things right, but she didn't know how many obstacles had been thrown in my way. But she wasn't the only one grieving here. If she stopped for a second she would see that these amateur dramatics weren't going to improve anyone's state of mind. And they certainly wouldn't make it easier for me to talk sensibly to my wife, not if every time I turned my back Mary was being coached by a neighbour who had decided it was time for Ray Townes to be punished.

But I said none of those things. Because the sentiments would run into each other. I would stumble, trip over my words, make toffee of them. The blood rushing in my ears would deafen me to my own thoughts and I would become confused. I would jump back and forth, stutter and redden and hyperventilate, right there in front of her. When what I really needed to do was fix a decent drink and pull the house together and wait for Mare to get home so I could say to her, "Look, I know I screwed up. Everyone keeps telling me so, and anyway I see the evidence all around me. I've got you and everybody else running away from me, or dying because of me. And I'm sorry, okay? I'm broken in half by what I've done, and not just to you. To this woman who I thought was dead, okay, and who's out there running some-where, just trying to get away from me." I wouldn't try to elicit sympathy from Mary, but I did want to demonstrate that what had happened, what I had done and not done, had not been able to do, had had several effects on the world, and not just caused the temporary (I hoped) implosion of our marriage.

"I'm at the centre of a hurricane," I wanted to say to her and have her understand that, rather than look at me strangely and then cry, or shut herself in the bathroom, or rush around to Gina's.

So there were a thousand and one things I wanted to say and not a single one of them was likely to coalesce in a way that pleased me or satisfied the angry woman in front of me. And so I said, "Gina, do yourself a favour; go back inside," and then I spat lustily onto the face of my own driveway.

I ran a bath for my wife. My hope was that Mary would arrive home just as I closed off the taps, just as I achieved the perfect temperature. When that didn't happen I undressed and lowered myself into the water. Then I climbed out again and walked, dripping, to the liquor supply downstairs and poured myself a modest whisky, splashed in some soda and took it upstairs. The house was clean, I'd seen to that, and I'd made a salad too, with a dressing of oil and vinegar, with a little honey mixed in, and some sesame seeds, because that was what Mary liked. I had also cut some brown bread into cubes and hardened them in the oven. I grated some parmesan cheese and I straightened the covers on the sofa and cleaned the mirror in the downstairs bathroom, which was when the idea for the bath had come to me.

I lay for a long time in the water with the Scotch resting untouched up on the soap dish. I listened. I waited. And when the water grew too cold for me to stand it anymore, and I was tired of topping it up and hearing water gurgle down the overflow, I wrapped myself in a large towel I had never seen before and padded into the second bedroom to get dressed.

When the doorbell rang I thought it was her. I thought she had forgotten her key. I nearly flew the thirteen steps. But it was Gina. "What are you doing still here?" she screamed.

I looked at her, water still in my ears.

"You should be with her!"

I shook my head.

"Ray! You've got to go to the hospital. How can you just stay here?"

"The hospital?" I had no idea what I'd done.

And when she told me it was too late.

237

MARY

I was standing at the brink — as close as the barricades would allow anyone to get to the brink anyhow — and trying to remember how it had gone: that speech at the start of the film. I acted it out for Michael, stomping left and right, like a child playing at being a monster. He was laughing at me. Our faces were wet from all the spray coming over the railing in lacy waves. "Why should the Falls drag me down here?" I intoned. "To show me how big they are, and how small I am? To remind me they can get along without any help? Well all right they've proved it. But why not? They've had 10,000 years to get independent. What's so wonderful about that?"

"Bravo!" He clapped and whistled. Another couple stopped holding hands long enough to join in with his applause. Everyone was all smiles, including me. I laughed. "It gives me shivers," I said, and proved it by shuddering for them.

Michael suggested we ride the Maid of the Mist. "Can you stomach it?" he said. I suspected he was trying to create a perfect day, concocting an antidote from the materials at hand. I had mentioned to him the boat's appearance in *Niagara* and he had probably assumed I would want to reenact that too.

"No," I said, "I want to find the Rainbow Cabins. Is that okay? Will you be terribly disappointed?" I hung off his arm, and why not? "It looked as if they must be up that way." I pointed over the young trees that were just as I remembered them, pruned into cubes and spheres, and the spray-dappled parking lot that was full of brilliant spotless cars.

"Let's go."

He really was being the perfect gentleman, granting my every wish. A prince. The whole afternoon I was amazed that he had asked me to go away with him, even if it was just for a few hours. How difficult that must have been for him, how risky it must have felt. I was almost as amazed at myself for saying yes, but with the baby gone I felt everything had changed: my marriage, my life, all the rules.

We weaved through the cars in the wet parking lot. The roar of the Falls was in my ears, but also in my legs and my chest, my stomach. The world roared its approval.

"They must have to lay down new roads every year," I said.

"Yes, I've heard they rebuild the whole town every year as soon as the Falls freeze." He pointed out licence plates as we went: New York and Ohio, Oregon and Florida, Ontario and New Brunswick.

At the bottom of the hill, where the road turned its back on the water, we stopped a while. I was out of breath. It didn't matter that the child was gone, exertion was still difficult. It was as if my lungs had shrunk to accommodate its bulk and had yet to expand again.

"What will you do next?" Michael wondered. "We can't come here every day and pretend it's not happening."

"We should just move here," I announced blithely. "Then we won't have to worry about the coming here part."

I sounded foolish but I let the suggestion hang in the air with the mist. Not as a proposition, not at all — and he knew that, I was sure he did — but as a small evidence that I still had a sense of humour. Not every small inquiry was going to send me over my own Falls and into some flashing pool of doubt and uncertainty, some unholy swirl of Ray and his foolishness.

"We should find a realtor," Michael suggested. "Have him show us around."

I took his arm to climb the hill, but around the first curve the road narrowed sharply and we had to walk in single file.

The Rainbow Cabins were very real, only they bore a different name now, and a new sign. "Pineview?" Michael said. "Well isn't that the silliest name you ever heard. One of the natural wonders of the world fogging up everything for miles and they name it Pineview."

I was distracted, though, by the strange conflation in my head of what I remembered seeing up on the screen that long-ago afternoon (the same day I met Michael; the same day Marilyn Bell swam clear across Lake Ontario) and the hard reality of it here in front of me. "It's so close," I whispered, and put a hand against one of the pillars. The rock was warm and I imagined myself at the centre of the world, with these hard columns holding up not only the green felt roofs on the dozen cottages spread around, but also the continents themselves.

"I'll have a word with them," Michael said, "about the name." He strolled off towards the office. I assumed this was part of his performance, his low-grade comedy routine, but then he went inside and I saw him gesticulating through the window. There was soft wet moss on the north-facing wall of the cabin and I pressed a hand into it. Michael opened the door suddenly and I thought at first he was angry. A panic moved through me. Had something set him off? Was he the same as Ray after all? Michael, though, raised an arm to show me something that dangled from his hand. The sun had thrown him into silhouette and I had trouble making him out. I heard something. He had bought me a bell, had he? A memento.

"Number 8," he announced. "I'm told it was Number 8 they used." I squinted harder as he came down the steps and strode, grinning, towards me. "Want to take a look?"

He had a key to the room, a key on a pale blue plastic fob and he was twirling it around one finger, obviously delighted with himself.

"How did you do that?"

"It's ours until five," he told me. "We got a good rate."

I turned a fierce red, I saw it even at my wrists. "What do they think we're going to *do* in there? Dear God. You just rented a room by the hour."

"I told him you were tired. I told him I was a doctor and that you needed to rest for a while. I told him Marilyn Monroe was your favourite."

"And what did he think I was doing here at the Falls with my doctor?"

"I told him I was also your husband."

"Sweet Jesus!"

But I laughed, too, and wobbled a bit from the way the Falls were vibrating in my legs.

"You're a religious person, then," Michael said, leading the way. "I didn't know that about you."

I swiped at his back with my purse and he stumbled — play-acting more convincingly than I had down there at the railing — into the door of the same cabin Marilyn must have entered and exited a hundred times last year.

He worked the key into the lock. The door on its inside face was a pale institutional green. We might have been letting ourselves into a private room at the hospital. "If people could see us now . . ." I said.

"Yes, quite."

I took off my shoes and when I came out of the bathroom I sat on the edge of the bed. Michael was filling a kettle with water. "Apparently there's some tea in one of these cupboards. Would you like one?"

I nodded. "The linen's all different," I said. "The furniture's the same but the linen's different. I suppose she would insist on something like that."

"It's a different world she lives in," Michael said.

I wasn't so sure. I told him Marilyn and Joe's marriage had just ended. "That has to feel the same for everyone."

He brought me a cup — white with *Pineview* written in black italics and a tall pine tree stretching from top to bottom — and asked me if I thought my own marriage had ended.

I said I didn't know. This Marilyn thing was just a distraction. A way of putting everything somewhere else. I hadn't thought about it too hard, didn't want to.

"I mean you may be right. It is sort of odd, isn't it? A grown woman and yet here I am sitting on a bed purely because a film star was in it."

Michael said he didn't think it was odd at all. "You found a way to cope, that's all."

"He'll be so worried," I said. "In his way, Ray will be frantic."

"And so he should be."

It was the first time Michael had allowed his bias to show. I was grateful; it was the right time.

"How's it going with your singer?" I asked him. I pulled my feet up onto the bed. "What is her name? Did you tell me? I've been so self-absorbed, haven't I? I need to think about someone else for a minute at least or you'll be sending me home on a bus."

"Her name is Rebecca. *Was* Rebecca. It didn't work out."

"I'm so sorry."

"I had to let her go."

"You did?"

"It felt sort of good actually. I was convinced she would tire of me, but it was the other way around and I sort of like that."

"That's good. I'm glad, then. But still, you must be sad."

He insisted he wasn't, though I thought I saw a hesitation in him. He had his work, he said. And he had learned a lot about himself lately. "I learned that I hate jazz," he said, looking up. "How's that for starters?"

Michael was funny. I hadn't really seen that before. I think I said that it wouldn't be long before a comedian like him found someone new.

"I'll wait," he said. "It's okay."

I let my head settle into the pillow.

"You're tired," he told me.

"You're a hypnotist as well, are you?"

But I *was* tired. My feet and hands felt swollen. When he told me I should close my eyes I did so gladly. It felt a little as if the room was moving, as if I was in a cabin aboard a yacht anchored in a gently heaving harbour somewhere much warmer. The sensation was pleasant, not at all nauseating, which had been my fear when it began. I remembered what Marilyn Monroe had done, in this bed, when her husband returned from his early morning walk. She had rolled rudely away from him. There was that beautiful glimpse of her back before she tugged the sheets around her neck and pretended to be asleep. I'd known immediately the onscreen marriage was doomed. My own life had felt so perfect back then. I tried to identify the subsequent moment when my marriage to Ray had seemed doomed, but nothing would quite separate itself from the snuffling pack. I thought dreamily that the reason for this was that I hadn't given up yet.

Just before I met Ray there had been an opportunity to move away. I could have gone to Africa for a year or two (I told

Jenny this story for the first time last week and I think she liked it, which pleased me immensely, to think that she wasn't disappointed to have followed in my footsteps, footsteps I might have taken anyway). I had considered it seriously. But then it occurred to me that when I returned my parents would have separated. I was the glue that held them together. The offer had been made again the next year. But by then there was Ray. I wished it was possible to know whether my parents would be happier apart. Whether I had done them, and myself, a disservice. But then — drifting, drifting — I was glad that sort of knowledge was impossible outside of the movies.

I felt myself slide still further into sleep — any second it would be irrevocable — but I jerked awake. Michael was perched on a stool, working through a pile of glossy pamphlets: a cable car, the boat, a steak dinner on offer for $2.95. I saw them fanned out on his leg before he looked up and told me to relax, to close my eyes, he was fine. "Don't worry about me."

I dreamed of sunlight, of cloud and sun taking turns to wrap me up. There was a child and I thought it was my own, but then the little boy ran squealing into the arms of a woman sitting on a low stool near a small square window. The woman buried her face in the boy's neck and I was filled with a muted sort of joy.

When I awoke it was dark outside and Michael told me I had been out for three hours. "I've seen less successful anaesthetics in surgery," he said. "But I thought you needed it. I paid them a little more; I think they were happy to see their little place be so useful."

I wiped at my eyes. I sat up but the sleep was still in me. My arms were deliciously thick with it, and it was around my head like a fuzz, a pleasant static. "Is that them?" I said. "Is that the Falls? That's wonderful."

"It is. I've been concentrating on it for a while now. I think there's a sort of pulse to it. An ebb and flow. Either that or it's my own heart. Try it. Concentrate."

I swallowed to clear my ears, and then did as he asked. I listened to Niagara Falls, and though I couldn't hear the effect he had noticed, I was immensely happy at the thought of all that water just flowing downhill, the certainty of it, the unignorable fact that it would pour over the cliff for so much longer than I would care about anything at all. Whatever happened, no one was going to take away Niagara Falls.

Michael said, "What do you want to do? We could —"

"Let's go home," I said. "It's time." I swung my feet over the edge of the bed. They didn't quite reach the ground.

Michael rubbed his hands together. "Okay, then."

"Good." I smiled at him.

"Are you sure?"

"I am. Thank you so much."

"I can wait in the car," he said. "If you like."

"No," I told him. "I'm ready now," and with that I stepped calmly into my shoes.

I'm sure I've got it wrong, but it seemed like they were stabbing Ray with every needle they had in their armory today, trying anything to gain him another five minutes. And it felt like they did that for an hour, with increasing urgency, as if his death was a personal affront to all their education and skills. It seemed nearly a contest, a hockey game that might yet be pulled out in overtime, and when it became unbearable I closed my eyes and there he was, as fresh as if time had folded neatly on itself, like a sheet of new wallpaper waiting to be hung. It was Michael, with Niagara Falls shimmering like a silver curtain behind him.

He wouldn't have had me. I've told myself that so many

times. But it's a lie. He thought I should leave Ray; and the implication that I should take up with him instead was quite clear. I was wrong, he believed, to be so consumed by the idea of duty. There is no way of knowing how things would have turned out. I didn't want to think about it.

Jenny. Jenny is the answer to all the questions. Children are the answer. Children who wouldn't have been born without our forbearance or our outright misery. There might have been other children, of course, even Michael's, but to me they are unimaginable, just phantoms, and as far as I'm concerned a life spent hunting for those ghosts is no different than a life spent weeping in cobwebbed rooms. There is no light in a life like that, none.

And there have been brighter moments with Ray. Some of them quite protracted, lasting several months at a time. No two people can hate each other continuously for fifty years and stay together. There were times when it just didn't seem worth the energy it required. And other times when he was considerate and devoted; when our finances were no worry; when the garden seemed spectacular; and when Jenny had accomplished something marvelous at school or in her career. Any and all of those things were capable of lifting the veil. I also remember rare moments when Ray and I caught each other's eye across a quiet room and regarded each other knowingly, regretfully, before burying ourselves once more in a book or the television or a whisky or a chardonnay or, most often, in the deep wormy mess our marriage had become because I could never forget that he had been unfaithful to me more than once and had caused the death of a child.

I don't care how ruinous a view that seems, or how pathetic; it's too damn late to change anything. We will think what we need to think. I am no exception. And watching them unplug him just now, disengage him from all the hoses and the steel needles I used to recognize and know the names for, as well as several new and gleaming tools that are unfamiliar to me, and watching them roll him onto his side so they could remove the wet and discolored sheet from beneath him, I needed more than anything to think this: *Good, he is gone.*

RAY

I have almost no memory of where I last left off. An hour ago, for long seconds, I couldn't even come up with my own name. I was completely unmoored, consisted of only a black panic bobbing through a luminous swirl of disconnected moments. I am intermittently aware now of being attended to by my doctor, and that to him I am little more at this point than a fish he would haul heroically to the surface so I might asphyxiate, wide-eyed and fearful, in front of him and my wife. Leave me be, I wish to tell them, although I cannot (for the life of me) speak. For pity's sake, unhand me.

Unhand me. Unhand me. I have heard that archaic phrase before. It was Alice, way back in 1974. Odd how it has lodged in the grate. She had just moved back to Toronto after nearly twenty years in Alberta. She was a waitress, recently separated, she said, from her husband. It was the first time I had seen her since October 15th, 1954, and they were nearly her first words.

I had discovered her presence in the city quite by chance. I was checking the operating license of a strip club (one of many that had appeared along Yonge Street in the sweaty aftermath of the 1960s), and trying not to take too much priapic delight in my work. The manager (he had a tattoo of a whale on his arm, a leviathan pushing through torrid seas, that impressed me mightily) had offered a drink while he searched through his filing cabinets for the official paperwork that should, he knew, have been framed and hung on the wall. It was a suddenly middle-aged Alice who arrived with my ounce and a half of vodka, the split of tonic.

I already knew she was alive. Had known since she wrote to me in February of 1955 (*Dear Ray, You complete heel, you absolute monster, you dirty rat! It's me. How are you?*), concealing word of her Phoenix-like rising in an innocuous Alberta Police Association envelope. For weeks afterwards I was giddy with it — the impossible fact of her survival. Mary must have thought I had won the lottery and was keeping it from her. I wrote back quickly (Alice had included an address, made clear that it was safe to do so, saying her husband was "a trusting dolt"). I said that I was thrilled to hear from her (of course I was: much of my guilt disappeared overnight; I was a free man again; one who had made mistakes, sure, but not one who might wind up in jail). But why hadn't she written sooner? Had she understood the awful state I had been in. *I imagined the worst, Alice. Over and again, the worst.* And I also told her, warned her, that Mary and I were trying hard to be good to each other, that a reappearance, a rekindling of any sort was impossible. *It's too dangerous*, I wrote, and yet I thrilled, stiffened at the thought of such peril.

She wrote again late in the spring to say she was not interested in the slightest in seeing me again. *In your dreams!* she said. I could imagine her laughing. *I've let you off the hook, Ray, that's all. Punishing you was taking too much out of me. I meant it when I said you were a monster. You nearly killed me. Don't ever ever forget that.*

And so I tried to forget her. In most ways it was the perfect resolution, I thought. The gods had granted me a pardon.

At least they had until I arrived at the Zanzibar that morning. One instant I was staring hard and with a regretful fascination at the small brown body of an Asian woman as she writhed atop ragged sheepskin (I was fifty years old by then, and softening, anonymous again in the world), and the next I was reaching for the outstretched hand (and looking into the eyes) of a woman I had last seen on the collapsing bank of the Humber River. Instinctively I clutched at her wrist.

"Unhand me," she demanded. "This second." It was a comical outburst, particularly in that monosyllabic room, and it drew plenty of attention. And so I released her, gladly, but minutes later she was back at my side.

And we began again. We began again, with bitterness and recriminations, with wild swinging attacks that left hard-to-explain bruises, and with torrents of tears. With immediate regret and with incredible heat. With a real certainty that this, this fresh and frantic fucking and pushing and hating and swearing and fucking again, just as hard, marked the real escalation, the real descent into hell for us, and not those adolescent long-ago grapplings in department store elevators, when we were young and foolish, and everything was, if not forgivable, then banal and common enough to be unremarkable. We began again, because she was right and so was Mary, when each said I was a monster, a rapacious carnivore. I am still.

MARY

The house is so quiet now I have it to myself.

Jenny and Sharon left this morning. They bundled down-stairs so enthusiastically, so noisily, they might have been three years old, their suitcases bulging with the latest Hotwheels and stretchable rubber dinosaurs, instead of passports and vaccination records and mosquito nets. It is a war zone they are flying into, a war waged between disease and men (and women) but they don't need me to say so. They lowered their voices when they saw me and I think Sharon might even have mumbled an apology. I served them eggs at the kitchen table. I made theirs and then I made some for me too. Not because I was hungry but because the occasion demanded that there be food.

I told them I missed them already (which was true, but I was also looking forward to the absence of people, the solitude, the freedom and time to decide what to do with the rest of my days). "You'll be done in the spring?" I asked them.

"We hope so," Jenny said. "They want us in Libya for the summer."

"Libya. My God. I thought that was one of those countries like North Korea or Iran." She'll die, I thought to myself.

They'll both be killed. Raped and killed.

"That's the Axis of Evil," Sharon said.

"I know, but I thought Libya was like that too, off-limits."

Jenny laughed at me. "Not so much anymore." I sensed one of them tapping the other under the table with a socked foot and was delighted, frankly, at how I amused them. I am ancient, it seems, and completely, laughably, out of touch.

I suppose the globe looks very different to them. Ray and I hardly traveled. A morning now and again in Little India, across the great divide that was Yonge Street always felt like a holiday abroad. We went to Florida every second year, and Ray spent most of those fortnights strapped into a golf cart. In 1986 we spent a month in Mexico, but the food made Ray sick and that was enough for him to swear off Latin America altogether. We did Venice in '87 (and fought the whole time), France in '88 and '89 (the wine) and Germany in '90 (again, wine). In 1992 we signed up for a bus tour through Britain, beginning in Glasgow and ending in London, with side trips to Devon and Cornwall, the fens of East Anglia. It wasn't bad, but it made me feel extraordinarily feeble, trying to climb up those frightful bus stairs every four hours, either after a ten-minute viewing at a magnificent cathedral or a twenty-minute bathroom stop at some poorly covered pit. I have been as far west as Seattle (to see Jenny), and as far east as Berlin. Shame on me.

I drove them to the airport (I can still drive, there is that at least), thinking on how I'd heard them in their room last night, making love. I tried not to listen, and I also strained to hear every sigh. Their murmurings and acquiescences seemed gentler than anything I have ever experienced. And no, I didn't put that down to their both being women, I put it down to my limited experience.

Which is to say he was the only man I ever slept with. The only man I ever will sleep with, I suspect. I thought of my inexperience as a gift, a gift that he discarded, incidentally, as casually as if it was a pair of socks he didn't need. After telling him (after the first time, because it was painful and I had cried out; because I was embarrassed, self-conscious about my performance) I think the fact of my virginity probably lived in his brain for maybe a week. After that it was gone, wiped away completely.

I followed Jenny and Sharon into the terminal, trundling behind them like another piece of luggage. Sharon is the taller of the two, by a fraction. I also noted how confidently they moved through the terminal, with that sense of entitlement that comes from extreme familiarity, and, perhaps, from a decent enough upbringing. When we stopped in line they held hands, or rather they entwined their little fingers, and I couldn't remember ever seeing them do anything like that before.

I made her take his journal. Read it or don't, I said. Burn it or don't. Bury it somewhere. I don't care. I just want it a world away.

"I'll read it on the plane," she said. "He wrote all this since I arrived?"

I told Jenny to wait a while. Wait until it doesn't matter so much what he says in there. She regarded me quizzically, as if seeing something in me for the first time. Pain, perhaps.

From the lounge I watched their plane climb heavily into a patchwork sky. In case they could make me out — the red-hatted, eccentric little ant behind the glass — I waved to them and then, when they were engulfed by cloud, I turned away.

So it is quiet. I spent the afternoon restoring the parlor. Pushing furniture across the floor (who cares about the deep scratches I made — the important thing is that I did the work myself). I pulled back heavy curtains that have been drawn since the spring. The birds have begun to sing again, and the last dead leaves skitter across the patio. I can hear again; I can see. One day soon I shall also feel. Tomorrow I'll make appointments to have my hair cut and my teeth cleaned. And also with my doctor. A full physical, I will tell her. Poke me, prod me, take my blood and spread my legs, if you must. Then send me to your specialists with their imaging machines, their godlike insights. I want to know: How long have I got? Give it to me straight.

We had a reception here after the funeral. Mostly it was neighbours who came and we served them tea, some pale sherry. Jenny and Sharon and I made like waitresses in an olde worlde teashop: "The shortbread is from Scotland," I caught myself saying. "You really should try it." We cut crusts from sandwiches in the kitchen, and gossiped while we were at it about Mrs. Deering's fur stole (*couldn't they have cut the head off, at least?*) and Mr. Barrett's breath (*my God, I know!*). Giggling through tears I couldn't have explained properly, even if you'd stretched me on a rack. "It's relief more than grief," I'd have tried, and left it at that, if I could.

There were a couple of men that Ray had worked with but whom I knew only vaguely. Whenever they had visited Ray took them down into the basement and derogatory laughter galloped up the stairs at regular intervals. Man talk. When he got too sick to manage the stairs they stopped coming. Elsie — she of the infamous brownies — came too and brought with her the Walker's shortbread, still sealed so that there would be no doubt as to its provenance.

Katie, from the newspaper, came to the door but she declined to join us. She is just a girl, I have decided, a girl trying to act very grown-up. She brought with her a laminated version of the story she had written and as soon as she left I ran a utility knife through it and shoved the two stiff halves into the garbage can.

Alice, though, was a no-show. Which is not a surprise, but the possibility that she might feel duty-bound to pay her respects had made me anxious the whole day. She lives just north of High Park now. Ray told me in 1958 that she had moved to Edmonton, as far as he knew. He wasn't in touch with her, he said, which was a lie, though it doesn't matter how I know that. Her move to Edmonton was real enough (she rented a telephone and so her name — I was so pleased to see it — showed up in a directory they keep onhand for reference at the post office. One day in 1985, though, I saw her in a pastry shop on Bloor Street. She was sitting with another woman and they were talking animatedly about their imminent retirement. "Oh Alice, I can't wait!"

It was as if I had heard my own name. I said to Ray that night, "How long has she been back?" and he feigned ignorance so poorly that his facial expression more closely resembled that of a man who has just suffered an aneurysm. His face filled with blood and his hands began to shake. Had he made for the liquor cabinet I would have cut him off and thumped him. "Oh her," he said eventually, after I had laboriously recounted my sighting and threatened him with a locksmith if he didn't come clean.

"How long, Ray?"

It turned out she had been back for more than a decade. "I thought it would upset you," he said meekly. "I didn't know myself for a long time. It's not like we have anything to talk about, so we don't really see each other."

I am convinced that never in the history of the world has so much untruth been collected into two sentences.

And so I stopped caring about her, as much as I could. What else was I to do? I contemplated demanding that we move to another city, but that was ridiculous. Had he been honest with me (that old story) I think I would have been able to forget about her, or nearly. And had Ray been a better liar I may have lived a very different life. Ignorance is bliss etc etc. But listen to me. I have begun to list the what-ifs again. It is time for me to stop.

I don't know how often he "ran into her," or what transpired at those meetings. Was he sleeping with her again? Did he give her money? Did they laugh together, or talk about me? Did he buy her presents on her birthday?

I don't know. I don't know. I don't know. I don't know.

And does it matter? I don't know that either. One can only hope.

NOTES AND ACKNOWLEDGEMENTS

I would like to thank retired nurses Marilyn Boston and Barb McNaughton for sharing their stories with me, as well as Paul Robertson, the curator at the Museum of Health Care at Kingston. At a vital moment Diana Lyon provided me with a place to write and to concentrate. Joanna Lyon, Samantha Mussells, Richard Cumyn, Merilyn Simonds, and Gil Adamson read the novel at various stages, and all of them made honest, insightful comments for which I am grateful. Many thanks also to The Canada Council for their assistance.

Of the books I read, *Copper Jack*, by Jack Webster with Rosemary Aubert (Dundurn, 1991), *Hurricane Hazel*, by Betty Kennedy (MacMillan, 1979), and *Hurricane Hazel*, by Jim Gifford (Dundurn, 2004) stand out as particularly helpful.

And finally, thanks to all at ECW for having me back, and especially to my wonderful editor, Michael Holmes.

This is a work of fiction. Although historical figures do appear in these pages, their actions are imagined.

BackLit
INSIGHTS FOR
READERS

DISCUSSION QUESTIONS

1. Sometimes setting is so prominent in a novel it becomes a character in its own right. As a character, how does the city of Toronto compare to Ray and Mary? How does its character change in the fifty-year span represented in *The Carnivore*?

2. Though Mary and Ray spend most of the novel at odds, what similarities do you perceive between them?

3. Mary's life with Ray is mostly miserable. And it's easy to say that she should have left him back in the 1950s, when she learned what he was capable of. But because she didn't leave, how much responsibility must she take for her own unhappiness? Is her inaction just as reprehensible as Ray's actions?

4. Ray argues with Alice on the shores of the Humber River as Hurricane Hazel rages in the city, and Alice is swept away. Ray is convinced for a while that Alice is dead. If he's right, is he guilty of any criminal act? Did you see him as a

murderer? How does the situation compare to his role in Mary losing the baby?

5. Although Mary lost the baby, we know that Mary and Ray did conceive a child. How did that knowledge alter your view of Mary and Ray's relationship?

6. During the flood, Ray recalls his time in the army during World War II. Yet despite being involved in such a horrific world event, the flood stays with him longer. Why do you think that's the case?

7. Though Ray's actions are reprehensible, does his last act of confession offer him some redemption in your eyes? Does the fact that he seems to still harbour some tenderness for Mary make him seem less of a monster?

8. Compare Alice and Mary. Though Alice is cast as somewhat villainous, is she just a version of Mary that is liberated from family and marriage? Would you choose to be Mary or Alice?

INTERVIEW WITH MARK SINNETT

BACKLIT: Tell us a little bit about *The Carnivore*.

MARK: *The Carnivore*, as I see it, is a book that details some of the inner workings of an unhappy marriage. Simple as that. Necessarily it also takes some time to examine notions of fidelity and duty and betrayal, life and death.

But that's probably not what you meant. And so to answer your question in another way, it's also a book that paints a picture of Toronto in 1954 and particularly the fall of that year when Hurricane Hazel barreled into the city. Ray Townes is a young cop who performs some heroic deeds during that storm, deeds which end up in the newspaper. His wife, Mary, is a nurse, and she does her own share of lifesaving too. In the aftermath of the storm, Mary comes to suspect that her husband isn't nearly the saint the city has painted him as. So it's a historical novel, and a bit of a mystery, and a bit of a tragedy too, some might say.

BACKLIT: What inspired you to write about Hurricane Hazel?

MARK: My plan, some seven or eight years ago, when I started this novel, was to write about another disaster, this one in Devon, England, in 1952. The river above the little town/village of Lynmouth burst its banks and caused a damage that, in pictures at least, is remarkably similar to that caused by Hazel in Toronto. I thought the 1950s would be an interesting time to write about. Queen Elizabeth II had just begun her reign, and Prince Phillip came to Lynmouth to survey the damage and he rode the cable car up and down the steep hill. There were passenger jets in the air for the first time, and television was creeping into living rooms. It was about ten years before I was born and I thought to survey the state of the world as it was just before I got here might be fun.

But at some point during my research for that book I came across pictures of Toronto after Hazel. And I began to wonder if it might not make more sense for me to write about the history of this country I now live in, to try to understand it better, rather than dwelling once again on England, where I was born and where I lived until I was sixteen or seventeen. For a long while now I've tended to look to the U.K. for the music I listen to, and the sport I watch (soccer) and the news I read (the BBC, the *Guardian*). There is an attachment still that strikes me sometimes as not the healthiest bond in the world. I worry that by looking always backwards, and to another place, I am denying myself the opportunity to live fully in this country. I don't want to end up hanging over the bar in a faux pub, lording it up with stories of when I was a lad, or waxing nostalgic about this or that glorious season in the Premiership.

So to ward off that future I began to read more about Toronto, and more about Hurricane Hazel. And a story began to form quite quickly. And documentation about that period was more readily available to me, and I could simply walk the streets and try to imagine the events unfolding. I could see some of what my characters saw. In short, it just made sense to change course.

BACKLIT: *The Carnivore* contains a wealth of historical detail. Was writing in a specific historical period more difficult that you anticipated? What kind of research was involved?

MARK: It was difficult in that I had to be careful not to have the characters listen to a song that hadn't been written yet, that sort of thing. So there was a lot of fact-checking going on (thank god for editors). And of course I needed to understand and absorb exactly how the storm had affected Toronto, both physically and, as much as possible, psychologically. There are an awful lot of people who remember retreating to their basements when the storm hit (or fleeing their basements when they filled with water) and I didn't want them shaking their heads, saying, No, it wasn't like this at all. I wanted to get it right. So I read everything I could find, and I talked to people who had lived through the storm, and also to nurses who had been active at that time and, as I say, I walked the streets to just get some sense of what is where. All told, I spent perhaps a year on the research. And then I just let it sit. I didn't want the research to show too much in the book. I didn't want the action to stop so I could describe at length how a bus ticket looked in 1954, for example. If I forgot something, I let it go. I mean, I don't know the names of all the councillors in Toronto now, so why would I half a century ago? The people in the book are allowed to get things wrong. So long as they don't pick up a BlackBerry, I'm okay; that's the principle I stuck with as much as possible.

BACKLIT: *The Carnivore* is told from two very distinct voices — Mary's and Ray's. Was one character more challenging to write? Was it difficult switching between the two as you wrote?

MARK: Yeah, this is the hardest part. It took me a long time to commit to this strategy. I was scared stiff (still am) that the characters would sound too much alike. Or that Mary wouldn't come alive for the reader. Or that they would both live in the mind of the reader, but one would be vastly more attractive, and so half the reading experience would be disappointing.

What was hardest was that I came to believe that after fifty years of living together, a married couple would sound quite similar. They would phrase things the same way. And I had to let that show in the writing, even though I expected to be accused of not making them individual enough.

But a few years ago I read the marvelous novel by Julian Barnes, *Talking It Over*, and he pulls off a similar feat, and I thought it was worth a try. And I love the idea that Ray and Mary can tell the same story from two points of view, and each of them tell it so passionately, or bitterly, or sadly and, for them, truthfully, and still not get it right. I am very fond of the notion that the true history is not contained in these pages, but lies somewhere between the two narratives. That's part of the reason I wrote their daughter into the novel. I think that even though she doesn't have much of a voice here, she is perhaps in possession of the truest portrait of this marriage. She's the mute witness.

BACKLIT: Both Mary and Ray are fairly unappealing, self-centered characters. How did you relate to them, and what was it like to inhabit their worlds while you wrote?

MARK: You think so? I think that's certainly true of Ray, but Mary does take her nursing seriously and does spend some serious time worrying about others in the world. It strikes me as an awful waste of a life that she stays with Ray, and perhaps that's what you're getting at. But her staying with him is the least self-centred thing she could do.

I found them both fascinating to write, to be honest. Ray tends to slip into his bad behaviours unwittingly. I don't see him as particularly venal. But he doesn't regret enough, or try to repair enough; he simply tries to hide his mistakes. It's a very superficial life he leads. Which is why it's so marvelous that at the end he tries to dig so deep, to really get to the root of things.

He's facing death and trying to make sense of everything. It's too damn late for that (I think that's Mary's opinion, especially when he rehashes some lies for the reporter), but it's what people do. And you know, I think it actually happens for most people a lot earlier than it does in this novel. I'm in my mid-forties now and I know that I'm aware much more intensely the last couple of years that death and maybe sickness are on the (hopefully distant) horizon, and so I've begun fishing around in my past, trying to get a clearer sense of myself. A lot of my friends would admit to the same thing. And writing this book was part of that process.

BACKLIT: *The Carnivore* is deeply invested in notions of guilt and responsibility. How important do you think each of these factors is to Ray and Mary's relationship? How much do they colour the way Ray and Mary remember the events surrounding Hazel?

MARK: Mary stays with Ray out of a misplaced sense of duty, no doubt about it. She thinks it's her responsibility, and I've talked a bit about that already. And you're right, guilt and responsibility are the twin engines that drive these people. But man, it's complicated. I don't think either of them can see clearly the role that these play in their lives. I don't even know that they use either word in the book. I think I could go on for hours but I'll stop there.

BACKLIT: Your previous novel before *The Carnivore*, *The Border Guards*, was a thriller. What connections do you see between it and *The Carnivore*? When you set out to write a "literary" novel, did you find the writing process different?

MARK: I think *The Carnivore* has a real plot and real dramatic arc to it, and that links it to *The Border Guards*. A lot of so-called literary novels are largely plotless, and plot is thought by some to be antithetical to the whole idea of writing a literary novel. But I don't buy that. I wanted there to be some momentum to this story, some pace, and for it not to get bogged down by its structure. After all, what you've got here is two elderly people waxing nostalgic, waxing bitter, and without a good story to hang their reminiscences on, I think I might have been in trouble. I'm no Richard Ford, that's what I'm saying. I'm not skilled enough to transfix you for days on end with only interior thought on display.

But I did want this to be a more serious novel. I wrote *The Border Guards* because I know damn well that my dad doesn't read my poetry. And I wrote *The Carnivore* to see just what I'm capable of. And the process is different, yes. You dig deeper. You don't need a car chase every ten pages. You can digress a bit. Explore language and metaphor, character. Edit and polish for years.

BACKLIT: Though your last couple publications have been fiction, you're also an accomplished poet (*The Landing*, which won the Gerald Lampert Memorial Award, and *Some Late Adventure of the Feelings*) How does being a poet affect the way you approach writing fiction? Do you have any plans to publish another collection of poetry?

MARK: I want to write more poetry, yes, and I do have half a collection sitting in a drawer. But there is little time for me to write these days, and I have other novels I'd like to work on, so I really don't know when or even if it'll happen.

I don't know how the poetry affects the way I approach my fiction writing. I do know that having worked for weeks, months sometimes, on the arrangement of words in a single sentence must have made me a better writer. I can better see the possibilities of a few words, and I can see how best to sort them on a page. I find editing to be the most rewarding part of the writing process. That's where I can make it sing. But does that make my prose poetic? I don't know. Some reviewers have described it that way, but maybe they just knew a bit about my background.

I've also seen the language described as plain and flat and unadorned.

BACKLIT: Which writers have inspired you or influenced your craft?

MARK: Well, Don Coles is as good a poet as we've ever had, and I still hope to write just one poem as strong as any of his. And I think Ted Hughes was really marvelous, and Seamus Heaney amazes me. Karen Solie's a pretty special young Canadian poet too. So any of those.

As for fiction, I grew up in England and I'm still drawn most to the middle-aged white guys from that country: Martin Amis, Ian McEwan, Julian Barnes, Tim Parks. I'm reading David Mitchell's *Cloud Atlas* right now and that is a pretty amazing feat of storytelling too.

I grew up reading a lot of Graham Greene and though it's not a Catholic guilt in *The Carnivore*, I do think Greene's way of moving characters around to make a point about the universe, or the human condition, impressed me mightily at first. Ironically, I now find his novels a bit diagrammatic.

BACKLIT: If Hurricane Hazel hit again, and you could save one book from the advancing waters, which one would it be?

MARK: *Moby Dick.* Wish I could come up with another title. Something to raise an eyebrow, or create an audience for something woefully underappreciated, but truth is, if I could only cart around one book, this is the one I'd choose. It's maddening and lumpy, and even tedious for stretches. But it's also as thrilling a book as I can think of, deeper and wider than any other.

SNAPSHOTS FROM
HURRICANE HAZEL

On October 15, 1954, 300 million tonnes of rain and 110 kilo-metre-per-hour winds battered Toronto, flooding rivers, washing out bridges and streets, and sweeping homes and trailers into Lake Ontario. Eighty-one people died in Canada's most infamous hurricane, and 1,868 Torontonians were left homeless.

We've selected a few photographs from the City of Toronto Archives* to illustrate the storm's destruction, as well as the spirit and resilience of Torontonians in Hurricane Hazel's wake.

*Images credited to City of Toronto Archives, Fonds 1257, Series 1057; item numbers appear with photographs.

[#2000]

[#2011]

SOUNDTRACK FOR
THE CARNIVORE

by Mark Sinnett

I don't suppose I'm very different from most other writers in
that, at idle moments, moments when I should really be writing,
or plotting, or fixing something in the house, I'll laze around
trying to imagine what sort of film my books would make. And
in the case of *The Carnivore*, the short answer, of course, is that
it would make a damn good one, and so I move on quickly to
casting decisions and budget considerations. And then, inevit-
ably, I work on the soundtrack.

I long ago decided that I wasn't going to use much period
music, not even for the scenes set in 1954. Mostly that's because
I just don't know what the music scene was like then. I mean, I
can look up the charts of the period and then populate the film
with that music, but I'm not sure I want my characters to be that
easily swayed by current fad and fashion. My house sure doesn't
pulse with Bieber and Gaga, so why should Ray and Mary have
moved to "Mr. Sandman"? And I just don't know whether Ray's
a Sinatra guy, or a Miles Davis fan. Would he and Mary, or he
and Alice, have sung along with Rosemary Clooney? I think

that if I tried to make these decisions, with my limited know-ledge, I'd have been unfair and untrue to the characters. I would have been guessing, and also would have saddled them with too much mid-century baggage.

And so I decided to use music that I love, timeless music that means the world to me, and music that, if I were in Ray's shoes, or Mary's, I'd want in the background, salting down from the leaden clouds.

I hear Gillian Welch singing *Time (The Revelator)* over the titles. "I'm not what I'm supposed to be / But who could know if I'm a traitor?" At least that's what I hear. And that about sums it up.

Bonnie "Prince" Billy will sing "Cold & Wet," and he could do it just about anywhere, but I hear it as Ray drags his sorry self home after that long night of the storm, like a rat through the bedraggled streets. A nearly comic effect would be achieved, I think. And I do think there is a dark dark humour at work for long moments in this book. I seem to be the only one to think that, mind you.

And when Alice slips into the water and is carried away, it's "The Drowning Man" by The Cure. Google those lyrics and you'll see why. But it's also about the heavy dark drift of the music, which is so purely evocative of the river the way I imagined it while writing those chapters.

Damien Jurado has a hundred sad and haunted songs that I hear coming out of the wooden cabinets in Alice's seedy digs above the furniture shop. But if I'm going to pick one for the scene in which she and Ray cast off their clothes it would be "What Were the Chances," from his *And Now That I'm in Your Shadow* album.

The great Toronto singer/songwriter Hayden has a great song called "Starting Over," which is hushed and melancholy, ill and wan somehow, and yet also quite fierce, and full of sexual longing. I see Ray wrapped in his blankets, gnawing on his dinner, or sipping at his booze, lifting a knee softly to this.

Nouvelle Vague cover the old Visage new-wave thriller, "Fade to Grey" in a cool way. and I think of this song whenever I think of Mary, newly pregnant and walking Yonge Street, or on a streetcar along Queen. I don't know why, really, and I've edited this paragraph out three times now, but it's a persistent association so finally I'm going to leave it alone.

Mark Kozelek has written some truly miserable songs, and I'm fond of them all. His "All Mixed Up" (with Red House Painters) is a must in the aftermath of the storm. And works for Ray and for Mary, I think.

Jessica Lea Mayfield is very young but sings as if she's borne witness to every one of the awful moments in the fifty years Ray and Mary endure in this book. "I'll Be the One You Want Someday" should play over the credits, in my humble opinion.

And that's about it for now. By the time they make the film (got to think positively) I'll have a whole new list. But let me quickly just add this. For all the incidental music, for the general atmospherics, I chose the work of two composers. First, there's Max Richter, a German-born U.K. artist. He writes mostly for the piano, but he also incorporates found sound and prose fragments, burbling fluid electronica and hissing (and somehow consoling) drifts of static. His latest, *Infra*, is one of the two perfect albums for this story. The second is by an Icelandic woman, Hildur Guðnadóttir, who mines some of the same ground as Richter, but works with a cello (among many other instruments) and creates much bleaker music, but also very beautiful. And it's these wild drones of hers that would fill the film if Edward Burtynsky filmed the book and took the river as its main character, rather than Ray and Mary. *Without Sinking* is the name of the album that tears me apart.

ABOUT THE AUTHOR

Mark Sinnett is the author of *The Landing* (Carleton University Press, 1997), poetry, winner of the Gerald Lampert Memorial Award; *Bull* (Insomniac Press, 1998), short stories; *Some Late Adventure of the Feelings* (ECW Press, 2000), poetry; and *The Border Guards* (Harper Collins, 2004), a novel/thriller, shortlisted for the Arthur Ellis award. He lives in Kingston, Ontario.